THE BLACK CIRCLE

AND OTHER ELDRITCH EPISODES

DEREK HUTCHINS

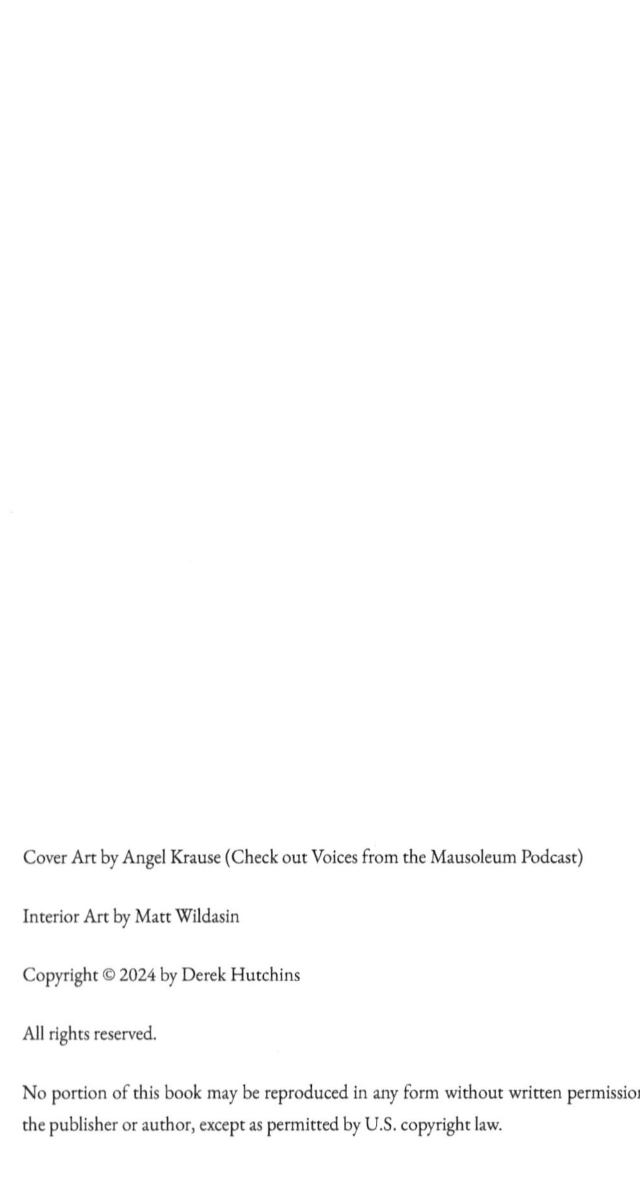

Cover Art by Angel Krause (Check out Voices from the Mausoleum Podcast)

Interior Art by Matt Wildasin

For Taylor

Contents

BEYOND THE GLOAM OF endless sleep
    An endless cycle shall repeat.

    The sleeping dead again shall rise
    Who fell from unknown, cosmic skies,

    And with our doom their souls are fed;
    All dead, to rest, in endless peace.

THE BLACK CIRCLE: PART ONE

I

WHEN MARCUS BROWN DECIDED to stop at that haggard road-side inn, with slouching roof and aura of squalor, he had no idea that his life was about to change forever. The inn rested beside a graveyard, one for the poor, marked only by slanting wooden crosses thrust haphazardly into the dirt. But a graveyard is a grave-yard, and just because those inhabiting it were poor didn't mean they were any less dead or any less ghoulish than the residents of a more ostentatious cemetery, and Marcus whistled as he drug his weary feet and travel-stained boots up the trail to his destination.

A pair of women, dressed in handspun rags, gazed down their bulbous noses at Marcus as he neared the doorway. *A cheery welcome for a cheery folk*, Marcus thought, and returned their disdain with a merry, sardonic grin, and tip of his imaginary hat, which earned him an ugly sneer.

He strode into the inn not meaning to draw attention, but attention was drawn regardless. As soon as he stepped through that flimsy excuse for a door, all twenty or so eyes of the inn's occupants, mostly local villagers who were stopping by for a cheap dinner or pint of ale and broad company, turned to Marcus.

You see, Marcus Brown was a sellsword, and being a sellsword not only required a general grimy disposition, which he had, and the ability to fight (and win) which he also had, but it also required the carrying of an actual weapon. In Marcus' case, a steel longsword, unsheathed, hanging from his belt, its sheen dulled from its many battles. And it was mainly this detail that caused the supper hounds to look at Marcus so fixedly.

Now, sellswords are often maligned and generally untrusted due to their traditionally selfish and opportunist philosophy, Marcus being no exception, but in a small inn like this, where locals clung to their hovels like flies to dung, the only excitement in their lives and only news from the outside world came from travelers, some of whom happened to be sellswords.

So, as Marcus took his seat at the nearest table and allowed his rucksack to plop on the ground beside him, it came as no surprise to him that one of the men who was staring at him in the candlelit gloom, managed to overcome his hesitation and fear, and croak "Buy you a drink, stranger?"

"I'd welcome it," was Marcus' curt reply. The local man, who had a frizzled tangle of beard and a horribly unsightly goiter that bloated the flesh beneath his chin, hollered to the innkeep for two pints of ale and when the cup was set in front of Marcus a moment later, he requested a meal as well, handing the innkeep a faded coin. The innkeep flashed a false grin before crossing the dirt, hay-strewn floor to the kitchen, muttering to herself.

Once Marcus had taken a sip of his ale, which wasn't the worst ale he'd ever had, but nowhere near the best, his new, unsightly friend determined it was appropriate to re-engage Marcus in conversation.

"So, what news of the outside world?"

In truth, Marcus did not have much to offer in this regard. He paid little heed to the affairs of kings and church, fashions and trite gossip did not interest him, but what he did know about was war, and bits of information he had picked up along the way. "It seems the English and French have managed to establish peace, but no one expects it to last long. A marriage has been proposed between two children under three years of age. God willing, they'll live long enough to consummate their holy union."

The goitered man spat in the dirt. "Marryin' chillins. It's a shame, aye, that's the way of it. You wouldn't hear of anything like that going on round here, I'll tell you what."

No, I hear round here you like to eat them, Marcus thought, though he managed to keep his mouth shut.

A straw haired lad of eight or nine set a hearty bowl of stew before him, along with a wooden spoon. "Did you fight in the crusades, ser?"

Marcus could not help but smile at the boy. He too, had once been a poor child like this, and had once looked upon warriors as the noblest of heroes. It wasn't until he'd actually become one that he'd realized how wrong he'd been to idolize them. "I did," he answered. "In the year of our Lord, Eleven Hundred and Forty Seven, I joined the second crusade. Traveled to Portugal to retake Lisbon." He purposefully failed to mention their utter embarrassment and defeat in Hungary and Jerusalem, details with which the boy need not concern himself.

The boy's eyes grew wide. Marcus knew the names meant nothing to them, and that's why he'd said them. He could just as easily have said, the land of Snodgrass, and they wouldn't have known any differently.

One of the men cackled from somewhere in the room, Marcus assumed at his comment, but he paid him no heed, and dipped his spoon into his soup.

"And where come ye from?" one of the Germanic villagers asked in a dialect that was so garbled Marcus almost didn't understand him.

"England," he lied. Truthfully, he'd spent the last eight months in France, but he'd fled to Germania to escape a gambling debt he'd accrued. Work had been scarce since he'd returned from war, and life had not been kind to Marcus. He had no family to speak of, no friends (none he could trust, at least), and since that time he'd wandered, working when he could and stealing when he couldn't.

"And what is yer destination?" the same man wheezed.

"Wherever I can find someone to hire me," he replied truthfully.

"There's a group in the forest. Guarding summin', but they won't let no one get close enough to see what it is." The comment came from a broad shouldered woman with a sagging stomach and a filthy tangle of hair who was collecting empty dishes off tables.

Marcus' interest was piqued. Private militaries were often recruiting soldiers to join their ranks, and he had more qualifications than most. "You speak in riddles, m'lady. Tell me clearly, what manner of group is this and where do they reside?"

"In the Black Forest. A few leagues east of here. Follow the road north, then take your third right. The road's overgrown. No one uses it anymore, not since they took to policing it. So mind you don't miss the turnoff."

Marcus made a mental note of the woman's instructions, then listened to a pale man with a pointed nose as he began to talk in a soft voice. "My friend, Verno, he said he snuck past the guard once. Made it all the way to a stone fortress before they found him."

"No, it's not a fortress," a fat man with a red face retorted, clumping his companion upside the head. "I heard it was a castle. A *witch's* castle."

"Castle, fortress, what's the difference? T'arent' no witches living round here."

"There's certainly a difference," Red face replied, eager to defend his honor, "And you'll understand what it is once I send you to meet your maker, you oaf!"

"Gentlemen, gentlemen," Marcus stood, quieting the uproar. "Thank you for our perspectives. I should very much like to visit this...place, be it castle or fortress. But for now, we shall enjoy one another's company. I have many stories to tell, and the more drinks I am provided, the longer I can talk."

Marcus regaled those who would listen for two hours, filling them with stories from his time in the seminary, to his crusades, to his adventures as a wanderer and sellsword, until they ran out of money to buy him drinks. He talked until the candles burned low and the chill of the outside air began to creep in through the space around the door. He talked of the women he'd bedded and the men he'd killed...and at last, when his belly was so full of sour ale that he could hardly contain his bladder any longer, he forked over another coin to the innkeep for a roof over his head, but only after he had failed to convince her to give it to him for free. Marcus even offered to share her bed, but she only laughed and said that even his sword couldn't save him from her husband's wrath if he tried such a thing, and thought he heard her mutter "Cheap bastard," as she left his company.

Marcus relieved himself in the woods, then found his room. His quarters were small, smelt of mold, and were devoid of furniture except for the straw bed and a small table upon which rested a single tallow candle. He kicked the bed and a mouse scampered out and into a hole in the wall.

As Marcus lay there, in the dying light, itching with fleas, he thought of the secrets that lay in the forest. He was less excited about the prospect of employment, and more excited about what it was these mysterious men were guarding, and how he might profit off of it. Was it treasure? There must be some kind of wealth involved, whether their own or of the man who was paying them.

He slept for for three hours, enough to replenish his stores, and awoke before dawn. A good sellsword is always on his guard, and Marcus had trained himself long ago to sleep lightly and wake whenever he wished.

He collected his scant belongings and crept, as silently as a spirit, down the stairs. He forced open the door into the innkeeper's residence, and explored in the dark until he found the small bag of coins he was looking for. He slipped it into a hidden pocket up his sleeve and then made his way out onto the lonely road, knowing that by the time they awoke, he would be several leagues away...in the Black Forest.

II

Marcus found the turnoff without difficulty, and trudged along the muddy trail until dawn broke, and still saw no sign of a fortress (or castle). The forest was mystical in its appearance, filled with shadows and a low hanging wall of mist that slowly faded as the day wore on. With the aid of the slanting lances of light breaking through the canopy, he was able to dig up some mushrooms, which satisfied as a vagabond's breakfast. He had hardly stood on his weary feet when it began to drizzle, and within moments his traveler's cloak was drenched, and he was shivering, wishing he had never left that flea infested sanctuary. At least there he could be dry and warm.

Marcus' feet came to an abrupt halt and his breath caught in his throat when he heard a deep voice speak clearly. "Turn back. This is private land."

Marcus looked up to see a fearsome, black cloaked figure barring his path. The man's face was hidden behind a featureless metal mask. Marcus' heart beat quickly. It was as if the man had appeared out of thin air. Perhaps Marcus' senses were growing weaker with age.

Marcus held up his gloved hands, a gesture that he meant no ill will. "It is for that very reason I have come, friend. I had dinner at the inn just down the road and the good people said your...liege...might be in need of fighting men."

The figure stood still, and Marcus found it infuriating that he could not read the man's features. If they required their men to wear masks, perhaps this work was not for him. But the man's sword lowered ever so slightly as he said, "Indeed, he is. But whether you are one of them is yet to be determined. Throw down your sword."

Marcus did not resist. Any true man of war had to be confident in his abilities with and without a sword. He drew his weapon and cast it down at the stranger's feet. He did not remove the knife hidden in his boot.

The man snorted and pulled a strip of dirt stained cloth from his pocket. He tossed it to Marcus. "Put that on. Round your eyes."

Marcus did as he was told, though he did not like it. Once he was blinded, he felt the man testing the cloth, adjusting it, to ensure he really couldn't see. His hands were pulled roughly in front of him and bound. Marcus felt a hard tug, as he was yanked forward, led blindly through the darkness.

He had only the sounds of the forest around him, though the songs of birds and rustling of leaves told him little he did not already know. A quarter of an hour later, he heard the man shout in a native dialect he did not understand, and heard the squeal of hinges as heavy doors were thrown open. He tripped as he stepped across the threshold and shuffled over stone, and through another doorway, trying to keep track of the turns in his mind in case he needed to make a sudden escape.

Finally, the blind was pulled from his eyes and he found that he was in a candlelit stone chamber. The space seemed to be some kind of meeting hall, as there was a long wooden table lined with benches. Tapestries covered three of the walls, though their details were shrouded in shadow. Across from the tapestries was a series of arched stained glass windows depicting religious figures caught up in epic transfigurations and battles. Along with the man who had brought him here, there were four others in the room. A nun and a priest dressed in black, and two well built guards who flanked their position at the table.

The priest had a series of books spread out in front of him he had apparently been studying. He turned to Marcus now, raising a candle to his face.

Marcus was surprised to find he knew the man. "Friar Rowe?"

"Marcus Brown." There was a demure look of satisfaction etched across the man's lined face. He was older than Marcus remembered. His hair was thinner and his beard was gray, but it was definitely the same man. "It would seem a great coincidence that we meet again in these dark times."

"Perhaps it is not a coincidence." Marcus cast his eyes around the space again, but did not see any religious iconography indicating a place of worship. "Is this a monastery?"

"Of a sort." Rowe stood, drew a knife, and cut Marcus' hands free. His guards stood ready to draw their swords. "It's all right," Rowe assured them. "Marcus is an old pupil of mine."

Once, before Marcus had joined the crusades, he had aspired to be a man of the cloth. For nearly two years he had studied at a seminary in Glasgow, under Friar William Rowe's tutelage. It had not taken Marcus long to realize that the restrictions and sacrifices a life of servitude required were not for him. He much preferred to fight for his sustenance. At least in a life of war he could take whatever spoils he could lay his hands on, and there were no restrictions on temperance or seeking pleasures of the flesh. He had joined the wars to fight for God, but along the way had lost his faith and himself. His skills were lethal, but he had forgotten what he had signed on for in the first place. "Well if it's not a monastery," Marcus addressed his former mentor, "What is it?"

"We are members of the Black Circle, a new order dedicated to protecting humanity from evil." It was the woman who spoke, her face devoid of humor or emotion.

Fanatics. That's what they were. A den of zealots. But zealots to what? And he couldn't understand what Rowe was doing among them. "I thought that was the Church's job."

"The Church fights a war against the devil," the woman clarified, unhelpfully, "We fight something else."

Marcus looked to Rowe for an explanation. "I don't understand. How did you get here, Rowe? What is this place?"

Rowe smiled, a thin grin which hid years of experience. "About eight years ago, I had an experience which changed my life. Because of it, I left my position as a friar, and started this new order. The Black Circle."

"So you no longer work for the church?"

"No, though we do occasionally work together. I have a new calling now."

Marcus regarded Rowe's weary features with empathy for the man who had once supported his own decision to find a new path. He had always imagined Rowe would serve in some abbey or another until he dropped dead. "What kind of experience? I refuse to leave this room until I hear it."

"Stewart, fetch some wine, and have Liana prepare us a meal."

The masked man bowed and left the room.

"Sit. The tale is long, but you shall hear it, every word," Rowe continued, "Though I suspect that after we are finished, you will wish you had never come here."

III

As Marcus ate a plateful of coarse bread, seasoned chicken breast with carrots and turnips, he nursed a cup of warm beer and listened to Rowe's tale.

Firelight spun around the room, cast forth from a great stone hearth that may have once warmed kings and queens, decorating their faces in an ever shifting pattern of shadow and light. It was in this atmosphere, his face half buried in darkness, that the former priest began his story:

"I was called to perform an exorcism about eight years ago in Norfolk. It was an affair shrouded in secrecy, a personal request from King Henry himself. The duke was the victim in question, and it was believed that after the untimely death of his wife the year prior, he was bereaved, and in this moment of weakness the devil seized him, as ever since the man had become a cruel ruler, sentencing men to death that had no reason to die, and exalting men that had no business providing their counsel. Norfolk, in less than a year, had become a den of debauchery and vice. Drunkenness and whores ruled the streets, and crime and murder were left unpunished. But the most recent crime, the one that infuriated the king the most, was that the duke had declared war on his neighboring fife. This was the situation into which I was dispatched, and the most difficult part was that the duke had no idea I was coming.

"So, what could I do? I set out with an escort of soldiers, the king's own men, to see the peculiar and dangerous business to its end.

"After an eight day journey to Norfolk through wind and hail, we arrived to an equally cold welcome. The duke received us into his hall, and we reported that we had been sent by the king as emissaries of the church, to visit with its congregants, and to perform a special sermon three days hence. The duke had no choice but to begrudgingly receive us. We were invited to eat in the royal hall that evening, though it was perhaps one of the most pitiful displays I have ever had the misfortune of witnessing. A drunken lute player entertained us with misplaced notes, and we ate in relative silence. The men, it seemed, were held captive by an oppressive atmosphere of fear. At one point, a man broke out in a fit of boisterous laughter and the duke rose in a burst of fury, pointed at the man, and shouted 'Seize him! The duchess orders him to be seized and beheaded this instant!'

"A number of soldiers rushed to follow the duke's command. They pulled the laughing man, kicking and fighting, from his seat, and cut off his head with an ax, right there in the hall where we sat eating.

"I was appalled, and fearing for my own life, waited until the duke had left the hall before I turned to the man next to me and asked him to explain the barbaric display of violence I had just witnessed.

"'It's the way round here, as of late,' the man explained, explaining absolutely nothing.

"'But he declared the late duchess ordered the execution, who left us nigh a year ago? What of it?' I replied.

"The man offered me a grimace, gesturing at a large, and prominently placed painting of a woman with flowing blond hair and a face as beautiful as a rose at dusk. 'Aye, that be her. No one right knows what foul influence she holds over this place. She weren't a wretch in life. Some think the duke's gone right mad. But I say it's her spirit, whispering orders in his ear, so I say.' He cast a furtive glance around, confirming I would be the lone recipient of his next utterance. 'And I seen't her, too. Wandering the halls late at night, when all others are asleep. Singing, she was, with the voice of an angel.'

"'You've seen her?' I asked fervently, incredulous as I was.

"The man nodded. 'Aye. But don't go talking about it, and don't bring her up to the duke. Talk of her is apt to see your head end up with that fellow's there.'

"I nodded, agreeing with my new friend's wisdom, shook his hand, and bid him adieu.

"We were shown to our humble chamber in the castle, and as its occupants prepared for the night, me and my companions waited. I instructed them that after our candles had burned low, we would pay a visit to the duke and rid him of the demon plaguing him once and for all.

"Patiently, we waited, and I spent the time in prayer, pleading for protection and power to perform the appointed deed. At last, the set hour arrived, and by candlelight, we explored those hollow, joyless halls until we arrived at a wooden door flanked by a pair of guards. I told them we were to pay an official visit to the duke, to which they scoffed and told us to wait until morning. I drew forth my official letter marked by the king, and ordered them to step aside, or we would resort to violence to see our mission complete.

"The two guards, who apparently had no great love for their fallen duke, fled, and we burst into the room. No sooner had the doors flung open, then I found myself looking upon the most bizarre scene. I gasped. My eyes hardly believed what I was seeing. The duke, reposed in his bed, and leaning over him, whispering into his ear, was the duchess in her sapphire gown, the very face I had seen in the painting!

"She lived! Or so I thought, and eager to expose what I believed to be some nefarious plot, I strode forward to seize the woman by the arm. But to my utter shock, my hand passed right through her flesh! It appeared my friend was right — *the duchess' spirit was haunting this place!*

"The Duchess reared back her youthful head and laughed, mirth born of derision and scorn at my inability to apprehend her.

"'What devilment is this?' I cried.

"To which she said, in a voice unlike her own, or any man I have ever known. 'Jump, my Duke. And join me in death...'

"At once the duke rose, and as if in a trance, stepped out onto his balcony and off the ledge, before we could stop him.

"A horrible wind rushed through the room, and before my eyes, the she-devil faded, her form rising from the ground, becoming that of a porous, crimson cloud.

"The cloud, as if with a mind of its own, flew through my guards, and they fell to the ground, senseless. I gave chase, not knowing what I would or could do, but only knowing that I could not allow this entity to escape while I had strength left to pursue it. Down, down, down I followed it, through hidden passageways and steep stair. I had the chilling thought that the cloud actually wanted me to follow, for at times it seemed to slow its pace so that I could catch up.

"Finally, our chase ended in some forgotten dungeon, where skeletons and vermin made their bed. Amidst the detritus I saw a large, floating sphere of the darkest black, hovering several feet above the ground. The cloud paused before it, and I watched as the cloud took the shape of another being — a crimson cloaked, human shaped fiend which sat upon a pile of tentacles and wore a face so heinous and ghastly that it will forever haunt my waking thoughts. It turned to me, grinning horribly, and in that awful voice, spoke. *'Once again, priest, you have failed to catch me in this world, as you did in the last. Forget what you have seen, that is best, for if you continue the hunt it will end as it always has, with me devouring the dust of your bones!'*

"And with that final riddle, he leaped into the black circle, tentacles spinning behind him, and he and the portal vanished from my sight.

"I spent many hours, months, searching the occult records for any mention I could find of this crimson beast. But over the course of my reading, I was able to learn but little, until I came across the writings of the mad Arab, Abdul Alhazred, who described a being, red in color, who journeyed from across the stars. He could appear as any personage or object he desired, and has long sought to rule the hearts of men, sewing chaos in their midst, for his hatred of their mortal flesh, of which he has none. No name was ascribed to this being, who is one of many, dwelling on, or slumbering beneath the Earth. But the Greek's referred to it as 'Pandemonius', for the horror he wrought among them. According to legend, he was there when the flood drowned the world, when Babylon was sacked, when Christ was crucified, and Rome burned. Rumor blames the plague of Justinian on his black soul, as witnesses claim a ship of rats arrived in Constantinople, driven by a captain dressed in red. I formally departed the church, in good fellowship, and began my hunt for this Pandemonius, harbinger of evil."

Rowe paused here, drinking deeply from his beer, and Marcus surmised it was his turn to speak. "So...did you find him?"

"Yes," was Rowe's rousing response. "What the devil do you think we're doing here? He's in an airtight cell down below. Never to see the light of day again."

IV

Marcus wasn't sure how to react. But his initial thoughts were draped in skepticism. Rowe was his mentor, or at least at one point he'd respected the man, but it just seemed impossible to accept this incredible story at face value. Yet Marcus was certain they were hiding something here, so the ghost story must be a cover. Still, if they were going to come up with a cover story, couldn't they have come up with something a little more plausible than that? Marcus wasn't fool enough to admit all this, however, Rowe had taken him in, fed him, and he was in no hurry to offend his host.

Rowe also was no fool, and seemed to read Marcus' thoughts without him having to speak them. "Of course, I don't expect you to believe me. If I hadn't witnessed what I had with my own eyes, I wouldn't believe it either. We've all seen horrors beyond our own imagining in our time in the Black Circle."

"Well, it seems a simple solution. You have this thing trapped down below. Show me."

Rowe seemed to shudder, as if the thought repulsed him. "I'm afraid that is out of the question. That door opens for no man, not even myself."

Marcus could have guessed as much. Rowe's response did nothing to dismiss Marcus' suspicions. They were hiding something. The question was: what? "I see."

"Now, regarding the reason for your visit. You seek employment. We need men. We do not simply guard locked rooms, but we send agents out to investigate and assess, and if necessary, eradicate further threats. Your expertise could be extraordinarily useful in this regard. So, old friend, now that you know what it is we do, what do you make of us? Do you wish to join us in our cause, and spend your life protecting the innocent? I assure you, there is no nobler endeavour. We could use a man like you."

Marcus smiled in pretended consideration, and raised his empty flaggard. "I have not had enough to drink to accept such a commitment so readily. I must have a night to think it over. I do not believe that is asking too much."

"Take as many nights as you need. We would rather have a fully committed man fight with us for a day, than a lukewarm one for a lifetime," Rowe replied, "We shall talk again in the morning. Helen, show Marcus here to one of the spare rooms."

The nun rose, and after bidding good night to Rowe, Marcus followed his candle bearing guide down an oppressively narrow stone passageway to a small chamber with a rug and wood framed bed and down mattress, a good deal more comfortable than his accommodations at the inn.

Marcus did not mean to fall asleep, but his wit fled the moment his head hit the pillow. He dreamed strange dreams. He dreamt a floating red cloud, pulsing with light, was guiding him through a series of tunnels and passageways. Down a flight of stairs, and to a doorway. All the while, a disembodied voice, the pleasing voice of a fair maiden, urged him on. "*Come, Marcus,*" she whispered seductively, "*Come, and collect your bounty. Come and collect what is rightfully yours.*"

The doorway before him swung open, and Marcus awoke in a cold sweat. The air was cool and he could see outside his window that the sun had not yet risen. How long had he slept? Surely, not more than an hour.

Still, there was not a moment to lose. He slipped into his boots, put on his coat, and lit the candle which rested on his bedside table.

He had a treasure to find.

Marcus shambled out of the room as silently as he could, leaving the door ajar. Like a phantom, he glided through stone halls, searching for the flight of stairs that would carry him down to the mysteries that lay below.

As he rounded a corner, he nearly ran straight on into the sallow faced nun he had met earlier.

"Christ, Almighty!" Marcus exclaimed.

"Long may he reign." Helen looked Marcus head to toe in a distasteful scowl. "Where are you going, Master Brown?"

"Just looking for the privy," he lied.

The nun's expression did not change. "Do you always carry your sword and rucksack to the privy?"

"You'd be surprised, I've fought many battles in privies." The nun did not laugh, so Marcus gave her a straight answer. "I carry my sword with me wherever I go, I am a stranger here."

She seemed even less pleased with his quick response, but stepped aside to allow him to pass. "Three doors down, on your right."

Marcus nodded his thanks and counted to the third door, then turned back — the nun was still watching him. He cursed his luck, then stepped inside, taking advantage of the moment to actually relieve himself. He waited until he could bear it no longer, and peeked back out into the hall.

The nun was gone.

Marcus pressed on. As he rounded the next bend, two thoughts arrived in his mind, one right after the other. The first was that this place was a maze, and he feared he would just end up going in circles. The second was that this passageway bore a striking resemblance to the one in his dream. Subconscious memory guided him from thereon out, and he felt himself being carried along, instinctively knowing which turns to make. He found the stair before long, and descended, then navigated his way through another underground maze, until he saw a light at the end of a tunnel.

A torch on a sconce illuminated a large iron door, in front of which stood a hulking guard. Marcus passed a pile of loose stones and mortar, as the guard noticed his presence.

"Who's there? Goggins, is that you?"

"No, it is not Goggins," Marcus stated, drawing his dirk. "I am merely a nameless spirit, and if you cry out, it will be the last sound you shall ever make."

Marcus saw the guard had a sword of his own, but wisely did not attempt to use it. He wore no mail or armor, and one thrust with his dagger could end the man before his sword could be drawn.

"W-what do you want?" the man stammered.

"I want you to turn around."

The man did so, and Marcus set to work tying the guard's hands with strong cord from his sack. He then tied the guard's feet, and his legs to his hands, so he couldn't run, then stuffed his mouth with an old rag.

Once the man was suitably restrained, Marcus plucked the keys from his waistband and set to work unlocking the twenty locks that held the great iron door closed, one by one.

The guard moaned and howled in muffled, unintelligible distress, to which Marcus' only response was to turn to him and say, "If you are trying to tell me which key goes where, I thank you, but I'm afraid I can't understand a word you're saying."

He turned the final key, slid the lock bar, and was met with a heavy metallic clanking, followed by a sinister hiss of compressed air.

Marcus pulled the door open, and stepped into the unimaginable darkness...

STORY NOTES

THERE WERE SEVERAL INSPIRATIONS for this story, which you have not yet finished. I grew up in Connecticut, a lover of folklore and scary stories. There is an abandoned village in central Connecticut called Dudleytown, which is patrolled by a mysterious group known as the Forest Society. The site is off limits to civilians, and no one knows why. I employed a similar device here with the Black Circle. Who are they and what are they guarding? Keep reading to find out.

The other inspiration is, strangely enough, the novelization of Once Upon a Time in Hollywood by Quentin Tarantino. I read it right before writing this story, and ended up using a similar tone. I thought it would be fun to use a similar voice for a story of cosmic horror, and while it's not exactly comedy, I do feel that Marcus' wit gives this story a much lighter tone than most in this book.

THE TOWER OF DOOM

Everything has its price. Yet for Alistair Barkley, purveyor of antiquities and scholar of mystic arts, no price was too steep. And yet despite all his acquired wealth and knowledge there was one thing that eluded him, one thing for which he would sell his soul if given the chance.

Immortality.

When the first signs of aging had revealed themselves, Alistair had a striking and terrifying realization, one that all mortals must at some point face: he was going to die. Not today, and probably not tomorrow, but eventually the sands of time would wear down his pulpy chassis and Alistair Barkley, the once significant and dapper man, would fade from glory and then blink out of existence like a distant, dying star.

That was inevitable. A scientific fact. And if science couldn't fix this particular problem, perhaps the cabalistic wisdom of the world could.

It was this particular end to which Alistair had devoted the last nineteen years of his life and as much wealth as he could spare. He'd staked his bet on acquiring as many ancient relics and purported claims of lost tomes which contained the secrets to prolonging life as he could get his hands on. Many, such as the ill fated *Lex Tenebrarum*, had eluded him. But at last he'd found a promising lead, one which might finally give him what he sought.

It was spoken of in the writings of Solomon Cross, a knight of an ancient order who'd studied and hunted many relics in his time. A staff of Egyptian origin, the scepter of Amun-Ra. The staff had been lost centuries before, last seen in Hungary. But during his research, Alistair had made a connection between a named owner of the staff, and a nameless castle not far from the city of Eger.

He had told no one of this discovery, but he was not the only one looking for the scepter. His notes regarding his research had mysteriously gone missing, and Alistair had no doubt his professional rival, Mme Monique Le Roux was the culprit. She'd no doubt paid a thief to break in and steal his papers. It would not be the first time she'd thwarted his work. After he'd deduced (from her own findings) the location of a sorcerer's shrine in Pakistan, she had taken it upon herself to sabotage his quest to find the dreaded skull of A'an Sh'bar.

He'd been left no choice but to leave immediately for the East, and so it was that he found himself trekking alone through the dreary trenches and lonely, mist shrouded hills of northern Hungary, bundled head to toe in furs, with his eyes and face hidden beneath a hood and goggles to shield himself from the cold.

Icy winds sliced at Alistair like daggers, and he felt the cold seeping into his extremities. Oh, did he feel it. But...to everything there is a price. He reminded himself of that morbid fact before readjusting the heavy pack on his shoulders and raising his electric lantern to illuminate his path through the treacherous and rocky slopes.

Unyielding, he pressed on, trudging down muddy, forlorn roads which had been forsaken centuries ago, and slipping his way up a slate slathered rise, until at last, arriving at its zenith, he gazed out at an enormous, black castle silhouetted against the last rays of a dying sun. Stretching below him was a vale hidden in mist. How deep that trench ran or what lay beyond that impregnable floor of fog, Alistair dared not guess. A narrow trail of rock wound its way up to the castle's gates, and he found his way to its entrance.

Alistair cautiously navigated this route, clinging to a rope-line which had been installed to make the journey easier. He did his best not to look over the edge and only failed once, when his foot slipped on wet shale, nearly sending him plummeting into unknowable depths. But he was able to hold onto that lifeline and resume his perilous quest.

Alistair arrived at the castle gate to find the high wooden doors and grated portcullis had been smashed inward to an irreparable degree, almost as if a giant had swung a mighty fist to breach the castle's defenses. Alistair did not dwell too long on this mystery, but taking advantage of the open door, stepped lightly over broken beams and twisted columns of metal into the stronghold's courtyard.

Here he paused, and took a moment to raise his head to examine the cascading layers of stone before him. The monolithic rises and frightening battlements were no longer decorated with flags, the fortress was entirely as bereft of life as a graveyard except for one small detail; one he had failed to notice previously:

In the window of the tallest tower a live flame flickered and flashed, as if from a homely hearth or candle.

A sickening dread creeped up Alistair's spine, spurring him to action. Some*thing* was here.

Good omen or foul was yet to be seen. If there was someone here, a caretaker or wanderer seeking refuge, perhaps they could tell him something of the scepter. And if they were an enemy, well, Alistair had learned long ago how to defend himself and the wisdom of never traveling weaponless. He knew not where the scepter would be, but he had all the time in the world to search the enormity of the castle's depths. His first order of business would be to visit the tower...then he would see what he would see.

Bearing his electric lantern, Alistair ventured forth into the crawling darkness of the castle's inner chambers, exploring the crumbling passageways and lichen covered walls, searching for the stair that would bring him ever closer to his goal.

He first passed through a great hall, which was barren now of any furnishings or decorations save for a single moth eaten tapestry hanging on his right hand. The image on the worn tapestry depicted a great beast of many wings and eyes, some used for flying and some used for shielding its body, which Alistair recognized as one of the Old Gods, in some circles known as the dreaded, many eyed Thrax, who is said to have ruled the world before man was. It is well documented in the writings of Solomon Cross and other occult historians that the high priest of Thrax was at one point in the possession of the scepter at Amun-Ra, and that the power imbuing him with eternal life flowed from this sacred trophy. It was widely theorized in occult circles that ancient Jews based their description of seraphim on records or personal experiences with Thrax, a conclusion derived from the similarities of their descriptions and appearance.

Alistair shivered, for of everything he'd read of Thrax, the rumor he had heard the most was how the God lay slumbering underneath his hidden pyramid, waiting for the hour when his high priest would call him forth to rule over earth once more.

Despite his fear, Alistair was elated to find the tapestry here, as it suggested another connection between this place and Rama Kimer, one of the last known possessors of the scepter.

A faint sound echoed throughout the chamber, as of some animal scuttling over stone, and Alistair turned to face the darkness.

There was the faintest suggestion of a pair of luminous eyes watching him from an unlit corner of the hall. But he blinked, and it was gone.

Alistair half thought to call out, but his voice caught in his throat, and he decided against it. If someone, or something, was out there, he wanted to keep his presence a secret for as long as possible, and certainly didn't want to impart the impression that he was scared, or at a disadvantage.

Alistair moved on into a narrow, elongated passageway where the air was suddenly incredibly warm and strangling, and he found himself sweating in his coat. He removed his hood and goggles and was greeted not by fresh relief, but by one of the foulest odors imaginable. It was the most unattractive combination of rotting, decomposing flesh and bile.

Alistair held his breath, traversing several interconnected spaces, each more insignificant than the last, until he emerged once more into a vaulted chamber and at once perceived the source of the abominable reek.

A series of corpulent, swollen sacks of moist greenish flesh hung suspended by vine-like lines, almost like some kind of web of living strings. The sacks weren't smooth, but covered in rounded ridges, almost like scales. Their size was greater than that of a man from top to bottom. How many there were, Alistair couldn't say, as they stretched out of sight, and many hung in groups, hiding others from his limited vantage point.

Disgusted, yet curious, Alistair approached one of these sacks, but withdrew in haste, when he saw the flesh bulge, as something inside pushed against the lining.

He hurriedly searched the rest of the chamber, and in the black, half hidden by a particularly grotesque sack, he found the stairs leading upward.

Alistair rushed the spiral stair like a madman, slipping his way upward, ever upward, until his legs cramped and he struggled to breath. Only then did he stop for a moment of respite.

Over his labored breaths and pounding heart, he thought for the briefest of moments that he could sense something else there in the darkness with him. Something living. There were other breaths besides his own, heaving —

Alistair cast his light upon the descending stair to reveal nothing but a puddle ridden gradation of cragged cement.

It was then that he felt something drip onto his shoulder and had the ghastly impression to look up —

Alistair caught a quick glimpse of leathery wings and taloned feet before they were retracted into the darkness above — but that look...that knowledge that he was, in fact, not alone, and that some unspeakable terror was stalking him in the darkness, was enough to cause him to resume his flight in earnest.

He did not climb, he scrambled up the stairs, one hand clutching his lantern, the other his dagger hilt, which hung from his hip.

Alistair Barkley did not dare to glance behind him, but ran onwards into the unknowable abyss until at last he found the tower door — thankfully unlocked — cast it open — and flung it closed behind him.

He pushed his fingers to the wood, so intent on holding the door closed that he did not even stop to look into the room.

"Hello, Alistair."

He spun at the voice and mention of his name, startled to find that the voice belonged to none other than Mme Monique Le Roux, his nemesis, sitting elegantly in a velvet lined armchair.

Le Roux was flanked by shadows and wrapped in a bodice of furs. To her left was a crackling fire in the hearth. She rose to greet him, a lordly smile painted upon her youthful face.

And in her left hand, she clutched the scepter.

The staff was more gorgeous than Alistair had imagined. A slender rod made of gold, decorated with arcane symbols, colorful vibrant hieroglyphics, and ornate etchings. Sitting atop the scepter was a golden, many eyed beast surrounded by an array of wings.

Thrax.

Le Roux grinned arrogantly as she watched Alistair digest the scene before him. "I've been waiting for your arrival. You've come for the scepter, I presume. Have a seat. We have much to talk about."

Instead of responding to her feigned politeness or heeding her invitation, Alistair was so filled with jealous indignation and confident in his moral and physical superiority that he immediately lunged across the room, tore his dagger from its scabbard, and plunged it deep into Le Roux's heart!

Stunned by his own action, and lack of defense instinct from Le Roux, Alistair stumbled back, ready to watch her crumble or cry out in pain.

Le Roux did neither of these things. Instead, she regarded Alistair with an eerily cool confidence, smirked devilishly, then reached up and plucked the blade from her breast as if it were a loose thread, and not a lethal weapon.

The dagger's blade was coated in a thick varnish of crimson blood.

"You have lost the game Alistair. I have found the scepter, and I alone have discovered the secret to immortality!"

"Damn you," Alistair whispered, then louder, "May all the Gods damn you"

Le Roux shouted authoritatively in a voice and language not her own, and one which Alistair could not place.

Immediately two winged beasts glided down from the unlit rafters, landing hard on either side of Alistair, and gripped his arms with malicious strength.

"Alistair, Alistair," Le Roux cooed, drawing closer. "Did you really think it would be so easy?"

The wicked things holding him were coated in a shiny luster. They were vaguely humanoid, with two legs, each with taloned feet, four arms, two great leathery wings springing from their backs, and heads that contained no discernible eyes, but an enormous mouth filled with razor sharp teeth.

"Not all is as it seems, Count Barkley," Le Roux whispered, and he thought he could sense a slight edge to her voice, a hopelessness in her eyes. "I found the scepter, but it does not come freely. To reap its reward, I must serve the Almighty Thrax as his High Priest and do his dark bidding. I am no more than a slave, no more than any of his blood wraiths, and yet I have committed myself willingly to his cause."

"And what does the great Thrax bid you to do?" Alistair words were laced with malice.

"Prepare the world for his coming, and build his army."

She spoke then to Alistair's captors, blood wraiths, as she'd called them, before turning her attention back to Alistair.

"Kill me!" He roared. "You've gloated enough. Kill me, and be done with it!"

"Count Barkley, I'm not going to kill you," Le Roux hissed. "You are far too valuable an asset. Did you notice the cocoons in the lower chamber? Those are how we transform normal men into blood wraiths. It's a very painful process. Men go in, blood wraiths come out. You will be sealed inside one of these cocoons, and in a fortnight, you will emerge, newly formed, baptized in blood, and with a desire to do nothing else but serve the Almighty Thrax, and no memory of your former self. Then, you shall have the immortality you seek. After all, Alistair, *everything has its price!*"

STORY NOTES

THERE ARE LOADS OF references for this short story, and I'll do my best to mention as many as I can remember. When I was in college my friend and I had an idea for a comic book about a character making his way through a blizzard, face hidden beneath a mask and goggles, toward a castle where he then battled some monstrosity. The comic book never materialized, but I borrowed that initial image for our story's beginning here.

Indiana Jones is a clear influence, with our character searching for a lost relic, fighting against time and professional nemeses. The film *Van Helsing* was probably an unconscious influence on the appearance of the cocoons. I was inspired by 80s body horror films, specifically *The Fly*, with the idea of physically transforming into a monster. I can't think of many fates more horrible than that.

The stories of fellow author Coy Hall gave me the inspiration to set more stories in Eastern Europe, which prompted the setting of Hungary, although he is much more versed in the actual history of the region than I. Go read his debut collection *The Grimoire of the Four Imposters*, it's fantastic.

Lovecraft is an influence on every story in this collection, but I think the melodramatic tone of this story specifically. He was my introduction to cosmic horror, and remains the master of the craft and genre. I have always been fascinated by castles, and always try to come up with reasons to write stories that are set in castles, so naturally I had to include at least one in this collection. And finally, perhaps my biggest inspiration as a writer is the television series *Lost*. I try to make *Lost* references as often as I can — in this story the moment Alistair plunges the dagger into Le Roux's heart to no effect is a direct reference to the moment Sayid stabs Fake-Locke in season six.

THE LUNATIC AND THE LIGHTHOUSE:

A Tale of Terror Torn From History

By Professor Everett Cobb

WHEN I FIRST HEARD the tale of the Lunatic and the Lighthouse I was at sea, crouched around a lantern deep within the bowels of a creaking naval warship on a rainy night. Exactly the right place for such a haunting yarn of ghosts and mystery to be spun and savored. Other stories were recounted that night by fellow mariners, but that was the keynote address. That pinnacle piece of American folklore ignited in my heart a burning passion for the legends and myths of the country where I was born and raised, eventually resulting in my receiving my Masters in American Folklore from Mystic River College.

I have listened to and read countless stories since then, and written numerous books about nautical lore and folk traditions and their place in history and modern culture, and few are closer to my heart than the tale of The Lunatic and the Lighthouse. For those interested in my analysis of the many variations of the legend and their historical significance, I invite you to read my book *They Swarmed from the Sea: American Maritime Folklore And its Warning of An Unknowable Abyss.*

After writing the book I symbolically laid my fascination to rest, having scrutinized and exhausted all known resources on the subject. Fortunately for myself, and for you, dear reader, fate has intervened and judiciously provided a historical piece of evidence to this case which is far more precious than rubies. I trust you will forgive the comparison, but to my eyes, this is the greatest treasure I could ever hope to obtain.

I had worked closely with the United States Lighthouse Historical Society while writing my book, and they had been extremely generous with their records and granting me access to otherwise off limit historical sites. So when board member Anna Rasmusson, who was familiar with my research, reached out to me earlier this year regarding an item that had come into their possession which 'might be of some interest to me', my curiosity was piqued. Imagine my surprise when I learned that the item in question claimed to be none other than the journal of one Irving Glass, a lighthouse keeper! The informant had found the journal while going through an old sea chest buried in a storage facility in Indiana, and had sent it to the Historical Society in the hopes that it might be of value and interest to them.

Reader, I fought to contain my excitement, but knowing the tale was well circulated I had to consider the possibility that the journal might be a hoax. I drove up to Massachusetts the following day to authenticate the record — and along with the assistance of the society's historians — can now safely declare that this indeed appears to be the long lost diary of Irving Glass, the "lunatic" referenced in the incident on George's Island.

The diary was everything I had hoped it would be and more, providing significant insight into Glass' mind at the time of writing, as well as a firsthand account of the events, as recorded by Glass. Whether or not they are factual is an entirely different matter and impossible to determine. A full transcript of the diary will soon be available on the historical society's website, but I will include here the fragments necessary for our evaluation of the legend. Please note that there will be missing words and phrases due to illegible handwriting or water damage to the original text as well as incorrect or antiquated spellings, but I have done my best to keep the integrity of the work intact during my transcription.

EXCERPTS FROM THE JOURNAL OF IRVING GLASS

3 November 1899

Wether is fare. Lorne ses a storm is brooding, he can feel it in his nee. I told him that was a lode of shite and he ses we will see. I gess we will.

The wind is biter but thank the lord the lighthouse establyshment has supplied us with cotten cotes. I kept the fire going all day to. That and several cups of coffee dos the trick.

Cleend the chimnees today and my hands are still blak from the sut. Diner tonite was beef and potato soup with biscuits and tea. I better lern to cook sumthing new on leve [leave] or I mite grow to bord to ete. I askd Lorne if he thot captin Kid's trezur was bareed [buried] here, on acownt of I herd it was bureed on an eyeland up north neer boston, and we are on an eyeland not a feyoo [few] hurs away. He neerly struck me I think. Dont go digging up my eyeland he sed, thers no trezur heer. I think I mite dig som holes wile hes sleeping!

I almost forgot. The lamper and inspector came today to visit. Daved Hodges is his name, and hes the one who hird me. A mity good fellow and a good christin. He sed us and owr lamp is the best hes seen in weeks and he wants to giv us a rase [raise]. I hope he dos becus 2 dollars a day is hardly a good living.

4 November 1899

Sumthing streng has hapend. Ther was a storm last nite, that fel upon us without warning. A hevy mist hid all from vew, and Lorne kept the lite burning well into the day. I was set to washing the windows and from my perch spyd a dark shape on the rocky shore belo [below].

Lorne sent me down to find out wut it was, and wut I found was a woman, neked as the day she was born, laying on the beech. She was breething okay and seemd confusd and did not anser my qweshtons [questions] or understand me. I gav her my cote and not seeing any sine of ship or others, brawt her up to the bunkhowse for a spot of coffee and sum warm bread.

The girl cud not hav bin more than 18 or 19 yeers, eyes as dark and bloo as the sea, which spat her owt. Hair as dark as the sky at nite, and skin as wite as perls. Finally after many qweshtons from us, she beegan to talk — at first in a streng tong [tongue], and then in sumthing resembelling english.

She informed us she had not been in a shipreck, as we had preveeosly suspeckted, but clamed [claimed] that she lived in the see itself. She also sed she belongd to the order of daygon and that she had been sent to us with a mesage from her see god. She told us that our lite must go owt, as he dosnt like it and it disturbs his slumber.

Lorne told me to take the bote acros the chanel and fetch the constable and establyshment for help. I did not want to make the jurny alone or in the curent choppy waters, but Lorne thretend violence upon me if I did not obey him, and feeling sympathee for this pore, wretched childe, I left, intent on finding help.

As I was redying the bote I herd a scream and new it was the girl in trubel [trouble]. I ran back up to the bunkhowse and burst in, finding Lorne with a bleeding face, and the girl withowt my cote, carreeing [carrying] a frying pan. It took no jeenus [genius] to see that Lorne had tryd to force himself upon her, and in his anger tryd once more to atack her and, I imagine, take her life for rejecting him.

Lorne is a bigger man than I, bilt of salt and eyern [iron], but I was abel to pry his fingers off her and told her to run. I held Lorne for as long as I cud but evenchooally [eventually] he broke free and went after her.

The streng thing is she was nower [nowhere] to be fownd. We serchd the eyeland hi and lo but by nitefall, she was gawn.

Tyerd as he was from manning the lite, Lorne told me to take over tonite, so he cud sleep. So here I am, alone in the tower, wondering in myself wut has becum of her. Did she fall from the eestern bluff? Or was she even heer at all?

5 November 1899

Clowdee skys today and trubld [troubled] sees [seas]. Lorne will stil not tawk to me. I have tuk [took] to carreeing a nife on my person and wen I slept today I lockd my dor. Lorne bares a scar were [where] the woman struck him, a nasty gash running sideways acrost his nose. He has not botherd to tend to it.

I spent most of my time in solitud, polishing the brasswork with a roten stone and tending to the wicks. I walkd the eyeland before sundown, partlee to stretch my legs but also to see if I cud find any sine of wut hapend to the gurl. I had neerly walkd the shore wen I came acost a set of footprints in the sand. They were too small to belong to Lorne, and the weerd thing was they wer leeding into the water.

I puzeld [puzzled] over this disckovery over diner, but I did not breeth a word of it to my companyon. I made super [supper] tonite, a paltree dish of rice and beans and salted pork. I returnd to bed and

Lorne to the lite, but try as I mite I cud not fall asleep so I stept owtside for a smoke.

As I stud [stood] in the biter breez on the ege [edge] of the overlook, watching the lite pass by in intervals, liting the space before me, I became aware of moovement on the beech. Grabbing my lantern, I set out to investigate — and wut I saw griped my hart with fere — for I saw 3 shadowee figurs waking [walking] abowt below! In the vag [vague] liting I thawt [thought] that the shapes, tho baring a human fisicke [physique] were strenglee alien and fishlike, with eyes that refleckted my own lite back to me like animals, and skin that shimerd like fish skales. I ran back to my bunkhowse to fetch a club, but wen I returnd the trespassers had fled.

I spent sum time patrolling the eyeland and fownd nuthing else. Evenchooalee [eventually] I gave up the serch and lockd myself in my room.

6 November 1899

Mor clowdy skys. The see is angree.

Lorne asked wut I was dooing last nite so I told him wut I sah [saw]. He sed he thinks I was dreeming. I thot maybe he was rite...until Lorne fownd a weerd thing on the beech... a grooping of brocken wood formed into some kind of simbal. I did not recognize it. Then we lernd were [where] they had got the wood — our bote! Torn to scrapwood. Now ther is no way to leve the eyeland.

Lorne thinks I was the won [one] hoo [who] did it and wut proof do I hav otherwise? He yelt after me for the beter part of an owr [hour]and I did not waver in my clame [claim] — I now wut I suh [saw]. I now I did not destroy owr bote.

Still Lorne dos [does] not beleeve me. We ate apart tonite.

I will lock my door agan [again.].

7 November 1899

By jove, wer do I beegin? I woke up last nite wile it was stil dark and after I had drank some water I reelized there was no lite pasing by my window.

The lite had gone owt!

I panicked, not wanting to put my job in jeprodee [jeopardy] or caws [cause] injuree to inosent [innocent] soles do to my...

[illegible].

...Up to the top of the litehouse and fownd the trap dore allredy open, but no Lorne. Working as qwicklee as I cud I reignited the wicks and got the lamp burning agan.

I manned the lite in Lorne's absents, and I determind to luk [look] for him as sun [soon] as the sun came up. But it turnt owt I wud not hav to wate that long.

In between the crashing of the wavs I herd a moning [moaning] sownd, and I lookt owt over the land beelow until I suh [saw] him.

Lorne was in the oshun [ocean] — tho he resisted beeing tost to and fro with the furor of the waves, as if he was held in place by some magick power. But upon closer inspeckshun [inspection] it was cleer he was tyd [tied] to a pole, the wavs rising and falling arownd him.

I admit that I hesitated, allowing myself for a feyoo [few] moments to indulg the thot of letting him drown. But the thot of beeing alone on this rock was even more intolerabel and I pracktickallee [pratically] ran down the stares and throo myself into the see. I chased thots of monsters from my mind as I swam threw the raging see owt to my overseyer [overseer] and cut him free with the nife that I held in my teeth.

Bringing him back to shore proved the mor dificult chaleng [challenge], but evenchooallee [eventually] we put owr [our] feet on land and I carryd mr. glunt up to the bunkhowse wer [where] I started a fire and put a blancket arownd him.

Rane pownded owr rufe as I atempted to get ansers owt of Lorne, but he only rambeld, haf [half] mad, and I cud not lern how he came to be straped to a pole in the water. Perhaps he did it himself, but I new that was not troo — do to its implasibilitee [implausibility] and the fact that ther ar much eesir [easier] ways to kil oneself, if that was his gole.

For sum time I sat in silens [silence], lisening [listening] to Lorne mumbel abowt a see god and the storm grow stronger arownd us.

A crack of thunder struck and Lorne shot to his feet, taking up a diner nife and swinging it for me, a glint of madnes in his eye.

Begone ye see devils, he rored, back to that hell from witch ye swam! I did my best to doge [dodge] his atacks, and having no wepon of my own, I fled.

Instincktivelee [instinctively] I ran to the one place I new I mite bee safe — up the stares.

But I had scarslee gon ten steps wen I herd the crash of the dore beelow and Lorne lumbering after me.

I did not luk back, but rased [raced] to the top, climbd into the beacon loft and threw down the hatch, locking it behind me.

Beelow I herd Lorne scratching and banging to get in, but I wud not desist and doo so. His sownds wer sudenlee cut short by a serees [series] of strangelld crys [strangled cries] — and then — silens [silence].

I herd not another sownd until morning, and only then did I atempt to open the hatch. Doing so I suh the stare was emptee. I desended as qietlee [quietly] as I cud and fownd my club — but as I lucked arownd the bunkhowse and arownd the eyeland, I did not find him.

Now nite is falling wons [once] more and I hav not slept a wink. I must sun [soon] asend the stare wons [once] more and keep the lite burning. Lest it fal and I meet the same fate as Lorne Glunt.

10 November 1899

I feel like 3 lifetimes have past sins [since] I last rote. Curentlee I am siting in a rented rum [room] in New London, and can no longer cal myself a wickee. I wil relate the events of the last feyoo [few] days as best I can remember, tho my memry surownding it all is cleer as haze and I cant onestlee [honestly] say if any of it reely hapend.

I manned the beecon as best I could that nite. Fere kept me awake tho I suspect I dozed of a feyoo [few] times and hoo [who] can blame me. As don [dawn] neerd I was startld by a feers [fierce] nocking on the hatch and I feered it were those kreechers hoo [who] dragged glunt to his untimelee end, but then I herd voyses [voices] — hewman [human] — and ones I new — the inspecktor and engineer. They had come to check in on us and to lern wy [why] the lite had gon out. I babld of sum lys [lies] as best I cud, not daring to tel them the trooth as I new they [illegible]

I spect they figgurd I kilt glunt, but after inspeckting and serching the hole eyeland twise over, fownd not a lick of evidens.

A bote was haled [hailed] and I was promtlee reeleevd of dutee for my neglijens [negligence]. Temporaree replasements wer eskorted to take over, and as nitefal neerd I boarded the bote to take me back to New London.

After all that I bin thru, I cant say I was sad abowt leeving that acursd ele [isle]. But meybe it wud hav bin beter if I stayd as daygons curse [illegible].

...the sun sank beelow the horizon and we wer cawt in [illegible] ...sum grate fors [force] beneeth us jolted the hole ship, and I fel to my nees — and the next thing I new the bote was sinking. No dowt [illegible]...underwater. I did my best to swim up torward the lite. The water arownd me beegan to glo, and I felt sumthing rap arownd my leg and pul me down — I fawt [fought] upwards, but it was for not and I new I wud sun [soon] run owt of are [air]. In my final moments I chansd [chanced] a luk down and wut I suh [saw] will hawnt me until the day I dye [die].

An armee of see beests in the apeerence [appearance] of man, but mor fish than man, with luminus eyes and tentackels insted of legs. Swarming mases of fish peepel, the girl who washd up on shore among them, calling me down to my deth. I neerly dyd [died] rite then — but I saw ther was sumthing even deeper —

Sanitee [sanity] fled as my mind tryd to axcept the site before me — the outline of sumthing so larg I cud scarslee imagin it — as if it wer so the hole see flore — and it was moveing — turning — reering its horibel hed — until I was gazing rite into a pare of striking eyes and a gaping mowth with teeth biger than myself... [illegible]... griped [gripped] owr sinking ship in its monstrus jaws — daygon himself, the see god of mith [myth].

I was doomd. Ther was no dowt in my mind — the only thing that saved me was the lite from our lighthouse turning on — they were afrade of it, see? And fled from its presents like children from work.

My mind went dark after that and the next thing I remember is waking up on the coneticut [Connecticut] shore and wawking [walk-ing] until I fownd my way in to town.

Now yu [you] now my tale. I sit her [here] in my lockd rum [room] witch I rented with the last of my paper, and I rite this so my tale can be told — and so others can now of wut lurks beelow the see — a kingdum beneeth a kingdum...is it the trooth? Its the only trooth I no [know]. I was mockd to scorn for teling my storee in a local tavern — fules mock, but they shal morn [mourn] — wen daygon reers his uglee hed and they find a way to darken the lite for gud [good].

I bot a gun and I hav baricaded myself in this rum and I dont think I shall ever leeve. I hav seen them, yu see? Lurking in the shadows of this citee, I hav herd ther futsteps slaping [slapping] over ston [stone] and seen ther glowing eyes. She is her [here]...com to drag me down to the deep to feed ther unholee king. But that wil not be my fate.

I can heer them now at the dore. I hav my pistol. My baricad wil not hold them forever. They shal not take me alive. They

[END OF TRANSCRIPTION]

That is where the journal of Irving Glass ends. Dramatic? Yes, who would continue to write while death nipped at their heels? Yet perhaps it is these peculiar details which lend some semblance of credence to the record. Truth is, after all, stranger than fiction.

What really happened to Irving Glass may never be known — as there is no known lighthouse record with which to corroborate his own, and no record of his death, or life after his dismissal from the Lighthouse Establishment for "delusions and suspicion of foul play" and the sinking of Glass' transport schooner tragically named *The Cleopatra*. Nor does there exist any record to inform us of how and why Lorne Glunt mysteriously vanished.

That is, until this journal resurfaced.

Many will no doubt scoff and balk at the document's absurd asser-
tions, and deem it nothing more than the ravings of a madman, but
between the lines of this tall tale there may lie kernels of truth. After
all, *something* happened to Glass and Glunt. Legends of the tragic
end that befell *The Cleopatra* and Glunt range from mermen to sea
monsters to more naturalistic conclusions such as murder and a leaky
ship. Was there ever any being known as Daygon? Well, obviously
the lighthouse still stands and no sea god has risen up to smite New
England...

But then again, the lighthouse has not been in operation since
1899...

So maybe the sea god got what he wanted after all.

STORY NOTES

The biggest inspiration for this story is Lovecraft's stories of *Dagon* and *The Shadow Over Innsmouth*. I wanted to tell a Lovecraftian story involving water and it seemed like it would be too much of a rip off to make my own water god, so instead I borrowed Dagon. I probably came up with this idea after watching *The Lighthouse* and thought that more stories should be set around New England lighthouse wickies. I may have gone a bit overboard with the poor spelling of the undereducated narrator, but it seemed like a good idea at the time.

SHIVER

I've been on my mission for nine months and haven't written in this journal once. Just not much of a journal writer I guess. But today something happened that I need to record. I'm never going to forget it, some things stick with you. I guess I'm writing this more because I need to just get it out.

I'm in the state of Minas Gerais in Brazil, my current area is called Nova Era, part of the city of Juiz de Fora. I've been here two weeks now, this is my first transfer as senior companion, and things have been rough so far. My companion, Elder Nascimento, (who, lucky for me, is a native Brazilian), has been here two transfers and so he kind of knows the area. They weren't really teaching anyone before I got here so we have spent the last two weeks knocking doors and talking to people in the street. I finally found a method that seems to work. When we knock on the door, we tell the person we have a free gift that can bless them and their family. Then we try to schedule a time to come back and give it to them. Who doesn't want a free gift? And who doesn't want their family to be blessed? We've gotten a few appointments that way, and given out some Book of Mormons. It's grueling work and we end each day exhausted, but I'm not here for me. All we can do is invite, right? We do have a few people here who accepted our invitation to come teach them, so I'm looking forward to that.

Okay, so there's this thing here in Brazil called *macumba*. It's some kind of voodoo devil worship from Africa that the slaves brought over. We see "offerings" all the time walking around. Usually they are just bowls of food left out on porches or in random spots on the street with candles around them, but sometimes I see flecks of blood as well, and one time Elder Nascimento says he saw a dead chicken as part of an offering too, some kind of sacrifice to whatever they worship. It's mad creepy.

Today Elder Nascimento and I were knocking doors before lunch and we climbed up this set of stone steps to this one house and saw a macumba offering on the porch. That may have turned some away, but not I. I'm here to give everyone a chance to hear our message. So we knocked, and when the door opened, we did what we usually do, explain we are missionaries from The Church of Jesus Christ of Latter-Day Saints and told the guy we had a message for him that could bless his life.

The guy's eyes lit up. He excitedly explained that he'd spoken with missionaries like us before and invited us in. As soon as we stepped inside, a wave of nausea hit me. I'd never seen anything like what I saw in this house, or what I *felt*. Every inch of the wall was covered with decoration or memorabilia of macumba. Framed pictures of Catholic saints hung from the wall beside pentagrams, surrounded by ornaments of symbols I didn't recognize and black candles that filled the place with a stifling aroma. A black book with writing I couldn't identify lay open on an altar. African dolls were arrayed on a shelf beside dirty glass jars filled with all kinds of strange fleshy decompositions.

I took all this in in a single moment, and all the while, the man watched us, smiling. It was a smile that was too big, like he wanted to eat us. No one ever smiled that big at us before, not even people about to be baptized. The man told us that the elders who had visited him before had left something with him and he excused himself to go get it, vanishing into a doorway veiled with strings of exotic wooden beads.

"This is a house of *Umbanda*," Elder Nascimento whispered, looking just as uneasy as I felt, "a macumba cult."

A macumba cult? Great. What could go wrong there? Instantly a raging headache exploded in my head, but it wasn't just a headache, it was a feeling. *Get out of here, you need to get out of here right now!* I'd never before felt an impression this strong, and whether it was from God or some primal response to danger, I *knew* I needed to leave that house ASAP or something very bad was going to happen. I noticed a detail then, as I was massaging my temples, trying to alleviate the crushing pressure, that I hadn't seen before, as I peeked through the rows of beads. There was a statue in the back room, shrouded in darkness, carved of some black stone. The statue was massive, nearly five feet tall, and sat atop a small table, so it stood taller than me. The figure had the face of a spider, with eight piercing eyes, and many arms protruding from its human-like torso, but it had no legs. Instead, the torso sat atop an enormous mass, like some freakish slug. I shivered involuntarily, as looking upon the thing, that grotesque abomination, forced my body to react.

I turned to my companion, "As soon as he comes back, we leave."

He nodded emphatically, not daring to argue. I knew that he must be feeling it too.

The man burst through the beads a moment later, still wearing that horrifying smile, and clutching a Book of Mormon proudly in his hand. The next few minutes were a blur. He invited us to go into the back room with him and chat. Instant red flags. I made up some excuse as to why we had to go, marked a passage in The Book of Mormon for him to read, invited him to church, and we took off. We speed walked until the house was out of sight. The headache left quickly, but it took a few minutes for the adrenaline to leave my system and my heartbeat to slow down.

Lunch today was with one of the local church members, Irma Teresinha, a widower who lives across town. We had to take a bus to get there (poor planning on my part), but we finally found her place, an unpainted red brick house squeezed in between two similar looking houses on a dirt street. The bricks they use here aren't like the bricks in America, they are large, almost like cinder blocks, but brittle, and all buildings are made of them.

She welcomed us inside and we sat at her kitchen table while she finished cooking, the fans blowing right in our faces to cool us from the infernal heat. Technically we shouldn't have been inside with her because we're not supposed to be inside with a woman unless another male is present, mission rule, but what were we supposed to do? If we told her we had to leave, we'd probably hurt her feelings. Not the first time I've bent this rule and it won't be the last. You've just got to use common sense. If the girl is taking her clothes off, maybe that's a cue to leave. Anyway, while she was finishing at the stove (clothes on), she asked how our day was going, so I told her about the macumba house.

"Cuidado, em?" She cautioned, without glancing over at us. "Those houses of Umbanda you should stay away from." She served us plates of chicken grilled in oil over rice and beans, with a traditional Brazilian salad of sliced lettuce with olive oil. That's my kind of salad.

I told her about the statue I saw, doing my best to describe its spindly arms and bulbous body in my limited Portuguese, but I think she understood, because as I was describing it her face grew dark.

"*Elbozra…*" she whispered, and a hint of the feeling of dread I experienced earlier returned, reaching its cold tendrils around my heart.

"What is it?" my companion asked.

"They say it came here long ago, from beyond the stars," she explained. "It's a monstrosity that dwells under the mountains, far from here, if you believe in the tales. A spider god from another world. There are some in the local community among Umbanda cults who worship it as a deity. Every so often there are disappearances. The cults take people and through some horrible process of dark magic they claim is from Elbozra, transform them into hideous were-beasts, minions of the spider god forevermore. Horrible things, covered in hair, like a wolf. But they walk on two legs. They are awful things. I've seen them, Elders, prowling the city at night. It's horrible…"

I did my best to translate and recall everything she said. I'm a skeptic by nature, and this was not the first time I'd encountered a superstitious Brazilian, even among members of the church, although this was definitely the most unique folklore I've heard yet.

Irma Teresinha seemed rather emotional about the whole thing, so I tried to lighten the mood and reassure her. "Sounds like they need the gospel. We must be in the right place. Maybe we'll be the first to baptize a wolf man."

"Ay, Elder!" Irma scolded. "This is no joking matter. I'm serious, you need to be careful out there. If you see a door with the eight circles on it, don't go in." She grabbed a napkin and sketched out a drawing of eight dots in a concentric pattern. "That's their mark," she warned, "beware the mark!"

We left her with a spiritual thought and prayer at the end of the meal, to help dispel some of the heavy subject matter of our conversation. Joking about wolf men, we headed to our next appointment, keeping to the shade as much as possible to avoid the blistering sun.

People believed all kinds of crazy things. But still, hadn't I felt something in that house? A power I couldn't explain? I tried to avoid the thought the rest of the afternoon while we taught a few lessons we had planned, one with a woman named Tatianna about the Plan of Salvation. She was brought to tears when we explained that families could be sealed together forever through priesthood authority that had been restored to the Earth. She lost a child a few years back and our message really struck a chord with her. She invited us back next week! The other lesson was with a guy who just wanted to debate scripture with us, particularly the meaning of James 1:5, my first real experience in a "Bible Bash." It went nowhere, you can't convince someone of something if they don't want to be convinced. Dinner was cheese and bread from a local bakery, then we headed off to the church where we taught an English class (and by we, I mean me, as Elder Nascimento knows about six words, God bless him), and we finished off our night visiting with Anderson, our ward mission leader.

Let me explain something about Anderson. He's a long talker, a nice guy, don't get me wrong, but what I've learned since being here is that getting out of any meeting with him in any kind of punctual manner is out of the question. I naively thought that by scheduling a meeting at the end of the day we might get out on time, since he knows we have a strict nine pm curfew. Oh, how wrong I was. And I paid for it later. What was supposed to be a one hour meeting quickly spiraled into a two and a half hour meeting. Yes, it was productive, but come on guy, we don't need to hear your life's story every time we get together.

At ten pm, after many failed attempts to excuse ourselves, and way past our curfew, we were finally able to hit the road. They sent us home with a plate of leftover food, so we were in a good mood despite the late meeting. It was a twelve minute walk back to our apartment in the dark, and even though we walked fast, we weren't able to beat the rain. Thick buckets poured from the heavens, pooling on the cobblestone streets and drenching us from head to toe. Of course, neither of us had brought an umbrella.

As we were nearing the corner to turn onto our street, a stray dog crossed into our path and began scrounging through an overturned trash can. We approached cautiously, as I'd already had run-ins with this particular dog, and knew that he was fond of American ankles. I looked around in the dark for a stone in case I needed to defend myself, when my companion grabbed me by the arm. He pulled me, nearly dragging me into a puddle, until we were hidden in an alley between two buildings.

"It's just a dog!" I told him. But he only pointed, wide eyed with fear. I followed his gaze and saw that a dark shape was creeping out of an overgrown lot across the street. We could see it clearly under the lone streetlight, a hulking, wolfish creature that moved on all fours, but seemed larger, man sized, its body bone thin despite being mostly covered in hair. Needle-like fangs dripping with saliva protruded from its snout. The beast snuck up behind the dog. From our vantage point, hunkered behind a bush, we watched in open mouthed terror as the dog yipped twice, then was silenced with a sickening crunch as the wolf thing tore into its throat. We both crouched, shivering in the rain, unable to look away as the creature gorged itself, devouring the dog's innards and sucking the bones dry. When it was finished, it lifted its head, blood dripping from its gore soaked jaw, and I could see its fierce golden eyes searching the darkness, hollow, yet possessing an intense amount of intelligence. A predator's eyes. The thing stood up on its hind legs — *the wolf stood on two legs!* To the height of a man, not shaking or twitching with imbalance, and sniffed the air. I said an earnest prayer, hoping I wasn't dessert. The thing didn't bound, it walked back into the overgrown grass, disappearing to wherever it had come from. We waited, waiting to see if it would reappear. After about five minutes, having seen no sign of the creature, I nodded to my companion — there was only one thing to do — run!

We sprinted, splashing loudly down the wet streets, not stopping or looking back until we were at our apartment door. Only then, as Elder Nascimento fumbled with the keys, did I look back to see that we had not been followed, though I did not feel safe until I was inside my apartment with the door locked. And even then, was I really safe? That thing is still out there.

Now I'm sitting at my desk. It's almost one AM, my companion is sleeping, but I am wide awake. I don't know if I'll ever sleep again. What was it that I saw? A werewolf? A minion of the spider god? It fits the description of the thing Irma Teresinha described exactly. I didn't think such things could be real, yet how can I deny what I saw with my own eyes? In the mouth of two witnesses...And if that part is true, perhaps the rest of Irma's story is as well. It's enough to drive me mad. And yet even the singular beast I could perhaps dismiss as a mistake of nature, a creature contrived by accident, that witnesses claim to be something it's not. But there is one thought I cannot dismiss — the most disturbing realization I've had since arriving home is regarding the warning I received earlier today, to leave the smiling man's house. No, the real thought keeping me from blessed sleep is knowing that if I hadn't left, *I'd have become one of those beasts too!*

STORY NOTES

This story is based on an actual experience I had while serving MY mission in Rio de Janeiro, Brazil. I was knocking doors one day with my companion and we were invited into this guy's house, and just like in the story it was filled with Umbanda memorabilia. That creepy guy with the smile that was too wide was real, and he really disappeared through his hanging beads and came back with a Book of Mormon. I can't say I've ever experienced anything supernatural, but that day was the closest I think I've ever come. My head hurt and I knew that I needed to leave that house. I've always wondered what would have happened if I had stayed. That question formed the basis of this story.

THE LOST TEMPLE OF V'RAZIS

The following is a transcript taken from the personal blog of Heather Maria Chaves, former professor of folklore and occult studies at Mystic River College. The blog post details a version of events she claims occurred during her explorative expedition to Cambodia in the spring of 2006, and gained popularity after her mysterious disappearance later that year. She has not been seen since.

BLOG POST TRANSCRIPT

6/16/2006

[Website redacted]

TRUTH REVEALED: AN OFFICIAL RECORD OF MY DOOMED QUEST
FOR THE *LEX TENEBRARUM*

I am writing this confession and claiming it as the true and definitive version of the events that occurred during my recent trip to Cambodia in search of the lost temple of *V'Razis*. For those news attentive readers, you may recall the flimsy story that was reported in papers, online articles, and media news outlets regarding my calamitous rescue and the investigation that followed. I am sorry to inform you that the reported version of events was a lie, a fable constructed even while I was wandering the sinister Cambodia jungle searching for civilization because I knew that the accurate and factual story would not be believed, and might have disastrous consequences, as you will later come to understand. I have never spoken a word of the truth to anyone in the month or so since my return, and my only hope is that my tale will find some level of credence and attention on the internet among the conspiratorially devout, and thus, circulated to a wider audience. My sincere desire is that others may be wiser than I have been, shun the nefarious curse of curiosity that led to my downfall, and by enlightening you to the truth, that you will carry this knowledge on so that future generations may avoid witnessing the nameless horrors and unfathomable abominations that I had the misfortune of seeing with my very eyes. As Prometheus, I reached for the sun, and I suffered the consequences.

Since my youth I have had a fascination with folklore, and it was with the study of folklore and mythology in mind that I entered my studies at Miskatonic University. It was there that I became interested in the lore of grimoires, and graduated with a focus in the occult and ancient, oft forbidden lore of mysticism and forgotten deities. While attending university, I sought out and studied as many grimoires as I could get my hands on. *The Necronomicon*, of which one of only a handful of copies was housed at the very library I called home, as well the Pnakotic manuscripts, *the Book of Eibon*, *De Vermis Mysteriis*, among others. For as many grimoires as I was able to obtain, there were just as many whose existence was only hinted at in legend, such as the mystic Coral Coated Book, that accursed tome that many say will drive one insane simply by laying eyes on its shell encrusted cover. But my obsession rested with another book, one which I deemed that I might more realistically acquire, the fabled *Lex Tenebrarum*, which for centuries no man has reportedly seen. Through my research I learned much of this ancient, enigmatic creation. Two ancient sources describe the book and claim that it was written in the Adamic language, and that the Jewish prophet Zenock carried it east from Babylon during the time of Abraham, but that it since has been lost to the world. Some would say that is a good thing, and that the arcane knowledge and corruptive texts it contains are dangerous. But not me. At least, not then. When I heard from an Islamic trader that for generations, his family has carried on the tradition that the *Lex Tenebrarum* contained hidden secrets, preternatural rites that can bring about miracles greater than deeds of which Mohammad is capable, I knew that I would devote my life to finding it. This narrative seemed to fit with the tradition that a Middle Eastern prophet hid the book from the world, confiscated perhaps out of jealousy or fear that it would corrupt his own divine mission.

It was during my time at Miskatonic and my study of the Necronomicon that I first learned of the Great Old Ones, and the dominance they are purported to have had over our natural world eons before our existence. Under the tutelage of my mentor, the distinguished Professor Petra L. Thanoy, I was informed of rumors that the final resting place of the *Lex Tenebrarum* was in the temple of the formless god V'Razis, whose location no man knows.

It was the first I had heard of V'Razis, a cosmic entity that even the mad Arab deemed too fearsome to include in his beloved *Necronomicon*, when he set pen to paper centuries ago. For years, I delved into digital archives and online databases, scouring the known world for any information on V'Razis that I could find. My search yielded no results, and I had almost given up when I stumbled upon an internet forum where a former Cambodian soldier mentioned finding a vine shrouded temple whose walls contain the name *Vo'asis* written on their ancient surface. It wasn't an exact match, but it was close, and I thought that perhaps the error might lay in translation, since I was no expert in Cambodian. With the assistance of my tech savvy acquaintance, I was able to track down the soldier, whose name I learned was Ponleak, or Pon, and questioned him about his experience. The digital conversation was challenging, as I was using an internet translator, but he verified everything he had said in the post, and even agreed to take me to the temple site if I could fund the journey.

Naturally, I was ecstatic, and immediately called my department head at Mystic River College in Rhode Island where I then worked as a Professor of Folklore and Occult Studies, and began attempts to put together an expedition. The college did not have assets to fund such a speculative venture, so any hope of fulfilling my dream would have to come from private investors. I had hardly begun my search when my dad called and said he had mentioned my proposed crusade to one of his business associates who was interested in meeting with me to discuss funding my expedition. It was all too perfect. However, at the time I was blind to any red flags and eagerly accepted their invitation to visit my dad's business associate, Horatio Barkley and his wife Victoria, at their sizable estate in the mountains of Utah. I was on a flight the following day and immediately upon arriving, Horatio whisked me off to his enormous library which housed a pretentious and laudable collection of rare occult volumes, including many grimoires with which I was familiar. He expressed excitement at my awe, and boasted at length about his keen interest in ancient tomes, and the lengths to which he had traveled to secure such a collection. I admit, I was impressed, but I was speechless when only minutes later, he agreed to fund my entire expedition!

What could I do but accept such a generous, and desired, offer? We retired to his study, and over drinks, finalized the terms of the deal.

Barkley already had the contract written. I needed only to sign. The terms were standard and fairly straightforward, the only detail worthy of note is the stipulation that if we were to locate the *Lex Tenebrarum*, the book was to reside in his private library after it had been sufficiently studied by myself, and other interested academics. I signed away my soul without blinking an eye.

My next task was to put together a team. Ponleak, of course, was essential, and because I did not speak Cambodian, a translator was needed. I contacted one of the college's Cambodian professors who recommended an acquaintance of hers, a woman by the name of Laura Stahl with whom she had worked while visiting Cambodia on several occasions. After a brief discussion and offer, Laura agreed to join the team. The other stipulation of Victoria and Horatio, (which was not written in the contract, but rather a request of my benefactor), was that an individual of their choosing be allowed to join the expedition. As much as I despised the idea of being babysat, I could not deny the generous terms of the offer, nor resent the Barkley's too harshly for simply trying to protect their charitable investment. Their selection was a rugged gentleman (I use the word gentlemen loosely here), Flint Augustine, an Australian who had spent his life hunting treasure, and possessed a significant depth of survivalist knowledge which could be useful in the wilds of the Cambodian jungle. Such was the cost of chasing my dream.

That made four, and I was content to keep our numbers at that. However, fate would not allow us to depart without adding one more to our group. Andy Fine, my boyfriend of three years and constantly patient supporter, asked to accompany me. I stubbornly and instinctively declined, despite his vexatious persistence, and should have stuck to my guns. Andy had been an avid backpacker, and traveled extensively, so he was not inexperienced in the adventure business, but in the last year and a half had contracted Multiple Sclerosis (MS) and as such his condition was unstable. Bringing him along would be a liability and risk that I did not want to be responsible for, to some degree because of the costs, but also because of my feelings for him. In recent months, his symptoms had been more manageable to the point where he could function almost normally, but there was no telling what disaster the stress of the journey and limited access to healthcare might bring about. Of course, I would have loved to have him alongside me, I always wanted him alongside me, but the rational part of my mind knew bringing him was not logical. However, Andy persisted in his efforts to convince me, justifying his request by explaining he had solicited a doctors note affirming that he was physically able to handle the rigors of the trek, and appealing to me emotionally by suggesting that it might be the last adventure he ever got to experience and that he wanted to be by my side while I made the greatest discovery of my life. I am a rational thinker, but in this instance, I allowed my emotions to control my decision, and against my better judgment, I booked Andy a ticket as the fifth member of ou r company.

I wanted that damned book more than I ever wanted anything, I think. Selfishly, I told myself it would be a career defining discovery. Of course, I was curious about the legends as well. If the place was real, and the book was real, then why couldn't the stories that were told about the secrets hidden in the book be real as well? And a small part of me, which I don't think I even accepted consciously at the time, had to find that power, had to hold it in my hands, because if that power was real, maybe, just maybe, there was a chance it could help Andy.

After a grueling flight halfway around the world, we met Pon at the Phnom Penh airport in the early morning on April 23rd. I don't know what I was expecting him to look like, but the man I greeted was older, in his fifties at least, with short gray hair and a rotund stomach from years of alcohol abuse. The skin on his face had begun to sag, but he seemed glad to be joining us, constantly flashing us a smile made of rotting teeth. The man had fought in the Cambodian Civil War against the dreaded Khmer Rouge over thirty years ago. He was a hero. I reminded myself of that and did my best to be gracious and trust in someone who, by appearance, did not look all that trustworthy.

We hailed a couple of taxis and as we drove Pon explained to the group that he had found the temple down an offshoot of the Stung Areng River while stationed near the western coast, not far from the small, riverside village of Trapeang Rung. We drove through the humid and sweltering country until we arrived at the impoverished fishing village. From there, Pon secured us three canoes and we loaded our belongings into the vessels, forced to make the remainder of our journey upriver. That first night, we camped along the river's edge just outside the village. The journey by river would take nearly two days, and the sun was already beginning to set. That was my last peaceful night of sleep.

We awoke to the crowing of a rooster before the sun and devoured a quick breakfast of fruit and bread, then took up our paddles and set to work. Andy and I shared a canoe, Laura and Flint were paired together, and Pon was deft and skilled enough that he maneuvered his own way on the water, as there was no room for him in the other boats along with our supplies. For the most part, our water voyage was peaceful and quiet. We enjoyed the colorful foliage and applied as much sunscreen as possible so we didn't bake in the unforgiving sun, and soon left all signs of civilization behind. That night we camped on a stony beach, which made for a fitful night sleep, but sleep was not to be had that night no matter where we were resting our heads, because no sooner had we extinguished the campfire than foreboding and frightening howls and screeches began echoing from the encroaching jungle growth. We had Laura ask Pon what was making all the racket, but he only shrugged, and encouraged us to stay inside our tents.

I thought I was capable of handling the rigorous life of adventure but the second day had me doubting myself. Already exhausted from lack of sleep, we continued carving our way upriver against the current, and I soon began to fall behind. I looked back and saw that Andy had given up paddling and was nodding off, his illness having sapped his remaining strength, and I was left to forge ahead on my own, paddling for the two of us. Pon was gracious enough to slow his pace so that we did not get separated from the group. After the sun had reached its zenith, I saw a large shadow pass overhead, relieving us from the overbearing sun, and was about to offer a prayer of thanks when I looked up and saw that it was not a cloud as I had thought, but a great company of bats! They swarmed above us in a wide group for what felt like several minutes before they passed on. At the time I remember thinking how breathtaking the sight was and how lucky I was to see it. Now, I believe it was an omen, a shape of dark things to com e.

By nightfall, Pon had steered us to the right hand shore where we left our canoes behind, strapped our gear to our sore backs, and pressed onward down a narrow trail into the wild jungle. Mosquitos swarmed us on every side, attracted to our flashlights, yet despite the spray we had applied, they were not deterred from feeding on our flesh. Twenty minutes of hell later we emerged into a small clearing where four or five huts had been constructed of bamboo with thatched roofs. A group of seven men were prepared to meet us, all brandishing assault weapons or machetes. They did not attack, but seemed understandably wary of our imposing upon their isolated community after dark. Pon entered into a heated exchange with their leader, giving me a chance to look around in the dark. Parked behind one of the houses I found a jeep, which seemed the oddest thing out here in the middle of nowhere. The vehicle was in questionable condition, but glancing down I saw that the keys were still in the ignition! Pon called us over and pointed down a dirt road that I had not noticed before where a metal gate blocked the road which continued into the forest ahead. As Pon talked, Laura explained that the villagers wanted us to go away. They were guardians of the temple, and no one was allowed to go there, hence the gate which barred our path. We circled up and discussed what to do. How could we get around this obstacle? Flint wanted to expose his own cache of weapons and threaten them, but I spoke against the idea, not wanting anyone to get hurt. I had noticed that the men had taken an interest in both myself and Laura, two foreign women who happened to be graced with a desired feminine shapeliness. I instructed Flint to go around the hut and start the jeep, while myself and Laura distracted the guards. Assuming the jeep worke d and had sufficient fuel, he would drive it around where the rest of us would then jump in, and use the jeep to break down the gate. It was a desperate plan, and full of holes and risk, but I was willing to try it to avoid bloodshed. No discovery was worth the shedding of innocent human life, and we were invading *their* territory.

Laura guided me over to the guards, smiling, we put on all our feminine charm. I was fairly useless as far as verbal communication went, but that didn't seem to matter. The guards were grinning brightly, happy just to stand in our presence and get a closer look at us. Laura began asking them questions, I assume about their village as she was motioning to the various huts, however their conversation didn't last long because only moments later the roar of a jeep engine ripped through the night like a bomb. The mechanics squealed as Flint swung the antique jeep out in our direction. Laura and I both turned to run.

I felt a quick hand slap down around my wrist, holding me back. I kicked my attacker with my boot, heard him grunt, and managing to avoid more grasping hands, rushed to the jeep and flung myself into the vehicle's bed. Everyone else was already inside, and Flint stomped the pedal to the floor as we rushed through the warm, jungle night, gaining speed as we hurled ourselves recklessly toward the imposing metal barrier. Gunshots sounded off, and we all ducked as several bullets grazed our vehicle, but none managed to injure any of its passengers or slow our incredible escape. The jeep jolted as we slammed our way through the gate's insufficient protective plating, the dented wall passed over our heads and landed with a crash behind us. The jeep pressed on as the villagers yelled and continued to fire until we were out of sight.

I don't know the distance, but we can't have traveled for more than a few minutes before Pon instructed Flint to pull over. Laura translated, as Pon informed us that our destination only lay a short walk down the road. We got out, leaving the vehicle for the village guards to find or for us to retrieve on our way back. Would they come after us? Arrest us at gunpoint or murder us for trespassing and our riotous theft? I shuddered, not allowing myself to dwell on the thought. I had risked everything to get this far, I was going to get to this temple. What happened after that I couldn't control.

We hastily made our way down the narrowing trail, winding its way up an embankment populated with gnarled roots and thick trunks of cyclopean trees that looked like something from another planet. At last we arrived at the top of the hill and my heart leapt as I gazed upon the destination I had dreamed of for years: the lost temple of V'Razis!

Dressed in majestic moonlight the temple, constructed entirely of sandstone, consisted of one central tower, surrounded by five, serpentine walls that curved outward like tentacles from the central body of the structure. The main tower stood at least fifty feet above our heads, stacked with ornate arches and topped with an impressively carved pyramidal structure, with levels that decreased in size, rising to a single peak. The five arms were solid walls of stone, themselves reaching a height of nearly twenty feet, and peaked with a mirrored pyramid at each wall's end. As we moved into the crevice between two arms, we saw that there were openings in the stone, allowing one to pass through each arm without having to go around the entire temple. Cracked steps ascended to an opening beneath the central spire. The entire temple was a crumbling ruin, in the process of being swallowed by the jungle itself. Cyprus trees were growing out of, and over the stone; their enormous roots appeared to almost be strangling the enormous construction. It was clear that the complex outdated the Khmer Empire. Most of the other temples in Cambodia were less than 1500 years old, but this temple appeared to have been sitting for thousands of years, slowly wasting away and disappearing.

We made our way over and under the sinuous maze of tree roots and up the moss covered temple steps. As I climbed, I noted that every inch of the walls of the arms and the temple itself was decorated with intricate carvings and bas-reliefs. I was beyond excited to study them in depth and rapidly snapped pictures of details as I went, but at the moment, my only objective was to make it to the central tower. I had to see what was inside.

My head rose above the lip of the main chamber and I pulled myself up and over the edge of the final step. The space before me was about twenty feet wide, with a similar opening directly across. To my right was a stone wall with an arched doorway, and to my left was a wall covered with hieroglyphics in some language that was foreign to me but not dissimilar to Cambodian, surrounding a central bas-relief of a skull like face, encompassed by five curved arms, almost like the structure of the temple itself. I assumed at the time that the image was meant to represent V'Razis. Clear water ran from the figure's gaping mouth into a small pool on the ground.

The rest of the team arrived one by one as they reached the peak of the steep ascent. Andy crawled toward me on his hands and knees, gasping, and I helped him sit and drink water. He was dizzy and the nerves in his legs were causing him immense pain. The main chamber was fascinating, but the tunnel door provided more possibilities. I turned to Pon and asked, "When you found this place, did you go down there?"

Pon gazed into the dark abyss of the tunnel and nodded. He beckoned me forward with a wave of his hand, and I assured Andy that we would be right back. Laura stayed with him as Pon led Flint and I down a sloping ramp through the narrow tunnel. I carried my flashlight in front of me, unconsciously checking my watch, wondering how much time I had before the denizens of the bizarre village caught up to us. We stepped carefully as we continued our descent into the heart of the temple. The ramp made a switchback, around a sharp corner. We must have walked for almost five minutes before we finally emerged into a small room. Directly in front of us was a mirror image of the bas-relief that we found in the main chamber, only no water was pouring from this face's mouth. Directly to either side of the relief were what appeared to be two tunnel entrances, leading deeper into the belly of the deceptively large structure. However, what caught my interest the most was the altar that sat in the center of the room, atop which rested a book of brass pages, connected by metal rings. A book, with hieroglyphics carved into the metal plates. My heart skipped a beat as I realized what I was looking at — the *Lex Tenebrarum!*

I inched forward with nervous excitement, gently caressing the brass pages as I gazed upon the object I had searched for my entire life. The writing on the pages was like no writing I had ever seen, glyphs and figures that were undoubtedly of some ancient origin. I delicately flipped through the pages, in awe at the miraculous preservation of the record. My first reaction was that it seemed strange that the book was not a physical book of paper and leather like other ancient grimoires, however I later concluded that perhaps this method of record keeping was wiser, as metal was easier to preserve than paper. As I flipped absently through the book that I could not read, Flint skirted around me toward the two tunnel entrances, and flashed his light over the strange and eldritch face on the wall. There was a frightening hiss, and I looked up to see a snake with shimmering green scales slither its way out of the face's mouth. Flint took a step back, and watched, not with fear, but curiosity, as the snake made its way along the floor and down the left hand tunnel.

Flint looked back to me and grinned. "Well, is that what you were looking for?"

"I believe so. I'll have to examine it further before I can be sure."

"Well, fantastic. I'm beat, how about we go set up camp, eh?"

I nodded, suddenly realizing how tired I was as well. As we turned to head back up the ramp, we froze as a musical tune consisting of five melodic notes reached our ears. I turned, listening carefully, and heard the sequence repeat, and realized with soul wrenching dread that *the music was coming from the tunnels!*

We stood in silence, waiting to hear if it would happen again. Flint inched closer to the arched doorways, but before any of us could speak, a cry echoed from the main chamber above, calling my name. It was Andy.

Immediately I knew something was wrong. Grabbing the brass book, I turned and fled up the stone ramp, slipping and stumbling on the broken bits of stone, scrambling my way upward as Andy's cries continued, mingled with Laura's. I arrived at the main chamber, and instantly recognized the cause for concern. The two entrances to the outside world had somehow been sealed by stone walls, leaving us trapped inside the temple!

Andy and Laura, babbling together, confirmed what I already guessed. As they were sitting, waiting for us to return, two stone walls had suddenly fallen over the entrances, sealing us in. Flint and Pon arrived behind me, and Pon began talking erratically, gesturing like a wild man at Laura. Flint, seemingly unworried about our new predicament, began prodding the stone walls, shoving his shoulder against them in an attempt to get them to move with brute force. Just looking at them, I knew his efforts would prove fruitless. I carefully wrapped the book in a cloth and set it down, and using my light, began to search the chamber for any kind of lever or switch which might trigger the doors into opening. I instructed Laura to ask Pon if this had happened to him before, but he said it hadn't, they were able to exit through the same way they had entered.

After nearly a half hour of searching, I had failed in finding any conceivable way of removing the great slabs of stone, and Flint's e-fforts had given him nothing but a sore shoulder. He drew his gun, a double barreled shotgun, and suggested that perhaps firing his weapon would scare the individual who closed the doors into opening them, but I forbid him from firing his weapon in those close quarters, as the risks far outweighed the potential benefit. We searched our backpacks and estimated that we had enough food to last two, maybe three days, with only meager portions, and with the water running from the figure's mouth and our filters, at least we wouldn't have to worry about dehydration. The rest of our supplies had been left at the bottom of the steps.

After a scanty meal, I determined the only options were to either wait for some divine deliverance, or attempt to find an answer to our problem from the inside. I set to work examining the carvings and hieroglyphics on the chamber walls, and asked Laura to assist me. She concluded, after several minutes of thoughtful inspection, that the writing was an ancient form of native Cambodian, entirely different from the language in which the *Lex Tenebrarum* had been recorded. The pictographs seemed to suggest some kind of sacrifice, with various images of a priest or priestess raising a knife, standing over another individual lying on a table. I tasked Laura with attempting to decipher the strange Cambodian dialect, to see if we could learn anything that might help us escape our current dilemma.

With Laura working, the only thing left for the rest of us to do was try and get some sleep. Cold bricks for our bed and no blankets, as well as the stress of the day's events, did not permit sleep to come easy for anyone except Andy. The intensity of the day had drained him of his strength, but he still tossed and turned as he slept, grumbling and moaning due to the nerve pain that must have been racking his body. At length I realized my brain would not rest and used what light I had to continue my examination of the record, and assisted Laura where possible. She had already made some progress, as many characters were similar to what she understood in modern Cambodian, and she had begun to form a key to help assist with translation. My study of the brass plates did not result in any insightful knowledge, as I knew nothing of the letters inscribed on the metal, all I could do was take some detailed photos and write in my field journal about the physical appearance, dimensions, and condition of the book itself.

At some point, my exhaustion caught up with me and I must have dozed off because the next thing I knew I was being shaken awake by Pon who was gibbering nervously in Cambodian. I waved him off, and shining my light around the chamber, perceived what must have worked him up into such a frenzied state: Laura was gone!

By that point Andy and Flint were already awake, but neither of them had seen what happened to Laura, and all Pon did was continuously point and gesture toward the tunnel. I called her name several times, but received no response, and with trepidation, Flint, Pon, and myself, ventured back down the sloping passageways.

We arrived in the chamber where the book had been found, and Flint spotted what appeared to be a smear of blood leading into the right hand tunnel. We followed behind Flint as we continued our rescue mission, although at the time we did not know if Laura needed rescue or not. The tunnel continued to slope downward, cutting back and forth in switchbacks as we descended, narrowing and widening at various points, but at last we found the target for which we had been searching. Laura's mangled body lay before us on the stone floor, her abdomen had been torn open by what looked like a wild animal, and which had then abandoned her, perhaps frightened off by our approach before it could finish its grisly meal.

Despair choked in my throat. It was my fault Laura was dead, I had been the one to approach her and ask her to join the expedition. It was a hard blow to my mental stamina, and all I could do was balk as Flint examined the tunnel, seemingly unbothered by the appalling display of gore in front of him. Once I had calmed to a level of functioning, I led Pon and Flint back up to the lower chamber, where they left Laura's body. We had nowhere else to leave it except for the upper chamber, and that would have been too much for our already fragile minds to handle, yet we couldn't leave her in the tunnels.

The mission had shifted from one of exploration to one of desperation. No longer was our goal simply to learn, we needed to abandon the temple as soon as we could. The one silver lining from Laura's unfortunate death was Flint's observation that if an animal had made its home in the lower tunnels, perhaps it meant there was another way out.

Pon had folded his legs to his chest and was rocking back and forth, muttering incoherently to himself in Cambodian. Sadly, there was little we could do to communicate with him without Laura. Flint was adamant that we return immediately and search the tunnels for another exit. Andy was still too weak to move, and I realized then that it had been a mistake to bring him. I told Flint to wait and noticed Laura's notebook on the ground near where she had been working. Pouring over the document, I saw that Laura had succeeded not quite in translating the passage into English, but she had written out a sequence of phrases phonetically in English letters. Stumbling over the words, I did my best to read the strange and incoherent text: *Skree Skree, V'Razis hypjet djo manat qarat jak nusu khjum wydwf...*

Immediately after reading the passage, a strange thing happened. I found myself no longer in the Cambodian temple, but surrounded by a wall of mist. As the mist cleared, I saw that I was in a spacious throne room. Hideously deformed creatures depicted in towering sculptures lined the vaulted hall, leading toward a throne of human skulls at the far end of the room. A line of religious figures in black robes walked in a harrowing procession toward the throne, and I found that I was one of them! Words escaped my lips that at first I did not understand, but I soon recognized them as the same words that Laura had transcribed. Though I did not know their exact translation, my mind gleaned their meaning, intelligence leaked into my mind like a plant soaking up water. We were priests offering a prayer to our God, V'Razis. The high priest descended from the throne of bones, his skin sunburnt and dark, a wicked gleam in his shining eyes. We surrounded an altar on which lay a weeping Cambodian woman. Our chanting ceased at once and the high priest looked to me and without speaking, I knew what

I had to do. I stepped forward, removing a knife from my cloak, and raised it high above my head. Taking my place at the altar, I cried out the prayer one more time, and plunged the dagger downward into the doomed woman's breast —

I awoke at once, and quickly realized I was once again lying on the floor of the main chamber of the temple in the dark, restored to my own body. Someone was screaming, and I soon realized it was not the Cambodian woman, but Pon. I reached for my flashlight and illuminated the horrible scene before me. A hunched figure was looming over Pon in the corner of the room, tearing at him and strangling him by his neck!

Andy and Flint had been on the floor beside me, also sleeping. My body was frozen, I had no time to react and frankly, didn't know how to proceed or even what threat I was facing. Pon's neck snapped in a sickening crunch, and his limp body dropped to the floor. The creature turned toward us, and my jaw hung loose from my face as I realized the thing that had just murdered Pon was not a deformed monster, but Laura!

But how? She was dead! Even as I then looked at the thing, I could see the gaping hole in her abdomen still dripping blood onto the floor, there was no way she was *alive*, at least in the way we understood the term. Some mystical element must have been responsible for her awakening, and I sensed it was connected with the passage I had read from her notebook, that I had unwittingly awakened her! She lumbered toward us, fingers outstretched, searching for her next victim. Her eyes were dull and lacked intelligence, like an animal. That some diabolic power had reanimated or seized control of Laura's corpse was the only explanation.

As she was stumbling toward me, Flint was the first to snap out of his shock and pull his gun. For the first time, I was glad he had brought it. He fired four bullets into Laura's already decaying body, the final shot blasting away a portion of her skull. She growled, but whatever energy had caused her to operate fled, and Laura's body once again dropped and ceased to move.

Flint inspected the corpse with the barrel of his gun as I turned to Andy and asked what happened earlier. He explained that after I had read the passage, I had fainted, and both Andy and Flint had been unable to wake me. Eventually they had fallen asleep as well, and all awoke to hear Pon's death cries. I had never wanted to crawl into a hole and die more than in that moment, when I first realized the supernatural stakes of what we were dealing with. Powers outside our control of which we had limited to no understanding. Who was V'Razis? What had killed Laura? What had caused her to reanimate and then kill Pon? What was it I had witnessed in my dream? Was it a vision, or a memory as I feared?

I supposed that the answers, if there were any to be found, awaited us in the foreboding darkness below our very feet. I did not want to go down there, in fact I dreaded it, but our situation left us with little alternative. I kissed Andy goodbye once again and he entered into one of his fits, a symptom of his illness sometimes would manifest as uncontrollable laughter. He laughed, a disturbing sound which started as a childish giggle, then grew into a high pitched cackle. There was no stopping him once he started, the thing simply had to run its course. And on that note I left him, and followed Flint back into the unknown, hoping that we would find some form of salvation, Andy's unnerving laugher echoing after us. This time, Flint carried his gun at the ready.

Carefully, I went with Flint into the abyss, with nothing but a pocket knife as protection against whatever foul beast lurked down there in the dark. We arrived at the lower chamber and moved down the right hand tunnel, since that was where we had found Laura's body, and our reasoning was that if there was a way out, the animal would use it. Before long we heard the five musical notes whistling upward through the musty tunnels. The tunnel widened, opening up into a wider room, no longer made of carved blocks of stone but a natural cave, with jagged walls and stalagmites reaching up out of the floor like skeletons reaching out of the grave. As we continued, the repeating musical notes grew louder, and the chamber grew larger. We saw many paths branching off in various directions, and soon realized that this was not one singular chamber, but an interconnected cave system, the depth and length of which we had no possible way of knowing. For all we knew it could have been endless. A cool breeze moved past us, lifting our spirits. If there was a breeze, it meant there was a way out! We began to follow the air, deeper into the subterranean cavern.

No sooner had we located the tunnel from which the air blew, then my flashlight began to dim, and then, left us in absolute darkness. I had no replacement batteries on me, only a set of matches in my pocket. As I dug my hand into my pocket to get them, I heard a sickening sound of moisture, and felt a slimy appendage wrap around my ankle. I pulled away, fumbling with the matches. Striking one, I gasped, what I saw in the blazing night will forever stay with me.

A hideous monstrosity, an indescribable mass of formless flesh, with one gaping mouth of thousands of sharpened teeth, held off the ground by an army of writhing tentacles which it used as arms and legs. I screamed as the mass pulsed, and then hundreds of tiny holes opened in the creature's glistening flesh, and the musical notes we had been hearing echoed throughout the cavern. I theorized that the holes must have been connected to the thing's lung system, but I am no biologist. The movement of air caused the match to extinguish, plunging us into darkness again. Two gunshots racked my eardrums, followed by an unholy screeching. In the momentary bursts of light caused by the bullets, I saw Flint being dragged by oozing tentacles into the mouth of the beast. Staggering blindly backward I struck another match and saw the creature for the final time — human blood ran from its gaping mouth, but there was no sign of Flint — the thing had devoured him whole! I turned and ran, lost at first, but then I glimpsed the entrance of the tunnel and quickened my pace. As I moved into the tight tunnel, the match died again. I no longer needed matches and felt the wall with my hands, moving as quickly as I could through the tunnels. I could hear the musical notes sounding behind me, but as I moved upward, the sounds gradually faded.

At last I arrived back in the main chamber, where Andy held the last working flashlight which illuminated my grimy clothes and utter dishevelment. I collapsed into his arms and cried until I was able to explain what I had witnessed. We were trapped in here, and that monster was guarding the only way out!

I gazed again upon the relief protruding from the wall behind Andy, depicting an inhuman skull surrounded by curling arms. I knew, not from study or empirical fact, but from knowledge leached into my mind from my own supernatural experiences, that the image was depicting the monster we had met in the temple's dungeon. It was not V'Razis, she was formless and dwelt in the cosmos, no, the thing we had the misfortune of meeting was merely one of her children. How many of them lurked down there in the dark? Surely, that couldn't be the only one.

I stood up and ran my fingers over the carvings on the metal plates. As I did, a power came over me and I saw letters and phrases appear before me in my mind's eye, phrases I did not have the ability to translate, but which I empirically understood enough to speak. *"V'Razis is the escape, but blood is the key. V'Razis is the escape, but blood is the key."*

I muttered the words aloud without understanding their meaning. It was Andy who figured it out. "V'Razis wants blood. He wants sacrifice, like you saw in your dream. In order for the gates to open, we have to sacrifice someone in V'Razis' name."

As soon as the horrible words left Andy's mouth, I felt them resounding truthfully in my soul. "One of us," I realized, we were the only ones left. My eyes found the image of the human sacrifice on the wall.

This place was evil. The book was evil. Guilt rose up inside me, filling me to the brim of my skull. My own stupidity and pride had led us to this point.

"It has to be me," Andy said, fatigue ringing in every syllable. "But you have to do it. You have to sacrifice me. Get out, make sure no one ever finds this place or that book again."

I immediately protested, "No! Andy, no. There's no way I'm going to do that. You can't ask me to do that. There's another way out, down below. I'll go that way and get help —"

"Then you'll die too!" He sat up, straighter now, using all the strength he had left to take me by the hands, looking me in the eyes. "I can't even walk. My days are already numbered. I'm not making it out of here. I either die, knowing you went free, or you go down below and that thing gets me later. There's no hope for me, there is for you."

Before I could stop him, Andy drove a pen into his forearm and tore it through his flesh, pulling it vertically up his arm. He seethed, and I watched in horror as blood began to ooze out in thick lines. "Now you have to do it... or I die for nothing."

I could have died with him. But what good would that have done? He sacrificed himself for me, and to die would be to waste that sacrifice. With tears leaking down my face, I took the sheathed blade from Laura's pack and knelt beside Andy. He positioned himself so he was lying flat on the ground, looking upward. A sudden pang of fear ran through me. "What if it doesn't work?"

With all the finality and confidence of a prophet, he gazed into my soul. "It'll work."

Either from my dream, or some other means, I had gained a heightened supernatural awareness, which spoke to me, placed words in my head, and caused sensations to flood throughout my body, giving me knowledge beyond my ability to gather myself. In that moment, I felt a chilling cold, like an icy tentacle, curling its way into my chest, and I knew that the sacrifice would work. That was the only thing that drove me to do it. Somehow V'Razis was speaking to me, she was telling me to go through with it. But could I fully trust in her promises? After the horror's I'd seen?

I had no other choice. Andy had forced my hand, either he died for nothing or he helped me escape. I grabbed Andy's hand and kissed him, professed my undying love, and before I could second guess myself, raised the knife above my head and spoke the words of the prayer which coursed through my mind. *"Skree, Skree! V'Razis plyotef sanas ey jari phlu khet djas ma'nuwet!"* Then I thrust the dagger into Andy's heart.

He gasped, I watched as the blood drained from his features, and he exhaled his final breath. For a moment I sat there, alone in the silence with my dead lover, and then the ground began to rumble beneath me, and the stone walls on either side lifted. Moonlight illuminated the chamber and I realized that I had no idea how long I had been trapped. I went to grab Andy's body, intent on carrying him back with me, but the gods forbade me, instructing me to leave him be, to complete the ritual.

With a broken heart, I left and scurried down the steps before I could once again be sealed inside. I crept back down the road and around the small village to the river, to our boats, which I used to travel downriver until I reached a town with electricity and could call for help.

There are reports about the incident in papers and news, but as I mentioned before, they are false. They claim we were attacked by an indigenous tribe, and I was the only one who managed to escape, but there was no cannibalistic tribe that we encountered. We found something much worse.

After returning to the states, and fulfilling my role in the investigation that followed, I, understandably I think, stepped down from my role at the College and went into reclusion. I have ignored all attempts at contact from the media and even the Barkley's, who at this point must assume that no book was discovered. I am writing this memoir to reveal the truth. Though I was driven to the edge of insanity and gazed into the mouth of madness, I am of sound mind. I have the *Lex Tenebrarum* here in my possession, I could not risk it falling into the wrong hands. The book is evil, and I am going to destroy it so it can never be used for the nefarious purposes for which it was created. In my search for this book I lost everything that I had hoped to save. Anyone else who seeks it can expect a similar fate.

There is darkness in this world that will devour you if you let it, that will drain all hope from your body and soul, and make you question the very threads that hold the fabric of your world together. Don't let it. This is what we were born to fight.

After the book is gone, no one will see or hear from me again. I can feel V'Razis' anger with my intentions, and I can sense the looming attempts she will raise to stop me. I pray I won't be too late. I pray the SEO's I have embedded and internet algorithms will lead any who search for V'Razis or the *Lex Tenebrarum* to this site, where they can read my story. I have done all I can, so I leave with you my final warning. Do not try to find it. You will regret it. The thing is cursed. Adieu.

Heather Chaves

I DATED A GIRL from Cambodia who introduced me to Cambodian history and its wonderful ruins. They're beautiful, and I've always wanted to visit them and set a story around those ruins. I don't have much to say about this story other than that it was greatly inspired by Lovecraft. I decided to create my own grimoire, and so I needed an origin story of sorts for it. There is a reference in this story to the Coral Coated Book, which is author Kyle J. Durrant's cursed tome that populates his stories. I thought it would be fun if, like Lovecraft and his cronies, we shared story elements and references. I highly recommend reading his collections of cosmic horror tales, staring with Beyond Dimensional Veils.

THE SPECTACLE AT VANDERBERG MANOR

SCAR'S OLD PICK-UP JOLTED wildly as it careened down a winding and forested hill at illegal speeds, causing Cliff to throw his arms up to keep from being hurled across the backseat. "Watch it!"

Scar only snickered. The truck's bolts groaned as it began to drag itself up another steep incline. The Connecticut woods were full of them. Beside Scar in the passenger seat was Cliff's older sister Willow, two dark braids cascading from underneath her bandana like theatrical tassels. She turned around to face him, her undecorated face simultaneously bearing signs of disappointment and amusement. "Shut up, you little bitch. You wanna join the club, you gotta pass through the gauntlet."

"Is the ride part of the gauntlet?" There were no seatbelts in the backseat of the truck, forcing Cliff to brace himself using his legs and arms. A car on the opposite side of the road flew past them, swerving to avoid a collision and laying on their horn.

"The ride *is* the gauntlet, kid." Scar drove with one hand on the wheel, the other hanging out the window. It was too straight edge to drive with two hands. "If you survive this, the real fun begins."

Cliff's stomach rolled, and he looked back behind him to see if he could glimpse the towering emerald roofs of Foxwoods Casino in the distance, but all he could see were the gnarled slumbering corpses of wintered trees, and the remains of fallen stone walls that used to mean something to someone. Probably the colonial farmers, who had taken their land.

Scar was Willow's boyfriend. His real name wasn't Scar, it was Kevin or some shit like that, but he'd been Scar for as long as Cliff has known him. He had an inch-long scar that ran vertically down his chin, which he claimed he'd received in an underground fight club he'd attended in New London, but Cliff secretly suspected that was a lie. His other identifying mark lay on his ankle, an amateur tattoo of an eye, which he ensured was always visible by wearing pants that were too short. Scar was the leader of the Rez Cats, a gang made exclusively of those who lived on the Pequot Reservation. Willow was the only female member of the gang, an honor she'd snagged for herself as a perk of dating Scar, and now that Cliff was seventeen, it was his turn to step up and join the ranks. That was, if he could pass the initiation.

What that was exactly, Cliff had not been told. Scar liked keeping his initiates in the dark as long as possible. Cliff had been speculating about what it could be for over a week now, his stomach growing constantly tighter as his nerves came to a climax and the date finally arrived. He curled his hands into fists and dug his nails into his skin. He hated going off the reservation. There was irony in there somewhere, as his dad had barely qualified for the reservation's heritage standards, being only 1/16th Native. There were many who claimed that the entire reservation was a fraud and no one there was even descended from the original Pequot tribe. Cliff could continue living there as long as he lived with his parents, but he couldn't buy property of his own. His mom was completely white too, which wasn't strange for members of the reservation, many of them married non-Natives, but it put Cliff in a strange position. He didn't look Native at all except that his skin was a slightly darker shade than most of his friends at school, and yet he'd grown up as part of this tribe and felt connected to this Native identity as it was what he'd been surrounded with and labeled as his entire life. The hardest part was he knew one day he'd have to step away from all that. Joining this gang was both a desperate attempt to cling to his Native identity and also Cliff simply living up to what was expected of him. He'd been hanging out with the gang for years ever since his sister joined, so it had always been his path once he was old enough. Even though Willow treated him like shit and threatened him if he embarrassed her in front of her friends, Cliff wanted to be like her.

Gravel skidded under the truck's flat tires as Scar steered his vehicle off to the side of the road and onto a small dirt turnabout. "Alright, hot stuff. We walk from here."

Cliff was glad to be out of the car. He wasn't a fan of Scar and he liked his driving even less. The November air was brisk as he followed Scar and Willow down a dirt path into the winding woods. Cliff zipped up his plaid jacket and kept his hands shoved into his armpits, keeping his eyes on his sister. Scar happened to glance back and grinned like the devil. "Yo, keep your eyes off my girl's ass, freak." He slid his arm around Willow's butt and squeezed.

Willow elbowed him, but that only encouraged Scar to squeeze harder. "Hey, this is my ass. What are you trying to pull?"

"She's my sister," Cliff muttered under his breath, but he didn't dare speak any louder. They followed the trail beneath a cloudy sky that masked the sun's descent until Cliff could distinguish a structure up ahead. As they grew closer, the details became clear: it was a house, a Queen Anne Victorian house to be exact, painted in fading red and trimmed with white. Gutters were hanging from the sagging roof and the lichen-eaten walls were in dire need of a good power washing, but Cliff still found himself in awe at the ramshackle grandeur of the edifice and imagined how glorious it must have been years ago.

"What an eyesore," Scar scoffed. "Leave it to the crackers to build something as shitty as this. Their buildings are a wound to our land."

And what is Foxwoods, Cliff thought, *is that what our ancestors would have wanted?* Scar was black, but his mom claimed Native heritage. His pretended pride in his Native ancestry was something that irked Cliff to no end. He just as native as Cliff, yet Scar was far more vocal about it.

They were approaching the house from behind, but Cliff could see a gravel driveway snaking its way through the leafless trees, with branches stretching up to the ashy sky like witches fingers. All of a sudden Scar and Willow dove behind a moss covered rock wall, and Cliff followed their lead. Crouching on the damp covering of leaves, he peeked through the rocks to see an elderly woman with flowing white hair in a tan cardigan smoking a cigarette on the back steps.

Cliff's heart began to pound. What if they wanted him to hurt this old lady? They were on her property now. Cliff wanted to prove himself and join the gang, but he didn't want to end up in jail in the process!

The scent of tobacco smoke wafted through the air. "Man, I could use one of those right now." Willow hunkered down against the wall, trying to stay warm.

Cliff kept his eyes on the woman until she stomped out her cigarette and stepped inside through a billowing sheer curtain.

"Perfect," Scar hissed. "She left the door wide open." He turned to Cliff. "Here's what you gotta do, little man. Sneak inside and take something from that house. It's gotta be valuable, something we can sell. You gotta choose wisely, cuz if you pick something that ain't worth shit, it don't count."

Cliff looked to Willow, whose eyes actually expressed a gleam of sympathy. "That's it?" He asked. "Just take something, and I'm in?"

"That's it," Scar confirmed. "Easy, peezy, right?"

Cliff took a deep breath. He had no weapons on him, that was part of the deal. If they got nabbed for trespassing, he didn't want to add being armed to the charges anyway.

"Don't piss your pants, squirt. We're coming in too," Willow gave Cliff a dead arm.

"Really?"

"You don't think we'd let you go in on your own, do you? We gotta protect our investment, plus there might be more shit we can steal. First thing you gotta learn about the Rez Cats is we stick together. That being said, first sign of danger, we outta there. You fall behind, you're on your own, cuz." Scar clapped Cliff on the back, then hopped over the wall.

Willow crept after Scar, and Cliff followed behind them. He kept his eyes on the ground, doing his best to avoid crunching leaves. Scar peeked in through the open back door, curtain billowing in the crisp breeze, then beckoned for them to follow as he slipped inside. Cliff scraped his boots on the stone steps, took a deep breath, and forced himself to step into the void.

At first, Cliff couldn't see anything. Heavy curtains were pulled over all the windows, and no lights were turned on in the house, filling his view with a stagnant gloom, causing his eyes to play tricks on him. There were several moments when he thought he saw inhuman faces peering at him from the darkness. Then, gradually, his vision began to adjust and he noticed that he was in a cramped hallway with intricate wood trimming and a crimson red patterned wallpaper.

Willow glanced over her shoulder at Cliff, noticing the force with which he was clenching his jaw. "You good, homes?"

"Yeah," Cliff managed to mutter. "Just feels wrong, ya know?"

"It's not wrong," Scar hissed. "This land belongs to us, so does everything on it."

Scar stopped, then rotated on his heels, facing Willow and Cliff. "I'm gonna go ahead, scope the place out. You two check these rooms on the right." He motioned to a couple of doorways that they had walked past but Cliff had completely missed, caught up in his own thoughts, then Scar vanished into another room.

"You and me, chump," Willow whispered, not trying at all to hide her disdain at her predicament of being stuck with Cliff. "Check that table."

Before Cliff could protest, Willow was moving into one of the rooms. Cliff turned and spotted a small table against the wall of the hallway. Atop it sat an old lamp and several unopened letters. There was one small drawer in the table, and Cliff checked there first. The drawer was empty except for a six inch long sword. In reality it was a letter opener, but Cliff just assumed it was a toy or replica and shoved it into his pocket. As he did he felt the tip and winced, as a single drop of blood ran down his finger. He sucked on his finger while he rummaged through the pile of mail. There were bills, magazines, and other papers, all addressed to Morgan or Katrina Vanderberg. Not finding anything particularly interesting, Cliff moved on, stopping to examine a series of framed photographs hung on the wall. There were two young blonde girls, one lithe and thin, the other curvy with wide hips. They had their arms around each other, and as Cliff ran his eyes across the photos, he could almost see them aging, it was like watching a lifetime play out before him.

THUMP! Cliff nearly jumped out of his skin. He scurried after Willow, passing through a sitting room, and found himself in another hall. This place was a lot bigger inside than it looked. There was an alcove directly in front of him, not quite a room, as there was no door, but large enough that it had its own ceiling and a few feet of space to maneuver. Cliff was drawn to the alcove by the overhead light that shone down on the space's central display: a petrified mummy resting upright in a stone sarcophagus, sealed behind a glass case.

"Whoa." Cliff had never seen a real mummy before. The corpse was massive, even in death, it towered over Cliff. He could only imagine how large the figure must have been in life. He found himself studying the creature's face, unable to look away, the shriveled features and sunken eyes, the jaw warped eternally open as if in a scream of agony. Poking out from a small tear in the cloth was what Cliff could only assume was a human tooth, a glimpse behind the veil of this horrific monstrosity. He shivered involuntarily and remembered that he still had to find Willow. He had to find some kind of object and ditch this house of horrors. What kind of freak would want something like that displayed in their home?

Cliff followed the hall and stopped abruptly when a staircase opened on his right, leading up to the second story. Listening closely, Cliff heard muttering voices, and thinking that it might be Willow and Scar, he ascended, stepping lightly to mask his presence.

The voices were coming from a door that was cracked open along the upper hall. Cliff loitered outside the door, straining to catch what was being said.

"This life is beginning to wear on me, sister. I must confess that I do not believe we will see their return in the flesh..."

"It was promised, my dear. The Great Old Ones do not go back on their promises. They will reward us for our service."

"I want that day to come, and I want you by my side when it does."

"Always, my love. We are one."

Cliff peered through the crack and saw the old woman from before kneeling in front of another gray haired woman in a rocking chair. He watched as their lips met in a sensuous embrace, before the kneeling woman's eyes flickered to the doorway and met his own. Cliff instinctively pulled away and pressed his back flat to the wall, but it was too little too late. There was a shrill cry from the room and Cliff scrambled, hunting for a way out.

He tore open a door around the corner and pulled it mostly closed. He was in some kind of stuffy closet, something warm and itchy pressed itself against the back of his neck and he found it hard to breathe, but Cliff stood still as a statue, praying that he wouldn't be discovered. This was not what he had signed up for!

"*Skree Skree, Shub Niggurath!* An intruder! Quickly, we must perform the ritual!"

"No, there must be another way."

"There is no other way, sister. Give me your hand."

There was a sharp cry, followed by chanting in a language that Cliff did not understand. He heard shuffling, a door open and close, and then a flurry of footsteps descending the stairs.

Instead of coming after him, they were leaving! This was his lucky break. Cliff slid out of the closet and poked his head back into the room where the sisters had been. There was a dagger lying on the chair, tip painted with blood, and on the floor were strange runes and symbols which appeared to have been hastily scrawled in the same substance.

The scene before him began to vanish before his eyes, as a thick cloud of mist seemed to enter the room. At first, Cliff assumed it must be smoke from a fire, but the cloud did not smell like smoke, rather it had a musty and moist odor, as if he were standing in a swamp. Within seconds, his visibility shrank to only a foot or two in front of him.

What was this witchery? Cliff felt his way blindly for the stairs and descended. He heard his name being called and followed the sound, turning corners and entering rooms until he found Willow. She took his hands and pulled him into an adjacent room, then shut the door. The fog was not so thick here, and there appeared to be only one entrance.

"I saw someone. Two old hags, upstairs. They were talking in another language!"

Willow's eyes momentarily displayed her concern, but she wiped it away as she waved the smoke from her face and motioned around the room. "Whatever. Just grab something and we'll bail. Look."

Cliff took in his surroundings for the first time and saw that they were in some kind of occult museum. The room was large, at least forty feet across and thirty wide. There were shelves and glass display cases hosting all kinds of curiosities and strange items, bookcases overflowing with ancient tomes written in forgotten languages and paintings hanging on the wall depicting carnivorous dog creatures and macabre monstrosities too horrible to describe. Cliff passed through the room, a stranger in a strange land, observing each mist shrouded commodity with curiosity and a glimmer of fear. The billowing cloud gave this space an otherworldly atmosphere, and Cliff felt as if he were walking through a dream. He scanned the titles of several leather bound books displayed under a glass case, reading the names to himself as his eyes scanned the words, *The Necronomicon, Lex Tenebrarum, The Book of Eibon*...some of the books looked like they might be worth something, but he wasn't sure. He passed by a statue of a faceless figure in a dark robe, tentacles protruding from the bottom where its feet should be and realized he was getting a headache. Was it the mist or the stress? Maybe both. Cliff arrived at an open shelf with several shimmering objects and decided to grab something, this was as good as it was going to get. He tried to appraise the things in his mind, but had no idea what a black trapezohedron, a brain in a cylinder, or a tarnished silver key would be worth. What he ended up selecting was a palm sized gold jewel carved intricately into the shape of an eye.

He took the eye because he knew the value of gold, but after looking at it, he saw that it was in fact quite beautiful. The eye was simple enough, a pupil and iris gazing forever outwards, causing Cliff to grow increasingly uncomfortable until he turned the thing over. There was no eyelid, but around the eye, and on the backside were complex and labyrinthine carvings, symbols and hieroglyphics interwoven with decorative flourishes and pictures of nameless beasts. The eye was mesmerizing, and when he looked again into its lidless face Cliff also felt as if it were gazing back into him. He shuddered, suddenly feeling vulnerable and violated.

His trance was broken by the shattering of glass. Cliff pocketed the eye and rushed out the door to find shards of jagged glass scattered across the carpeted floor. His eyes followed the trail to its inevitable end...*an empty sarcophagus!*

Cliff turned to warn Willow, but there was already a hand extending toward her out of the fog. Cliff screamed —

As Scar's hand clamped down on her shoulder. Even Willow jumped. "Geez, Scar. You scared the shit outta me."

"What the hell's going on here? Did the old lady turn on a fog machine or something?" He smacked Cliff's shoulder with the back of his hand without waiting for an answer. "Did you get it?"

"Yeah."

"Good, let's get the hell outta here." Scar shoved Cliff aside, pushing past him down the hall.

There was something else, another sound that Cliff's mind had registered but hadn't paid any notice to yet. Footsteps, shuffling over carpet. Scar had hardly taken two steps when bandaged hands found his throat and shoved him hard back against the wall. Scar fought to break free, but the thing's hands were too powerful. Finally Scar managed to bring his leg up and kick the thing away from him. But it was only a momentary victory. The dark, looming shape wrenched Scar back as he attempted to flee and in one quick, violent motion, snapped Scar's neck!

Scar's limp body drooped and sunk to the floor. Willow's mouth hung agape, too terrified to scream. The shape stepped closer through the fog, continuing its morbid mission, and revealed itself to Cliff in its full and unholy form, though he already knew what it was: *a walking mummy.*

Cliff shoved Willow, forcing her feet to move, then allowed her to take his hand and pull him behind her as she fled down the hallway through a series of mist-shrouded rooms toward the back of the house. All the while Cliff listened, his ears grasping the shuffling of feet that still pursued them, though their attacker was no longer visible.

Willow burst into the back room, and flung herself at the door, only to be met with a resounding crash of a clattering metal gate that was blocking their escape. It was a security gate, not uncommon to have in one's house, but Cliff and the others had completely failed to notice it on their way in! Willow shook the gate violently, creating a loud ruckus, but the gate was locked tight. With that option unavailable, Cliff turned to the windows, only to find that they too, were blocked with security gates. Unbelievable!

Willow found Cliff in the dismal fog and took him by the shoulders. He looked into her eyes for the first time in months and saw real emotion, fear. "What is that thing?"

"A mummy," Cliff muttered. "I saw it earlier."

"You saw it walking around and you didn't say anything?"

"No, it wasn't walking around! It was dead!"

"Yeah, well clearly it *wasn't* dead!"

Cliff shoved her away. "Don't blame this on me! I'm not the one who chose this house with the reanimated mummy for my initiation! Nice one."

Willow wiped a tear from her cheek as she straightened her bandana. "Screw you. Scar is...he's..."

Cliff felt a rush of empathy as he remembered the tragic events which had happened only moments ago. "He's gone." He took a step toward his sister. "And we will be too if we don't get out of here. Come on, there's got to be another way."

As Cliff took Willow's hand, a malicious cackle rang throughout the house. From somewhere in the corpse haunted estate, a door slammed.

And there was another sound. The shuffling! The creature had finally caught up with them.

Emerging through the primordial mist like a being from another dimension, the mummy, arms stretched outward, descended upon Cliff and Willow. With all their exits blocked, Willow picked up a wicker chair and held the legs out at the creature. The mummy took hold of the legs, managing to rip the chair from Willow's grasp, but not before she used her momentum to spin around the mummy so that she and Cliff, who clung to her like a shadow, were now facing the entrance to the hallway. The mummy hurled the chair against the wall, but Willow and Cliff were already running blindly through the ever thickening clouds.

"We're never going to find a way out of here!" Cliff wailed, hanging onto Willow's jean jacket.

"Shut up. In here, let's go." Willow shoved Cliff into a room and shut the door behind them. She fumbled with the doorknob, and cheered under her breath as she found that the door actually locked. They had managed to buy themselves some time, but they were also trapped, as Cliff realized by looking around at the small dining room. It was a dead end.

There was a single window against the opposite wall, which, surprise surprise, was covered by a metal cage. Cliff cut through the mist and inspected the cage more closely, looking for a weakness. Instead he found that the corners were bolted deep into the wall, without the proper tools, there would be no opening the cage. He slammed his fists against the cage in frustration, sending it rattling, and slumped down against the wall. Willow joined him, and for a moment they sat in silence, two siblings lost in their own existential thoughts, as they awaited their inevitable doom.

Finally, Willow broke the silence. "How long do you think we have before it finds us?"

Cliff snorted. "Minutes, maybe."

Willow stared off into space, clutching her legs to her chest, rocking slowly back and forth like a mental patient. "I'm sorry that Scar and I treated you like shit. I guess I haven't been very cool to you..."

Cliff had never heard his sister apologize to him before, not since they were little kids and their mom made them. This was sincere. "It's whatever," he said, trying to play it off. "Thanks for trying to get me into the Rez Cats."

Willow chuckled. "You shouldn't be thanking me for that. They're a joke."

"Yeah, well you were in it. I just wanted to be like you."

"You shouldn't always do everything I do. You're better off doing your own thing. For real. And now that Scar's gone...I guess I'm out too."

Cliff wasn't sure what to say for a moment. He'd imagined them together, chilling with the gang, for months. "Killed by a mummy... not how I thought I'd go out."

Willow laughed, it reminded Cliff of how she used to laugh when they were kids. "Right? Like, what the hell?"

The door thumped as something slammed on it from the other side. Slowly, Willow and Cliff rose in unison. She looked at Cliff and he looked at her, and he knew they were thinking the same damn thing. "You ready?" The slamming on the door grew more impetuous and frequent, and Cliff guessed they only had a few moments left.

"Yeah. Rez Cat's ain't going down without a fight. *Hoo-ah-hhhh!*" Willow raised her fists, sinking into a fighter's stance as the door burst open.

What happened next was a blur. Cliff and Willow both charged at the mummy, but all Cliff remembered was feeling strong hands hoist him by the shirt and fling him against the wall. He blacked out for a moment, and when he opened his eyes, he saw through blurred vision, Willow being dragged off by the monster, whose massive arm held her tightly against its torso. He saw her legs kick wildly, her fingers grasp for the doorframe and then tear free. Cliff heard his name being called in high pitched squeals as his panicked sister was ripped away from him.

Cliff struggled to his feet and immediately fell down, too dizzy to stand, his head throbbing where it had struck the wall. He could feel a bump forming and absently wondered if he had a con-cussion. He waited a moment for his head to calm, until he could wait no longer, and with his head still spinning, climbed carefully to his feet. He went slower this time, with one hand against the wall for balance he edged into the hall, gliding through the mist, not knowing his destination. There were no more screams. No footprints or signs to follow. He was lost in a maze that had no es cape.

After a few minutes of aimless searching, Cliff began to call Willow's name. There was no response. The witch sisters were gone, too. He was all alone.

Cliff sat on the floor, the fog crowding in around him, suffocating him like an airless tomb. With no other recourse he pulled out the golden eye and held it in his hand. There was no point in keeping it, it could not help him escape, and it could not help him join the Rez Cats, and it could not help him find his sister. All of this, his entire predicament, he blamed on the eye. He was about to cast it into the fog when he noticed that on one end there was a tiny clasp, a hinge, that allowed the eye to open lengthwise. Cliff carefully played with the eye until he managed to slide one half open, revealing a glowing stone, hidden inside the eye. The glow lit up the whole hallway, and seemed to dispel the mists of darkness. As he reached his finger out to touch the ancient form of illumination, his soul was rekindled with a feeling of hope, that perhaps things might be okay after all. The stone was warm to the touch, and he resolved that he was going to keep searching. This must be some kind of sign. *Don't give up on her. Don't give up on you.*

Raised voices and mechanical slamming reached his ears, and Cliff took the stone and used it to guide himself toward the sounds. They led him to a sealed gate, but on the other side he saw a set of stairs descending down into some kind of basement. He sensed intrinsically that Willow was down there, and that was where he had to go. The gate was locked, Cliff had been here before. But with no other option, and his sister on the line, Cliff backed up against the wall and flung himself against the metal gate. The gate rattled, but did not give way. Undeterred, Cliff tried again, throwing his body as hard as he could against the gate, until miraculously, the gate itself broke, and Cliff's body fell through it, tumbling down the stairs to the cold stone floor.

There was no longer any hope of surprising whoever was down there, as his fall no doubt alerted them of his arrival. Before he could even stand up, bandaged hands grabbed Cliff and restrained his arms, then proceeded to drag him down a dark subterranean passage. The stone had fallen from his hand, and he watched as the light diminished the further they traveled. The tunnel was made of rock, that much he could tell; the ceiling was arched, and water dripped on him occasionally, and he could feel his shoes passing over cobbled stones. Whatever this place was, it was old.

At last Cliff saw light beginning to illuminate the passage again and he was pulled into a larger room, with torches on sconces lighting the ancient chamber. He had found Willow, but he was too late, as the Vanderberg sisters were in the process of wrapping her in burial rags, her body splayed out on an altar. Willow's eyes found Cliff's, pleading silently for assistance which he could not give. He jerked as hard as he could, but the mummy held him firm. If he didn't do something soon, these hags would soon have another mummy for their collection. As they worked, they chanted in a forgotten language, filling his soul with dread.

It was then, in his moment of utmost despair, that Cliff remembered the letter opener he had stashed in his pocket. His arms were pinned, but his right hand could almost reach his pocket where he could feel the sharp prick of the sword jabbing into his thigh. He repositioned himself, and gripped the sword. He spun the blade deftly in his fingers, and stabbed it into the mummy's hand. He wasn't sure if it caused the thing pain or not, but it was enough of a shock that it caused the mummy to let go of him for a moment, and that moment was all he needed. He burst free of his captor's grasp, spun, and rammed the letter opener into the mummy's eye socket. It flailed,

blindly attempting to pull the thing from its face with bandaged hand
s.

Cliff tore one of the torches off the wall and held it out in front of him, thrusting it at the mummy who was lumbering toward him, its ancient wrappings instantly going up in flame, turning it into an undead pyre.

Cliff swung the torch at the sisters, but they did not flinch. He moved around the burning mummy to his sister's side, who was using his diversion to pull her legs out of the wrapped cloth.

There was a shift in the language spoken by the old women, and Cliff sensed that they had begun to evoke a new evil. Slowly, as if by some unseen sorcery, Cliff's torch began to die. He had time to give Willow a look of utter and desperate terror before they were plunged into infinite darkness. The darkness of the pit, where no light could enter. They were deep underground, trapped with two dangerous witches, capable of unknowable magic. And now they were blind. What could they possibly do? Cliff and Willow found each other in the darkness and held each other tight.

Their world became a blur of sensual experiences of which Cliff had never before partaken, and never would again. Strange sounds that were unlike anything earthly rose to his ears, he felt something slimy run past his arm in the dark, something was there in the room with him, but there was no way of knowing what it was. Light erupted into being, filling the room with a whirlwind of colors that Cliff did not know existed, the sisters were gone, as was the mummy, but in their place was something even more horrifying, something that caused his sister to scream. As Cliff looked at her, he saw only a reflection in her eye, the outline of an impossible shape that floated in the room several feet above the floor. Her eyes were wide with terror and awe, her mouth hanging open, unable to look away. Her entire body was quivering from the powerful experience, and Cliff had to physically pull her off the altar and force her to look at him, at which point she seemed to return to herself and together, they ran up a set of stairs on the far side of the room, the phantasmagorical colors still swirling around them, and arrived at a metal bulkhead door, which they threw open, permitting them to exit into the fresh air and free world.

The bulkhead door was in the middle of the woods, but eventually, after stumbling through the dark and cutting themselves on prickers, they found the Vanderberg house again and were able to make it back to the road.

As they hobbled back toward the reservation Willow at one point stopped, and the look of terror returned to her face as she gazed upon the road ahead of them.

"What's wrong?" Cliff asked.

"You don't see it?"

"See what?"

"The eye!" Willow's gaze was fixed before them, at the empty road. Cliff saw nothing. "It followed us, from that place..." She sank into an inconsolable babbling, and Cliff guided her around the invisible obstruction, forcing her to continue their trek, until she calmed down, and at last, they arrived at home.

They were done with the gang after that. Willow began going to therapy, but every so often he would find her staring off into the distance at nothing in particular. On multiple occasions he stumbled upon her late at night, scribbling in a notebook and muttering to herself. At one point curiosity got the better of him and he snuck into her room while she was out and opened one of the notebooks. It was the same line, written over and over again.

We are always being watched.

Eventually Willow left the reservation and Cliff stayed to care for their ailing dad. He didn't hear from her much after that, though on the rare occasions when he did she was kind to him. That night in the manor had repaired their relationship in a way that Cliff had never hoped for, unfortunately it had also broken Willow in a way he could never have imagined. Whatever she had seen, or thought she had seen, was haunting her. That much was clear. What little Cliff did know of his sister's whereabouts was mostly from postcards or late night phone calls that didn't last long. He knew she was traveling around, and he always encouraged her to come home.

"I can't." She would always say.

"Why not?"

"You know why."

Sometimes she would call him in the middle of a panic attack, and he would have to talk her down. He was the only one who could, the only one who would understand, even if he didn't truly understand.

Despite Willow's sporadic drifting and frequent panic attacks, Cliff had always remained optimistic about her future. He often thought about the light he had seen, and guessed that maybe the light had changed him, given him a glimpse of something pure and peaceful, something that might one day be but was not yet. Willow was out of the gang, she was out on her own, financially independent, and he hoped that one day she would settle down, and maybe therapy or medication would be able to help her mental state improve.

Which was why he was shocked when one morning he received a phone call informing him that Willow was dead.

Cliff flew out to Arizona later that day, where he met with local police, and identified her body at the hospital morgue. According to the report, she had been discovered by a maid, murdered in her hotel room. The police had no leads, other than their guess that the suspect was male. Willow had been strangled to death, and her neck bore deep bruises, the size of which suggested the killer had large hands. Only two other items were found in the room. One of them was a small piece of old linen cloth of questionable origin, perhaps torn from the attacker, though after observation, it was determined the cloth would not help them solve the murder.

The other item that was presented to Cliff was an envelope addressed to him. The police assured him they had not opened it, but were eager for him to do so, as they hoped that it might give them a clue as to what had occurred.

They left Cliff alone in a room at the police station with the letter. It was all that he had left of his sister, and Cliff took his time to open it, only to scoff at its contents, while at the same time, an icy claw of terror wormed its way into his heart.

The envelope contained a single sheet of paper, and as Cliff unfolded it, saw that it bore no words, but only a single, familiar image. It was the same image he thought he had seen reflected in Willow's pupils that night at Vanderberg manor, but which he had convinced himself had been a trick of the light.

It was the singular illustration, drawn by Willow's own hand, of a horrific, levitating eye.

STORY NOTES

THERE ARE A FEW inspirations for this story. The film *Don't Breathe* is one of them — I love the idea of thieves breaking into a house, only to find themselves trapped inside and at the mercy of some darker abomination. While reading Lovecraft and playing the Call of Cthulhu video game the idea grew in my mind that it would be interesting if these thieves came across a museum of Lovecraftian artifacts, and the owner of the house was a collector of supernatural objects. Naturally, their trespassing and tampering with these objects would awaken some horrific being which would terrorize them. I've always loved mummy stories and wanted to write one of my own, and the elements came together. I grew up near Foxwoods and the Pequot Reservation in Connecticut and heard about the Rez Cats, even went to school with some kids from the Reservation, and I thought they would make interesting characters. This story first appeared as an audio recording on the Lunatics Radio Hour Podcast in their episode featuring "Mummy Stories."

THE DRUMS

"Are you Richard Mathus?"

The man sitting in the flowery armchair by the window glanced up from his reverie to find a healthy looking woman standing before him. He hadn't seen a healthy looking woman in weeks. She had her curly hair pulled back into a bun, and was wearing a trench coat, drenched at the shoulders, which was currently draped over her body. Around her eyes she wore heavy eyeshadow that upon first impression, he felt made her look like a rockstar.

"Yes," the man called Richard Mathus whispered, his voice barely audible. "Who are you?"

"I'm Leslie Shaw, writer for the Ingram Investigator." She thrust forth a gloved hand, and Richard shook it limply. His eyes flickered to the visitor badge pinned to her coat. "I heard about you from a friend of mine who lives upstate." She thought the man in the chair was thin, perhaps dangerously so, with narrow fingers and a long face that was clean shaven and eyes that had seen too much. He wore a winter hat and was dressed in clothes that had once been white.

Richard regarded the woman in reluctant silence, like a cat arching its back, caught unawares and easily spooked, suspicious of any suggestion of movement. His fingers dug into the upholstery of the armchair.

"May I sit?" Without waiting for a reply, Leslie sat in the vacant armchair beside Richard. The chair was old and sagging, with gashes torn deep in the lining, but Leslie didn't seem to mind. She crossed her legs and with her hands hidden beneath expensive leather gloves, removed a small notebook and pen while maintaining eye contact with Richard.

"You seem guarded. I'm not here to judge, Richard. Just understand."

"Are you a cop?" His nervous eyes never seemed to stop moving.

"No, just a reporter." Her smile was like soothing aloe on a sunburn.

"The cops didn't believe me."

"Well, I'll believe you," she assured him, though he didn't see how she could keep a promise like that.. "It must be hard, to have been through so much only to be ridiculed. A heavy burden to bear. I'll share that burden with you."

Richard's hands relaxed, and he folded his arms, another nervous tick. "Alright."

"Alright? Okay." The click of a pen. "How long have you been here, in Rock Harbor Hospital?"

"Just call it what it is — a loony bin." His eyes flashed conscientiously toward the other patients around the common area. Some were engaged in leisure activities like reading or games, but others, bearing the mark of their mental deficiencies, were fidgeting strangely, wandering aimlessly, or uttering nonsense that no one but themselves could understand.

"I'm not calling it that, because that's not what it is. It's a hospital for sick people. Now, how long have you been here?"

Richard shook his head, glancing out the window at the overcast sky. "I came here in February. What's the date today?"

"October tenth. It is my understanding that you are being hunted, and that you hear things, things no one else can hear. Is that correct?"

Richard nodded, his face scrunching with emotion.

"What do you hear, Richard?"

For the first time he looked her directly in the eyes, and as he spoke, felt the burden of loneliness lift ever so slightly. "Drums. I hear drums. Pounding, always pounding, like some tribal horde is about to descend upon me."

Leslie scribbled like a madwoman. "When did you first hear them? Tell me everything."

Richard did.

"I don't remember the day, or the month, or even the year. I don't remember anything before it started, or even after, since arriving here. My life is one great blur and I lack the glasses to see it clear. But this much I can tell you — it began in dreams.

"The dreams I can recall clearly, though I wish very much that I could forget. I can see the stark, unblemished details now in my mind's eye, and I wish there was a way for me to share the memories with you, as no words can possibly hope to do the thing justice.

"But you asked for everything, and so I will do my best. You are the only visitor I have had in all my time here, and I do not want to disappoint you.

"The dreams were the same every night. Countless journeys I made into that foul, nameless abyss, and countless nights I lay awake, dreading my inevitable return.

"Every night I found myself flying over a crimson sea, dark, tumultuous waves licking up to drag me down to the depths. And before me, stretched an endless wall of featureless rock. No cliff in life has ever been so devoid of life and signs of natural erosion, but I know what I saw.

"And atop this impossible plateau, sat the city. Half hidden by an undead mist, towers and battlements protruding at odd angles, a city that stretched beyond imagining, out of sight. I have never seen architecture like it, no, not in this world.

"And it is from this haunted city that the drums called to me.

"I do not know their source, and do not wish to know, for I know that if I were to glimpse it, my mind would truly be gone. From which wicked chasm doth foul protuberance ring? I only know that that place is evil. That place is death. There are powers in this world of which humanity is wholly ignorant. This world is not our own, no matter how much we may think it is so. I have stepped beyond the veil, unwillingly, and glimpsed horrors that haunt my every waking moment, and I have felt the terrible isolation that comes with this knowledge. Even if I tell others of my tale, they do not believe me, and even if they did believe me, they would wish they had never known me. I have thought of taking my life, and even tried a time or two, but those blasted orderlies are too good at their jobs. I'm sorry, I've lost focus. You don't want to hear about this. I dare not tell you what else I see in my dreams. But it is not merely in the sleeping world that my suffering has taken shape.

"Whether on the first night, or the hundredth, I became aware that the drums had followed me out of my dreams and into the waking world. They were not my constant companions, at least, not at first. The occurrences were random, and gradually I began to stay inside out of fear of being assaulted by phantom abominations.

"It's funny, the more I speak of it, the more I seem to remember. I remember walking down a puddle ridden forest road, and nearly jumping out of my skin as the fierce beating began. The noise nearly gave me a heart attack. I turned, but there was nothing behind me — no source for the sound which was so loud and clear that I had no choice but to assume that its source was hidden. I ran for home, locking the door behind me.

"Then again, at the university while in the middle of a lecture, I heard them return, suddenly and without warning. Irritably, I asked for whoever was making that racket if they would please stop. All I received in return was blank faces.

"'What racket?' One student dared to ask.

"'The drums!' I cried, 'Those infernal drums!'

"Those blank faces expressed concern, and it was then that I understood that I was the only one who could hear them!

"My reclusivity increased, foolishly I believed I would be safe in my home. Bah! It was there that I was least safe! It was there that I was closest to my bedroom, and in my bedroom, closest to my dreams!

"You think me mad? Perhaps I am. But I had enough cognizance left unhindered that I understood my mental state was on a downward spiral. Tormented by sleepless dreams and wracked by ceaseless horrors, even within the walls of my own home and sanctuary, I had no recourse left but to seek professional help.

"For the first time in my life I visited a psychiatrist. I had always thought they were money grubbing hacks, and I still share that opinion, but I knew no hospital could cure my symptoms — mine was a malady of the mind.

"During my first and only visit, I recounted my journeyings to that wretched city and the drums that would not give me peace. And what does the doctor say? She tells me that the dreams have no inherent meaning, but are most likely an indicator of my stress and anxiety-ridden mind, manifesting itself through my subconscious. And then she dismissed me with a prescription for sleeping pills!

"The insult! Sleeping pills? I tore the note to pieces the instant I stepped out the door. Indeed, I suffered from insomnia, but I had no desire to return to that city, nor meet its polluted denizens who dwelt there-in.

"No, more sleep was not the answer to my problem. If science could not help me, perhaps a solution could be found among the occult and pseudosciences. Not knowing much about these areas, I turned to the internet.

"I shared my story in several chatrooms and online forums, hoping a scattershot approach would yield some results. I received many responses and comments, most of them unhelpful. But there was one that seemed promising.

"She called herself Angelina, and shared with me her own experiences of how she had dreamed of a similar city, and how she was haunted not by drums, but by a mysterious and incessant chanting, as if a cacophony of voices were performing some kind of arcane ritual in a forgotten tongue.

A *summoning*, she called it.

We exchanged numbers and that night, we spoke on the phone for hours. Angelina lived across the country from me, in New England. She was a writer. She had been doing research of her own, checking out occult books from the library and consulting with those knowledgeable in the mystic arts and preternatural phenomena, though whom, she would not say. However, it was in a library archive that she had found her answers. The diary and papers of a deceased professor by the name of George Angell from 1926. The account detailed the man's research into the Cthulhu Cult and included a dream journal of people from across the globe, documenting in detail the vivid dreams of many whose nightly wanderings bore striking similarities to our own. Dreams of a cyclopean city with nonsensical geometry...

"*Cthulhu...*

"Why did that name strike such dread in my heart? Why did it feel so familiar yet so perverse?

"Angelina and I conversed a few more times, two isolated souls desperately clinging to driftwood in the undying storm. We talked at length about what that journal could mean. It meant that others had once experienced something similar, and there was some solace in that. As we continued to explore the legends and lore surrounding that dreadful city of R'lyeh and its abhorrent host, Cthulhu, we learned much and our utmost fear was that even a grain of it might be true.

"There is much I might tell you, though I dare not implicate you further. It is best that I harbor these nightmares and hidden secrets. Suffice it to say, that according to legend, Cthulhu is a god from another time and place, who once ruled over Earth from his throne in R'lyeh, eons before the first human ever stalked these haunted shores. He is said to be of unimaginable size, vaguely humanoid in shape with tentacles sprouting from his massive head, and a pair of bat-like wings protruding from his back. It is whispered that he still lies, slumbering under the sea, awaiting the day of his return. These are not well documented, but there are many supposed groups who know of this sleeping god, and worship him by offering sacrifices of flesh.

"As Angelina and I continued our discourse, our relationship and dependence on one another deepened, and the dreams and pounding of the drums grew worse and more intense.

"Then Angelina stopped answering my calls.

"She didn't respond to my many messages either, and fearing the worst, my one remaining beacon of hope torn so suddenly away from me, I sank into a decadent pit of alcoholism.

"Long I languored and languished there, until I determined that my soul would not rest until I knew what had happened to her. I sobered up, booked the next flight to New York, rented a car with my dwindling savings, and drove upstate to the address she had provided me.

"I found the front door ajar and the house, vacant. Small rodents who had taken up residence scurried out of sight upon my arrival, and a bird who must have entered through the entryway, fluttered frenziedly above my head. The front hall was a bed of leaves which had blown inside, letting me know she had not been back in some time. After I received no response to my shouts, I ventured inside uninvited and found an office upstairs where it was clear she had been doing her research. Hefty tomes lay open, heavily marked, and the walls were plentifully bestrewn with papers tacked over each other, bizarre, nonsensical scribblings and etchings of abominations too odious to describe.

"But it was a note, a single slip of paper, tucked between two books, that truly caught my attention.

"It was addressed to me.

"*Richard, do not fear him. We were wrong. A.*

"How many times I reread that message, trying to decipher its meaning, it's impossible to say. What had changed Angelina's mind regarding our shared tribulation? What had happened to her? And if she had learned something critical, why had she not told me?

"Questions. Questions that had no answers. Night had fallen around me and I did not perceive the change. I might have sat there the whole night long, if the familiar fleeting of those horrid drums had not brought me unkindly back to myself.

"*Those accursed drums!*

"Never had they felt closer, and yet more distant. I found a flashlight in the kitchen and followed the sound into the backyard, where there was a well trodden trail leading into the woods. I felt drawn down this path, as if all my life had been leading me to this crucial moment.

"Cautiously, I entered those woods, my light casting strangling shadows of gnarled branches and writhing limbs against the endless sea of leaves and hollows. Dimly I became aware of another sound intermingled with those drums.

"A chanting, a jarring rift of human voices, crying out inharmoniously into the void.

"And those drums, pounding, dancing, crashing, calling to me and leading me toward my doom. Beckoning me with *doom, doom, doom,* and yet my feet carried me on. I felt powerless to stop them. My will had become consumed into one greater than my own.

"Something wanted me there.

"*He* wanted me.

"The thought thrilled me and chilled me in equal measure. Gradually, I became aware of a faint glow through the trees, and I switched off my light, drawing close and crouching behind a bush.

"The light arose from a giant bonfire, and around it, the silhouettes of people. Some of them danced, flinging their arms toward the sky in a frightening ritual, others played the drums, though they did not look like any drums I had ever seen. I soon noticed that there were other shapes in the darkness as well. Human bodies had been hung upside down from tree branches surrounding the camp, their arms dangling earthward toward puddles of blood, their forms swinging uncannily in the evening breeze. The worshippers all stood beneath a flat rock face, thirty feet high, and on it was painted a horribly lifelike image of what I recognized instantly as Cthulhu.

"The drums stopped without warning, leaving me in a foreign silence. Only the crackling of the fire was left for my company. It was a silence I had not felt in what seemed many lifetimes.

"All the faces in the clearing were now looking in my direction. Looking at me. I realized this too late. My heart began to pound, but my feet were frozen to the ground.

"'Richard Mathus!' A female voice, cracked and guttural, called from the crowd. 'Come forth!'

"I had been found out! My mind was a rush of cluttered thoughts, and so anxious that I thought nothing as I stepped into the open and stood before the quorum of cloaked figures, whose faces I could not see.

"'You have been summoned by the great Cthulhu. Chosen in dream, to be one of his disciples, to help shape the world for his return.'

"The speaker stepped forward, and flinging back her hood, revealed her face.

"*Angelina!*

"My soul was struck as if by a dagger at her betrayal. I thought to berate her, but I was speechless. I was then wracked with another thought, even more terrifying. If they could convince her to join them, what was to stop them from convincing *me* as well?

"As if sensing my thoughts, she continued. 'He is the way, Richard. We were wrong to fear him. He offers us the honor of being his servants as he retakes the world. An eternal place at his side. You will see such wonders! I have never felt such physical pleasures as I now enjoy!' She bit her lip and moaned carnally, as she offered me a goblet filled with what I surmised was brackened seawater, which reeked of foul fish and rotting flesh. The liquid was black as the night that echoed around us. 'Drink, and join us. Join *me*. Worship him with us, and put your tortures to rest.'

"I took the cup. I cannot deny that I felt a tingle of attraction to the obscenities she was spewing. Angelina was my only friend, not unattractive as physical appearances go, and the idea of joining her was seductive, but what I desperately wished for more than anything was for there to be an end to my torment!

"I almost drank, if only to find peace. But at the last moment one of the other cultists twisted in the light from the raging fire, and I saw, glistening beneath their hood, a squirming tangle of tentacles!

"The horror of that image caused me to drop the cup, and I knew that my choice had been made. 'No. I can't,' I told them, 'I won't!'

"Angelina's face became a furrowed screen of anger. 'You cannot run,' she hissed, 'He has chosen you. He will not let you go!'

"The voices began chanting again. *'Ph'nglui mglw'nafh Cthulhu R'lyeh wgah'nagl fhtagn!'* I don't know what it means, or even if I'm saying it correctly. They strode toward me, grasping, hands trying to restrain me. I felt cold fingers curl around my arms as I turned to run, it was a grip so strong it left me bruised, but the hands were coated in a thick mucus, the curse of Cthulhu worship, and I was able to slip out of their grasp.

"I fled.

"What followed was a maddening race through the unlit forest, drums chasing me, spectres stalking me out of the corner of my eye.

"I went straight to the nearest police station. I was flustered, babbling. It didn't help my credibility. The cops took my story, assured me they would look into it, then dismissed me in an unpromising tone. Cast me out back into the wild with those beasts.

"I stepped out the front doors, wondering what in the world I was going to do next, when I saw them. Three hooded cultists, watching me from the sidewalk. Only feet away.

"They had found me.

"I ran back into the station and began throwing chairs against the wall. Two cops tried to drag me out onto the street. I knew that wouldn't do. I delivered a kick to one in the belly, then jumped on top of him. That did the trick. I worked with my lawyer for an insanity plea that got me sent here.

"That is my story. Maybe if we can get the word out, we can warn others of what's out there, lurking beneath the waves. With you on my side, maybe someone will believe us! Shhh. There they are. The drums! Yes, I still hear them. I still dream too. That is my cross to bear. Lately, I have found the dreams oddly comforting. Isn't that strange? Like I'm going home. I'm sorry, I've done enough talking. What do you think? Do you plan to publish this?"

Leslie smiled at Richard. A curious smile of one who is strangely satisfied after a full meal. She slipped the notebook in her jacket and plucked off her gloves, one by one, revealing moist hands, glistening with a clear layer of glassy slime that webbed between her delicate fingers.

"You know, it took us a while to find you. Being admitted under a different name, that was clever. I had to know what you know. Had to be sure, but you should have known you couldn't hide from us." Her eyes sparkled perversely as she drew forth a metal flask and unscrewed the lid. "Your life is not your own. He has chosen you. Claimed you. Fighting that is futile. So, end this torture once and for all my friend, *and drink!*"

STORY NOTES

THIS STORY IS COMPLETELY inspired by Lovecraft's *Call of Cthulhu*. Drums in movies have chilled me since I was a child watching the original *Jumanji*, which remains one of my favorite films. In *The Fellowship of the Ring*, drums are employed again to terrifying effect. One of my oldest ideas is for a story called The Drums, inspired by my fear of hearing drums pounding and not knowing where they are coming from. I have tried to write the story multiple times, including at least two separate screenplay versions. But none of them felt right. It wasn't until I started reading Lovecraft that I made the connection and was able to write the story. It was always meant to be this.

This is my personal favorite story from the collection.

THE GUNGYWAMP FILES

MISSING PERSON REPORT
Pursuant to Penal Code §13519.07(d)

[Print Form] [Save Form] [Clear Form]

☐ Adult ☒ Child	Date and Time of Report: 09.26.2017 @ 16:42	Date and Time of Last Contact: 09.23.2017 -- @ 15 00 [rough]	Report Number: 1978-03

Report Type: ☐ Runaway ☐ Voluntary Missing Adult ☐ Parental/Family Abduction ☐ Dependent Adult ☒ Unknown Circumstances ☐ Stranger Abduction ☐ Suspicious Circumstances ☐ Catastrophe ☐ Lost

Category: ☐ Prior Missing ☐ Sexual Exploitation ☐ Urgent Case ☐ Silver Alert ☐ Abducted During a Crime ☐ Amber Alert ☐ At Risk ☐ Endangered Missing Advisory

Missing Person Information

Name (Last, First, Middle): Durham, Alexander, Jacob

Sex: ☒ M ☐ F ☐ Unk

Race:
☐ A - Other Asian
☒ B - Black
☐ C - Chinese
☐ D - Cambodian
☐ F - Filipino
☐ G - Guamanian
☐ H - Hispanic/Latin/Mexican
☐ I - American Indian
☐ J - Japanese
☐ K - Korean
☐ L - Laotian
☐ O - Other
☐ P - Pacific Islander
☐ S - Samoan
☐ U - Hawaiian
☐ V - Vietnamese
☐ W - White
☐ X - Unknown
☐ Z - Asian Indian

Alias/Moniker/Nickname: Alex

DOB/Age: 17 // 06.15.2001 **Height:** 6'1 **Weight:** 180

Eye Color: BR **Facial Hair:** No **Corrective Lenses:** ☐ Glasses ☐ Contacts **Hair Color/Style:** shaved on sides. Inch on top

Scars/Marks/Tattoos: Scar on chin

Cell Phone Number: 860-891-3215

Residence Address, City, State, Zip Code: 108 Willow Lane, Gungywamp, CT

Residence Phone Number: 860-789-0100

Business Address, City, State, Zip Code:

Business Phone Number:

FBI Number: **Local Reference Number:** **CII Number:** **Social Security Number:** 801-80-7839 **Driver's License/ID Number:** Y1098765 **State:** CT

Email Address: ajddaps@gmail.com

Probation/Parole/Social Worker Name & Phone:

Clothing: blue jeans, black sneakers (nike), hoodie --gray

Social Networking Site(s) and Screen Name(s): Insta: go.wit.theflo // snapchat: mister_dude_esq

Alcohol, Drug, Mental Health, or Medical Condition(s): No

Jewelry: No

Last Known Location/Activity (Description or Address, City, State, Zip Code): Gungywamp State Park trails (on black bike)

Possible Destination (Description or Address, City, State, Zip Code): MP habitually bikes trails after school then comes home

Known Associates and Lifestyle: was riding with Connor Fuches. Honor student. No record or history of substance abuse

X-rays Available Dental: ☒ Y ☐ N Skeletal: ☐ Y ☒ N | **Visible Dental Work** ☐ Y ☒ N If yes, describe: | **Dentures:** ☐ Upper ☐ Full ☐ Lower ☐ Partial | **Braces:** ☐ Upper ☐ Lower | **Dentist Name, Address, Phone Number:**

Photo Available: ☐ Y ☐ N **Age in Photo:** **Fingerprints:** ☐ Y ☐ N **Broken Bones / Missing Organs:** ☐ Y ☐ N If Yes, Describe: | **Medical Provider Name, Address, Phone Number:**

Vehicle Info.

Registered Owner: ☐ Missing Person ☐ Suspect **Color(s):** **Make:** **Model:** **Body Style:** **Veh. Year:** **VIN:**

Describe:

License Number: **State/Province/Country:** **Reg. Year:** **Operator:** ☐ Missing Person ☐ Suspect ☐ Other Describe: **Damage to Vehicle:**

Boat Info.

Operator: ☐ Missing Person ☐ Suspect ☐ Other Describe: **Registered Owner:** ☐ Missing Person ☐ Suspect ☐ Other Describe: **Damage to Boat:**

Boat Year: **Make:** **Model:** **Body Style:** **Color(s):** **Hull Number:** **State/Province/Country:** **Reg. Expiration:**

Suspect Info.

Name (Last, First, Middle): **Relationship to Missing:** **Sex:** ☐ M ☐ F ☐ Unk **Race:** **DOB/Age:**

Address, City, State, Zip Code: **Phone Number:** **E-Mail Address:**

Scars/Marks/Tattoos: **Clothing:**

Reporting

Name (Last, First, Middle): Morris, Ahsley, Mae **Relationship to Missing:** Mother **Sex:** ☐ M ☒ F ☐ Unk **Race:** Black **DOB/Age:** 48

Address, City, State, Zip Code: 108 Willow Lane, Gungywamp, CT **Phone Number:** 860-891-32 **E-Mail Address:** ashley.mae.morris72@gmail.com

FCN Number: **NIC Number:** M

MISSING PERSON REPORT
Pursuant to Penal Code §13519.07(d)

Print Form | Save Form | Clear Form

Missing Person's Name (Last, First, Middle):	DOB/Age:	Report Number:
Durham, Alexander Jacob	06.15.2001/17	1978-03

Narrative:

On 9.23.2017 Alex arrived home from school between 2:30 and 3. He told Ashley he would be meeting up with his friend Conner Fuches (also missing) and he took his bike and rode off into Gungywamp Park behind their property. This is an activity Alex often does, riding the trails in the state park, before returning home before 5PM for dinner. Only on the 23rd Alex did not return. When Ashley tried calling his cell phone it went straight to voicemail. She called the police later that evening, and she was informed that they would keep an eye out for him, but that they wouldn't do a missing person's report until he had been missing for more then 48 hours. The next day, Ashley went to scour the park land herself, and after hours of walking, found no sign of Alex or Connor. She contacted other known friends and aquaintances, but with no luck.

Reporting Officer:	ID/Badge #:	Date:	Investigating Agency Address and Phone Number:	Forward Copy of Report to: (per PC §14211(g)):
Natasha Rodriguez	672	9 26 17		gcpd@mail.com

Approving Officer:	ID/Badge #:	Date:		Internally Route to:
Henry Matheson	089	9.28.17		gcpd@mail.com

Authorization to release photo, dental treatment notes, and skeletal x-rays per PC §14212:

I am a family member, next-of-kin, or law enforcement official investigating the disappearance of the missing person, and I hereby authorize the release of all dental or skeletal x-rays and treatment notes, photographs, physical description, and circumstances surrounding the disappearance to assist law enforcement agencies in locating the above named missing person. This information may be used by the Department of Justice for inclusion in bulletins and posters.

☐ Yes ☐ No Initial ______

Authorization to release information to the National Missing and Unidentified Person System per PC §14209:

I am a family member, next-of-kin, or law enforcement official investigating the disappearance of the missing person and I hereby authorize the release of all dental or skeletal x-rays, photographs, physical description, and circumstances surrounding the disappearance to the National Missing and Unidentified Person System (NamUs) at http://namus.gov/.

☒ Yes ☐ No Initial ______

Authorization to refer missing juveniles who are the victims of sexual exploitation/human trafficking to victim advocacy groups and resources:

I am the parent or legal guardian of a missing juvenile believed to be the victim of sexual exploitation/human trafficking. I hereby authorize the law enforcement official investigating the disappearance, the power/right to refer the above named missing juvenile to the victim advocacy group(s) and/or resource of their choice.

☐ Yes ☐ No Initial ______

Name:	Signature:	Date:
Ashley Morris		9.26.17

Relationship to Missing Person:	Address:	City:	State:	Zip Code:	Phone Number:
Mother	108 Willow Lane	Gungywamp	CT	06336	

Testimony of Agent Jennifer Tang and her partner, Agent Hugo
Flores of the FBI in the Gungywamp Court Case dated 10.17.2017:

MR. PEARL:

Your Honor, we are ready to proceed.

MS. ZUCKERMAN:

Your Honor, Jasmine Zuckerman on behalf of the State.

THE COURT:

This is the matter of Kelvin Torrey versus the State of
Connecticut.

MR. PEARL:

Mr. Torrey is present in court and we are ready for motions.

THE COURT:

You may proceed with your first witness of the day.

MR. PEARL:

I'd like to invite Agent Hugo Flores of The Federal Bureau
of Investigation to take the stand.

DETECTIVE HUGO FLORES,
Federal Bureau of Investigation, after having been first duly sworn,
did testify as follows:

— DIRECT EXAMINATION —

BY MS. ZUCKERMAN:
Q. Could you please state your name for the record.
A. Agent Hugo Flores
Q. Agent, how are you employed?
A. FBI
Q. Agent Flores, can you state for the court the details of the case
you were assigned in Gungywamp?
A. Sure. Myself and Agent Tang were assigned to investigate a string
of various disappearances in the town.
Q. How many disappearances are we talking?
A. I believe there were twenty two missing person reports.

Q. And this is over what period of time, these disappearances?
A. Fourteen months.
Q. And these disappearances all appear to be have taken place in the
neighborhood of Gungywamp State Park, did they not?
A. They did. They were all reported to the Gungywamp Police.
Q. And upon arriving in town, what is the first thing you and your
partner did?
A. We went over the missing persons reports and reviewed the details
with those who filed, family members of those who had gone missing.
And as I checked with the surrounding towns, as Gungywamp Park shares
a border with multiple municipalities, I noticed there were even more
missing persons than we had originally thought.
Q. How many?
A. 59. All around the same park. That's what we in the biz call a
pattern.
Q. Okay. And how was it you first established contact with Mr.
Brombrine?
A. Well we knocked some doors of some of the neighbors of those in the
area to see if they might know anything or seen anything useful. We
ended up leaving our card. A couple of days later he gave us a call.
Q. And what did Mr. Brombrine say?
A. He called to report a bizarre visit from one of his neighbors, who
based on the description, we eventually determined was Kelvin Torrey.
Q. And how did you determine that?
A. Mr. Brombrine gave us the description and we talked to some of
their neighbors. They told us where Mr. Kelvin lived.
Q. And what exactly happened during Mr. Kelvin's first visit to the
Brombrine's?
A. Well, according to Mr. Brombrine, Kelvin just showed up at their
house and began knocking very erratically. He seemed very distressed,
and told Mr. Brombrine and his family that they needed to leave, that
they needed to leave their home and vacate the premises.
Q. And did Mr. Torrey give a reason for this bizarre demand?
A. He did. He said he was warning them. That there was some kind of
entity in the woods that posed a threat.
Q. And he blamed this entity for all the disappearances, did he not?
A. He did. And he also carried a large rock, he said he found it in
their yard, that it was a marker. And he seemed to believe this meant
Mr. Brombrine was being targeted. That whatever was out there was
going to come and eat them.

        MS. ZUCKERMAN We have that rock here.

[DISPLAYS EVIDENCE PHOTOGRAPH Z7748]

Q. So Mr. Torrey shows up uninvited carrying this rock, and
threatening this family. Whatever his motivations are, that's
aggression and deception. So, Agent Flores, you and your partner get
pointed to Kelvin's residence — and what did you find there?
A. Well, we found his house and knocked on his door, but there was no
answer. So we decide to have a neighborly look around his property. I
take one step around the side of his house and suddenly pain like I've
never felt before is raging from my leg. I look down and my ankle is
caught in a bear trap, you know the kind I'm talking about, the kind
for hunting. If it wasn't for Agent Tang, I'm not even sure I'd be
here today, I lost a lot of blood. She got me free and drove me to the
hospital, but that was pretty much the extent of my involvement in the
case, to be honest.
Q. Thank you, Agent Flores. One more question. In your professional
opinion, do you think that trap was placed there purposefully?
A. I don't think, I know. It was put there to prevent prowlers from
going around to the back of the house. They found loads more traps
like that all around the property.
Q. So we've established that this was done with intent. Intent to harm
others. Foresight. Planning. These are the actions of a criminal,
someone who seeks to purposefully inflict harm on others. A mentally
ill person, perhaps, but one with the mental fortitude and awareness
to successfully ensnare an FBI detective. And to do that, you have to
be smart. Thank you, your Honor. I tender the witness.

— CROSS-EXAMINATION —

BY MR. PEARL:

Q. I only have one question for Agent Flores. Just to clarify for the
jury, did you actually have any contact with Mr. Kelvin Torrey?
A. No, I never seen him in person before today.
Q. Thank you, I tender the witness, your Honor.

THE COURT:

        Next witness, Ms. Zuckerman.

MS. ZUCKERMAN:

        Yes, I'd like to call Agent Jennifer Tang to the stand.

— DIRECT EXAMINATION OF AGENT TANG —

BY MS. ZUCKERMAN:

Q. Could you please state your name for the record?
A. Agent Jennifer Tang.
Q. Agent, in what capacity are you employed?
A. I'm an agent for the Federal Bureau of Investigation.
Q. And you have some experience with serial killers, don't you Agent?
A. Yes. I do. Unfortunately. *
Q. Would you mind telling the jury about your experience?
A. Um, I'd rather —
Q. Would you mind if I do it?
A. Sure.
Q. Jennifer Tang was working as a private investigator in Los Angeles.
She was hired by Devlin Henne to find his missing fiance based on a
supposed snuff film he provided her. Agent Tang, all on her own, was
able to trace the origins of the tape to an abandoned property outside
the city limits, where an individual known as Pablo Jimenez was
kidnapping girls, torturing and killing them on camera, and then
distributing the footage. The girls were never seen again, and their
bodies were never recovered. Agent Tang was able to save his final
victim, and ended up killing Jimenez in self defense when he attacked
her.

MR. PEARL:

        Your Honor, I object. These details has not bearing on my
        client's case.

THE COURT:

        I'm going to permit this. These are vital details to framing
        Agent Tang's experience. Plus I want to know what happens
        next. Continue, counsel.

MS. ZUCKERMAN:

Thank you, your honor.

Q. Do I have it right so far, Agent?
A. Yeah. Yes.
Q. That's not the end of the story. The man who originally hired Ms.
Tang, the one who gave her the tape, Devlin Henne, he invites her over
for dinner to celebrate their success. He found his fiance's killer.
Only that girl wasn't really his fiance. See, this guy is a snuff tape
creator as well, and he had hired Ms. Tang to take out his

* see: 'The Undertaker and Other Macabre Tales' by Derek Hutchins
  A full account of Tang's history can be found in the
  story entitled "Snuff"

competition. Agent Tang is drugged and captured. Tortured. How long
did he hold you prisoner?
A. Almost two weeks.
Q. Two weeks. And again, due to her intelligence and perseverance,
Agent Tang manages to escape, and once again, bring two perverted
serial killers into custody. So… I think Agent Tang knows a thing or
two about serial killers. Back to the matter at hand. Even though you
were a rookie, you took lead of the investigation into Kelvin Torrey
after your partner's accident, is that correct?
A. That's correct.
Q. Do you have anything to add to Agent Flores' testimony of the
events up to this point?
A. No. Wait — there is one thing. When we were at Mr. Torrey's house,
I noticed a strange marking on his window.
Q. What kind of marking, can you describe it?
A. Um, like a rune. Like a letter, but in a language that doesn't
exist. It was painted onto the glass.
Q. Okay. So you bring your partner to the hospital. What happens next?
A. We reported the incident to headquarters. And my supervisor told me
to continue the investigation on my own. I returned to Kelvin Torrey's
property, this time with four local officers. Once again we did not
find Mr. Torrey at home, but we were able to secure a warrant from a
local judge granting us permission to enter his home. As my partner
reported, as we searched the property, we found several additional
booby traps. Inside, the place was filled with occult symbols and
charms hanging from the ceiling, more strange writing on the
walls…later we'd learn they were written in human blood. A lot of the
windows were painted red. There were also shelves full of ancient
texts…grimoires, older magicks. Beneath the house we found a bunker
filled with half empty cans of beans, and weapons. Lots of weapons.
Guns, knives with blood on them. . . then we found the body. It was an
old woman, she had been strung up by her feet, her body drained of
blood. In the same room, there were were plastic jugs full of blood.
Later, the police found the rest of the bodies. Buried in the
backyard.
Q. How many bodies did they find?
A. 34.
Q. Okay, but you weren't there for that.
A. No.
Q. Where were you?
A. Well, while we were searching the property I started to get this
bad feeling. This guy had visited the Brombrine family the other day
and threatened them, so I called a unit over to check on them. Then
after we found the body in the basement, I left to go check on them
myself. My plan was to escort them out of the home, but while I was

driving over I heard the unit I had sent report that they were
responding to a scream and gunshots in the home. I remember they said
there were multiple casualties, and they called for back-up.
Q. So you arrive at the Brombrine residence, and then what?
A. I walked in and immediately saw the bodies. The mother and son were
deceased with multiple gunshot wounds. The young girl appeared to be
unharmed, and the dad was wounded, but paramedics were tending to him.
The cops present reported that they had fired at the perpetrator, and
he had fled the scene. They described him as wearing a skull mask and
shirtless with his body painted green. I asked them which way he went
and then I went after him.
Q. You didn't wait for backup?
A. No.
Q. So what happened?
A. They told me he ran into the woods. I followed the trail. I had my
gun on me. I pretty much always do now. I hadn't gone too far when I
was fired upon. I took cover. While I was hiding, a couple of cops
arrived and they engaged the attacker in a firefight while I circled
around behind him. I tackled him from behind, stripped him of his
weapon, restrained him and walked him back to the house.
Q. And when you took the mask off...
A. It was Kelvin Torrey.
Q. Thank you, Agent. I tender the witness, your Honor.

THE COURT:

              Thank you, Defense, your witness.

           — EXAMINATION OF PATRICIA HUGHES, M.D. —

[REDACTED]

    *

    *

    *

BY MR. PEARL

Q. Doctor, state your name for the record, please.
A. Doctor Patricia Hughes, I'm a licensed psychiatrist.
Q. And how long have you been working in that profession?
A. Twenty two years.
Q. And in those twenty two years, how many cases of actual insanity
have you diagnosed?
A. Of psychosis? Not many.
Q. Two, by my accounting.

A. That sounds right.
Q. And one of those two is Kelvin Torrey, is it not?
A. It is.
Q. Can you explain for the judge and jury what led you to make that diagnosis?
A. Well, I've worked with the courts for many years, often conducting interviews with convicts in order to provide a professional accounting of the individual's mental state which may have relevance to their crime. Any undiagnosed mental illnesses, etcetera. And during my discussion with Mr. Torrey, it became incredibly clear very early on that something was wrong, that Mr. Torrey did not perceive reality in the same way that you or I perceive it.
Q. In what way?
A. He kept saying there were these portals in the woods. He mentioned a chapel of bones. He seemed to think that there was some existential threat out there in the woods and that he was actually doing these people a favor by killing them, that he was sparing them from some worse kind of. . . fate.
Q. Did Mr. Torrey exhibit any kind of remorse for his actions?
A. No, none at all.
Q. And what is your final diagnosis of Kelvin Torrey's mental condition?
A. In my professional opinion, Mr. Torrey is delusional. His mind has suffered a breach from reality, leading him to believe in perceived threats that aren't there, and to lash out violently. Obviously we've seen tragic evidence of that. It is my opinion that Kelvin Torrey represents a danger to himself and the general public, and that he needs professional treatment.
Q. And is Kelvin Torrey responsible for his actions?
A. No. His mind is in a state of psychosis, it's damaged, and as such, I don't believe he should be held responsible for his actions, no matter how atrocious they may seem to us.
Q. Thank you, Doctor.

[REDACTED]
*
*
*
*
*
*
*
*

THE FOLLOWING IS A LEAKED EXCERPT FROM THE INTERROGATION OF KELVIN
TORREY BY THE FEDERAL BUREAU OF INVESTIGATION. THE DATE OF THE
TRANSCRIPT AND ITS ORIGINS ARE UNKNOWN:

AGENT TANG: Kelvin, do you know who I am?

KELVIN TORREY: No.

AGENT TANG: My name is Agent Tang, I'm with the FBI. You've
                       been arrested. Do you remember what happened
                       tonight? What you did?

KELVIN TORREY: I saved people a lot of pain and suffering.

AGENT TANG: No, you caused a lot of pain and suffering, Mr.
                       Torrey. You destroyed a family. Two are dead,
                       another wounded. And there are more bodies on
                       your property, suggesting this is not the first
                       time you have harmed another human being.

KELVIN TORREY: No. Not the first time. Too many to count.

AGENT TANG: So you admit that you killed someone tonight?
                       Phillipa Brombine, and her six year old son,
                       Nick?

KELVIN TORREY: They're better off that way.

AGENT TANG: What does that mean, Kelvin? How could someone be
                       better off dead?

KELVIN TORREY: We're all better off dead.

AGENT TANG: Kelvin, I don't understand.

KELVIN TORREY: You saw it. I know you saw it.

AGENT TANG: I saw something. . .something I can't explain.
                       But nothing that justifies murder.

KELVIN TORREY: Did you gaze into the black circle? Into the pit
                       of despair? It seems beautiful at first, to draw

you in, and then it rips you apart. It ruined me.
I feel it, even now. Calling to me. Begging me to
spill blood and open the gate. But I'm not going
to do it.

AGENT TANG: I don't understand, Kelvin. What's this gate?

KELVIN TORREY: The gate...you need the key to open the gate. And
blood is the price. That's what he told me.

AGENT TANG: Who told you that?

KELVIN TORREY: DON'T OPEN THE GATE! WHATEVER YOU DO, DON'T
LISTEN TO HIM!

AGENT TANG: Listen to who?

KELVIN TORREY: It won't stop. Not until it's devoured our world.
It wants to feed, like an angler, it lures us in
with false promises. It's a deceiver. And it's
got a foothold in our world now. Don't you get
it? It's radius of influence is growing -- the
only way to stop it is to clear that whole area.
Get these people out of there. I tried, I tried
to tell them but they just wouldn't listen. . .

AGENT TANG: So you killed them because they wouldn't listen
to you? Is that it?

KELVIN TORREY: I didn't want to. But they wouldn't listen. I
couldn't make them understand. Dead is better. .
. Better than what they would become if they
heeded its call.

AGENT TANG: What would they become?

KELVIN TORREY: Servants. Prisoners to its will. I was almost one
myself, but I managed to fight it. But in return
it cursed me. I haven't slept in weeks, because
whenever I close my eyes, all I can see is the
black circle. . . and the horrors the lie within.
. .

AGENT TANG: Nightmares? Can you describe them for me?

KELVIN TORREY: Things that would make a lesser man blow his
                      brains out. Scenes of horror beyond description.
                      . .and I can't look away, no matter how hard I
                      try. No. It's too. . . too awful. I wouldn't want
                      to burden you. That's my cross to bear. Dez
                      Mogwool utr bachn prfgh leetsch.

AGENT TANG: What did you just say? Just now?

AGENT TANG: Kelvin?

[END OF TRANSCRIPT]

*I didn't include the first part of the interview, as it includes mostly redundant info from the trial.

DIRECTOR JOHN ZULU: OK, so you're at the house, the Brombrine residence. We received the police reports. We want to know about what you saw.

AGENT TANG: OK. Yeah. I asked the officers which way Torrey had gone and they pointed into the woods. So I went after him. Listen…I'm not even sure what really happened out there…

DIRECTOR JOHN ZULU: Well, what do you think happened? Or you don't remember?

AGENT TANG: It sounds crazy.

DIRECTOR JOHN ZULU: Agent Tang, we need to know what you experienced. What you saw…even if you're not sure it's real. The truth is often subjective. But that is what we're after, or as close as we can get to it. Truth. So tell me, Agent. . .what happened? I'm not here to judge, just to report facts.

AGENT TANG: OK. I chased Torrey into the woods. The first thing off I noticed were the lights. Floating orbs of light in the trees. They were colored but. . . I can't say for sure what color they were. . . or even if they were there at all. They were like those spots you get in your vision when you stare at the sun too long.

DIRECTOR JOHN ZULU: Keep going.

AGENT TANG: I was weirded out at first but kept going. I was aware of other movement too. Dark shapes, in the trees, just beyond my line of sight. I was paranoid -- I would see a shape - then shine my light at it, and it would be gone. I thought I was going crazy. Anyways, it felt like the lights were leading me somewhere.

DIRECTOR JOHN ZULU: Did you feel that it might be a trap?

AGENT TANG: Part of me did. Part of me didn't care. It was
                        the oddest thing.

DIRECTOR JOHN ZULU: Keep going.

AGENT TANG: I followed the lights until I arrived at a
                        chapel. I didn't realize it at first, but it was
                        made entirely of human bones. The light was
                        coming from the chapel. I had taken my light out
                        to shine at the shadows — the ones that weren't
                        there — stupid, I know — but I thought it might
                        be Torrey. But it wasn't and the light just put a
                        target on my back. Torrey fired at me. He missed,
                        and I evaded him — he fired until he went inside
                        the chapel, and I followed him. I'm sorry. . .

DIRECTOR JOHN ZULU: It's okay. Have some water.

AGENT TANG: Thanks. It's like I'm trying to remember a dream.

DIRECTOR JOHN ZULU: Take your time.

AGENT TANG: Inside the chapel there was a statue of a man at
                        the far end. Not much else. But Torrey was
                        inside, sitting at a table. He poured something
                        into two goblets and pushed one toward me. He
                        invited me to sit and drink with him. I told him
                        to get on the ground. He backed up against the
                        wall. Kept telling me that we should work
                        together. I didn't realize it before but one of
                        his bullets must have grazed me. I was bleeding.
                        A few drops of my blood fell onto the ground at
                        the base of the statue into some kind of dish.
                        And then it was like. . . it's gonna sound like I
                        was tripping balls, but this black circle, sprang
                        to life above the statue. . . like it was a
                        window to another world. It was like I was
                        flying. . . flying across a blue desert. . . it
                        was paradise. . . the highest high I've ever
                        felt. I wanted to climb into that world and live
                        there forever. Then we arrived a black fortress,
                        and I was filled with dread — the gate opened —

and a nightmare of flesh crawled out. A monster.
It was a gangly thing, with arms like sticks —
like that actually looked like they were made of
wood. So it had all these branching, slender
limbs — more than the normal amount. And a
terrible mouth . . . it tried to bite me, but I
don't think it could see me. It's head was
wrapped in bandages. It grabbed me. It wasn't
just a vision then, but it actually reached into
our world and took hold of me. It was trying to
bring me back — through the gate. And it would
have, if Torrey hadn't stopped it.

[handwritten: unable to find any info on SPRN or John Zulu in public record. Alias?]

DIRECTOR JOHN ZULU: *[circled]*   He helped you?

AGENT TANG: He saved my life. He hacked its arm off with an
                     ax. I fell to the ground and the portal closed.
                     It took me a minute to get over the shock of
                     everything, but when I did I told Kelvin to show
                     me his hands. He didn't resist, and I escorted
                     him back to the house.

[handwritten: not sure what to make of this...]

DIRECTOR JOHN ZULU: He say anything?

AGENT TANG: "Now you'll believe me. . ." So what do you
                     think? Do I belong in a mental institution?

DIRECTOR JOHN ZULU: I wouldn't say that. It's not the weirdest thing
                     I've ever heard. I work for SPRN — I hear this
                     kind shit everyday.

AGENT TANG: So. . . what is that place?

DIRECTOR JOHN ZULU: Well, that's classified.

AGENT TANG: But. . . I've seen it. I already know it's there.

DIRECTOR JOHN ZULU: You don't know anything. In fact, I need you to
                     sign this form, reaffirming your confidentiality.
                     You're going to need to testify in court so we'll
                     give you a cover story. But you are never to
                     breathe a word of this to anyone. Not to your
                     therapist, not to your deaf grandma, not to God
                     Himself — are we clear?

[handwritten: government bastards...]

AGENT TANG: Yes. You got a pen?

DIRECTOR JOHN ZULU: Here.

AGENT TANG: Thanks. Now what?

DIRECTOR JOHN ZULU: Now? You've got two options. Your life will never
                         be the same again. There are things out there the
                         public isn't ready to know. Things that would
                         shatter their perceptions of reality and plunge
                         this world into chaos -- we keep the flood at bay.
                         Seal up the cracks in the dam. You've seen
                         through the cracks — beyond the horizon of
                         science — so you can go back to your life, try to
                         forget, try to live and salvage whatever life you
                         have left by trying to suppress those memories --

AGENT TANG: Or?

DIRECTOR JOHN ZULU: Or — why don't we discuss that after the trial?

[END OF TRANSCRIPT]

Jennifer Tang vanishes from public
record after this. where did she go? It is
clear this organization, SPRN, is hiding
potentially earth shattering information —
How to access it??
More work to be done...

The form mentioned by Zulu during
his interview w/ Agent Tang

CASE BRIEFING ACKNOWLEDGMENT
ADDENDUM

AN AGREEMENT BETWEEN ___Jennifer Tang___ **AND THE UNITED STATES**

I have been reminded of my rights and obligations pursuant to the FBI Employment Agreement (FD-291), the Classified Information Nondisclosure Agreement (SF-312), and the Sensitive Compartmented Information Nondisclosure Agreement (Form 4144).

1. Intending to be legally bound, I hereby accept the obligations contained in this Agreement in consideration of my being granted access to classified information related to the Apprehension of Kelvin Torrey in the Gungywamp Case (F3252).

2. I hereby acknowledge that I have received a security indoctrination concerning the nature and protection of classified information, including the procedures to be followed in ascertaining whether other persons to whom I contemplate disclosing this information have been approved for access to it, and that I understand these procedures.

3. I have been advised that the unauthorized disclosure, unauthorized retention, or negligent handling of classified information by me could cause damage or irreparable injury to the United States or could be used to advantage by a foreign nation. I hereby agree that I will never divulge classified information to anyone unless: (a) I have officially verified that the recipient has been properly authorized by the United States Government to receive it; or (b) I have been given prior written notice of authorization from the United States Government Agency known as SPRN, by Director John Thaddeus Zulu (SPRN) or his equivalent, that such disclosure is permitted. In such a case, I acknowledge that I will be briefed as to what information will be permitted to be disclosed

4. I have been advised that any breach of this Agreement may result in the termination of any security clearances I hold; removal from any position of special confidence and trust requiring such clearances, or termination of my employment or other relationships with the Departments or Agencies that granted me security clearance or clearances. In addition, I have been advised that any unauthorized disclosure of classified information by me may constitute a violation, or violations, of United States criminal laws, including the provisions of sections 641, 793, 794, 798, *952, and 1924, title 18, United States Code; *the provisions of section 783(b), title 50, United States Code; and the provisions

of the Intelligence Identities Protection Act of 1982. I recognize that nothing in this agreement constitutes a waiver by the United States to prosecute me for any statutory violation.

5. I hereby assign to the United States Government all royalties, remunerations, and emoluments that have resulted, will result, or may result from any disclosure, publication, or revelation of classified information not consistent with the terms of this Agreement.

6. These provisions are consistent with and do not supercede, conflict with, or otherwise alter the employee obligations, rights, or liabilities created by existing statute or Executive Order relating to (1) classified information, (2) communications to Congress, (3) the reporting to an inspector General of a violation of any law, rule, or regulation, or mismanagement, a gross waste of funds, an abuse of authority, or a substantial and specific danger to public health or safety, or (4) any other whistleblower protection. The definitions, requirements, obligations, rights, sanctions, and liabilities created by controlling Executive orders and statutory provisions are incorporated into this agreement and are controlling.

7. These constrictions are consistent with and do not supercede, conflict with, or otherwise alter the employee obligations, rights, or liabilities created by Executive Order No. 13526 (75 Fed. Reg. 707), or any successor thereto section 7211 of title 5, United States Code (governing disclosures to Congress); section 1034 of title 10, United States code, as amended by the Military Whistleblower Protection Act (governing disclosures to congress by members of the military); section 2302(b) (8) of title 5, United States Code, as amended by the Whistleblower Protection Act of 1989 (governing disclosures of illegality, waste, fraud, abuse or public health or safety threats); the Intelligence Identities Protection Act of 1982 (50 U.S.C. 421 et seq.) (governing disclosures that could expose confidential Government agents); section 7(c) and 8H of the Inspector General Act of 1978 (5 U.S.C. App.) (relating to disclosures to an inspector general, the Inspectors general of the Intelligence Community, and Congress); Section 103H(g)(3) of the National Security Act of 1947 (50 U.S.C. 403-3h(g)(3) (relating to disclosures to the inspector general of the Intelligence Community); sections 17(d)(5) and 17(e)(3) of the Central Intelligence Agency Act of 1949 (50 U.S.C. 403g(d)(5) and 403q(e)(3)) (relating to disclosures to the Inspector General of the Central Intelligence Agency and Congress); and the statutes which protect against disclosure that may compromise the national security, including sections 641, 793, 794, 798, *952 and 1924 of Title 18, United States Code, and *section 4(b) of the Subversive Activities Control Act of 1950 (50 U.S.C. section 783(b)). The definitions, requirements, obligations, rights, sanctions, and liabilities created by said Executive Order and listed statutes are incorporated into this Agreement and are controlling.

8. I have read this Agreement carefully and my questions, if any, have been answered. I acknowledge that the briefing officer has made available to me the Executive Order and statues referenced in this Agreement and its implementing regulation (32 CFR Part 2001, Section 2001. 80(d)(2)) so that I may read them at this time, if I so choose.

EMPLOYEE   DATE

Jennifer Tang 10-05-2017

SPRN DIRECTOR   DATE

John Zahn Oct 5, 2017

FBI ASSISTANT DIRECTOR DATE

Abraham Hayes 10/5/2017

My brother, Clark Jimenez, was working for the
FBI when he went missing. They refuse to tell us what
happened to him, as no body was returned to us. In his
final phone call to me, he mentioned SPRN... something is
going on. I'm going to figure it out! Going Dark. If I vanish
too, I hope this finds the right hands. Finish the work I
started. EXPOSE SPRN — and whatever secrets they
harbor. — RSJ

[END OF DOCUMENTS]

STORY NOTES

The inspiration for this story came after reading books like House of Leaves and "S" (Ship of Theseus) by JJ Abrams where they do cool and unique things with the formatting of the book. I really enjoyed those books as its more of an experience that draws you in, a puzzle that you are a part of. I thought it would be fun to do something similar, but on a smaller scale.

A major theme in cosmic horror is characters going mad when they encounter beings or phenomena beyond their comprehension. I thought it would be interesting to take a character that actually went mad and see what they would do. In this case, he kills people because in his mind he is saving them from his own fate and having to face the impossible.

The character Jennifer Tang from my first collection was very popular, and I received multiple requests to revive her. She was left in a cliffhanger, but I brought her back for another round because I liked her too.

CHAPEL OF BONES

SOPHIE THOUGHT THAT THE bird sitting on her fence just outside her window was perhaps the most peculiar thing she'd ever seen. Its wings were featherless, black in color with tinges of red, the flesh ravaged as if it had been in a cockfight. It was a large beast, at least three feet in height, its hooked talons driven into the wooden beam upon which it was perched, and on its head there was only the smallest suggestion of a beak behind which rested a row of sharpened teeth which gleamed, twinkling maliciously in the moonlight. And was that fur riding down its back?

Sophie shivered, taking another sip of her chai tea. The bird, if it could be called a bird, looked as terrible as she felt. Her throat had been raped by chemotherapy, and despite her submission to that devil's bargain, life by death, she had come out the other side with a dire final prognosis: only months to live.

The pain, up till now, had been endurable. Yet the pain wasn't even the worst part. *The knowing* was the worst part, knowing that you were going to die, knowing that there was something growing inside you, eating you alive from the inside out. That knowledge was enough to make anyone go insane.

Her insomnia was as much due to *the knowing* as it was to the pain. And now she wasn't sure if this thing she was looking at was even real. Was she dreaming? Hallucinating from the lack of sleep? All possibilities.

But right now she was fascinated (and a bit scared) of the thing before her. Sophie tapped on the glass with her nail and the bird thing cried out, a chilling sound that made every nerve in her body tremble, informing her this thing was bad news, before it flapped its mighty wings and soared off above the trees.

Sophie stood by the window until her feet bade her to sit. She felt dirty. Wrong, somehow. As if being in the presence of that thing had soiled her soul. She hiked up the wooden stairs and filled the tub with hot, steaming water, then let a scented bath bomb tumble into the frothing cauldron, simmering and hissing as it melted into nothingness.

She slipped off her robe and stepped into the colored water, letting her blight roll off of her in calming, cleansing waves. The water rose to her throat, and for half a moment she courted the thought of allowing it to keep rising...to swallow her, so she could dissipate as well, end her suffering.

But she didn't.

Despite her lamentable predicament, there were things she enjoyed about this life. And she didn't *know* if anything came after. That thought curdled her blood, she was living out of fear, as well. Enjoying the days she had left, as best as she could.

As soon as she had been diagnosed, Sophie knew how she was going to spend her final days. She was going to give herself the life she'd always wanted, an early retirement, of sorts. So she'd rented a precious A-frame cabin in a secluded neck of the woods and removed herself from society to a life of peaceful seclusion. She maintained contact with her friends and family (the great irony of all this was that her parents were both lifelong smokers as well, and still in fantastic health), but she wanted to be alone. There was no significant other or children to messy things up. Just her.

And so Sophie had spent the last two weeks doing what she loved most: relaxing. Reading. Yoga. Watching movies and cooking meals she might never watch or eat again. It was a life of tranquility, with plenty of time to meditate and ruminate over her past, present, and future. The life of Sophie LeMann, a coda.

Sophie sighed; dimly aware that the bath bomb had stopped hissing.

Silence.

And in the silence...nothing.

How alone she was.

She had a brief lapse of nihilism, and in her panic (was it all truly meaningless?), she allowed herself to glance up at the cross hanging on the wall across the room.

Sophie had been raised a Methodist, and though she hadn't been the most devout Christian, she could honestly say that she'd put in effort. And as most dying people do, she had searched earnestly for some kind of meaning in the universe, and she'd started going to church again. More often and earnestly than she ever had in her life.

And she'd prayed. Oh God, she'd prayed. Pleading with the man behind the curtain to take away her suffering. To give her another chance. She was only forty six after all, didn't she deserve another chance?

And despite her pastor's insistence that sometimes God doesn't save us, despite our prayers and righteous living (such actions are God's infinite wisdom and we must do our best to accept it), she felt her prayers had been working, at least for a while. At least until she was told her condition definitely *hadn't* improved, as they'd thought, and she was definitely *much worse*.

Dying, in fact.

Terminal.

A horrible word. A horrible word for a horrible thing.

Sophie LeMann's newfound faith had been shattered that day. Broken into a million infinitesimal pieces. And she hadn't bothered to pray since.

At long last, the bath water grew frigid, and Sophie dragged her drooping body out of the tub and into a satin bathrobe, attire fit for royalty. If Sophie would never truly be rich, she could, at least for a few months, pretend. Her meager life's savings would get her that far.

In the nuclear glow of the dawning light, Sophie, eyes pulling for sleep, finally allowed herself to retire to bed where she, at least for a time, gave up the ghost and the burden of consciousness.

●

Sophie awoke, her head was a dull cacophony of incoherent thoughts. The fog of sleep. Had she dreamed that devil bird, or had it actually been there, perched upon her fence?

Her throat burned with raging fire, as it often did these days, and she tried to douse it with water and tea — but it only diminished the pain. Nothing could put it out permanently, nothing but death.

That grim thought followed her like a cloud. She did her best to block it out — meditate — distract herself with books and puzzles

— but the ominous threat of death clung to her like a frightened cat, sinking its claws into her flesh and drawing blood.

The sky was overcast as Sophie set out on her daily walk. Even the earth mourned with her. As she returned, stepping once again into her temporary home in her temporary life, she clocked the shotgun that hung above her door. Her brother had insisted she take it when she told him she was going to be living alone in the woods, though she hadn't brought herself to so much as touch it. A dark reminder that death hangs over all our heads. Only an arm's length away.

The day passed away as if it were a dream. Sophie lived in a constant stupor these days, increasingly exhausted and never able to get back to her full high. Everyday she could feel her mental state draw taut, one robust twist at a time. A mind could only take so much pressure before it snapped.

And, though time dwindled on, in the end Sophie managed to kill it, as all do, if they only wait long enough. Light gave up the ghost and darkness claimed its rightful throne. Sophie lay down and closed her eyes, knowing full well she wouldn't sleep, and trying her damndest anyway. Eventually she admitted defeat and descended from the loft for her witching hour tea.

She stood by the window, as was her ritual, and allowed her thoughts to wander as she waited for the tea to cool enough to drink. The mug warmed her hands wonderfully. She enjoyed the sensation. *There. That was a positive thought. Stay positive.*

She was brought sharply back to reality as her mind picked up something — movement out there — in the darkness.

Lights.

Dancing.

Ethereal.

Yes, she thought, squinting, there were lights out there. A series of bright, swirling colors. A phantasmagoric trance. What in the world could be going on out there? At first she thought it might be a party, but there was no blasting music. The air was as still and silent as a tomb.

No, there was no explanation. There was no need for one. Some things simply just were. And wasn't that enough? To just be? Sophie sipped her tea and felt her spirit lift as she watched the sensual way the colors curled in and out of each other, taking solace in the idea that the lights existed only for her in this moment.

And right here, now, she rejoiced to be alive.

Then something else caught her eye.

A movement — this one subtler, so subtle in fact she almost missed it, and later wished she had.

There was something gliding through the trees, away from the light. A shadowy figure on two legs, only these legs were abnormally long and the thing's torso was abnormally stout. Two spindly arms swung on a pendulum as it walked. Sophie watched it for a heartbeat, until it was lost to the night.

She sat there, rigid, once again feeling threatened almost enough to grab the shotgun above her door and maybe use it, but not quite. The thing was gone, wasn't it? If it had even been real.

Sophie sat there as the minutes passed. Feeling not quite so blissful as she had before. Until finally the lights faded too, plunging her world and mind back into a frightening darkness from which she saw no way out.

She climbed up to her room, (locking the door behind her), and lay in bed, anxiously wondering if she was safe and then telling herself it didn't matter anyway, she was dying. And then rebutting that cancer was a better death than being ripped to shreds by some monster. Or was it? Maybe it was better to get it over with all at once? And so forth, until sleep took her in its eternal snare.

The following day as soon as Sophie had showered and eaten (with what little appetite she had left), she donned her pea coat and went out for a stroll. With light came reason, and she had no reason to fear strange creatures or lights she may or may not have even seen. Her memory of the previous night's events was vivid. Her course, direct. She trudged through the snow, which rose several inches on her winter boots, until she saw something of consequence.

In this case it was a deer. Only its side had been gored, its entrails torn from its rib cage with abhorrent disregard and, Sophie guessed, devoured. There was blood staining the snow around her in a Pollock-esque display, and strange footprints as well. Twice the size of her own.

Her logical mind was appalled at the scene before her, and she wondered if she should call someone. The police? No, they dealt in human death, not animal. Her mind grew grave as she was forced to conclude that not only had she seen something last night stalking through the woods, but that it ate raw meat, and was not afraid to kill to get it.

Sophie shivered and was about to turn back when she noticed something else. A large structure half buried behind the thick tree coverage of the area.

Forgetting herself, she stepped forward, moving as if possessed, to find out what it was.

What she found, as she came into view of the thing, was not what she expected.

Not that Sophie had any exclusive expectations, but the towering house in front of her, as big as a barn with vaulted ceilings, defied logic. And the most illogical part of it all was that it was made entirely of bones.

Bones heaped upon bones, and most, from what she could tell, appeared human. The bones were stacked and sealed with some kind of white cement. Skulls leered out at her, set and arrayed in stark architectural patterns, giving the building a perverse symmetry and unassailable beauty. There were even windows along each wall and a doorway that arched several feet above her head, though no door, to block out the elements or animal life.

Immediately Sophie knew this place was somehow the source of the bizarre light spectacle she had seen last night, and despite the grisly horror of the unholy edifice, she could not deny there was a power emanating from this place, a power she struggled to resist, summoning her inside.

Surely, a peek was in order. After all, it wasn't everyday you stumbled across a chapel of bones in the woods. And a chapel it was, as Sophie realized as she stepped across the threshold. Stained glass windows lined the walls on either side of her. There were no pews, but there was a stone floor, littered with leaves and dirt, and at the head of the open space, a stone statue of the most beautiful man Sophie had ever laid eyes on. A face and jaw justly angled, hair with wavy tendrils running past his shoulders, a body without a scrap of clothing with muscles chiseled by the gods. He knelt on one knee, both hands raised to the height of his head, as if he were Atlas, holding the world, but there was no world to hold. And by his feet sat a gold plated dish, in the center of which was a tiny black hole, which Sophie surmised was some kind of drain.

Sophie could certainly see why someone would want to worship this man. His demeanor and physique had sex appeal and carnal beauty written all over them. Yet she could not deny she found the whole setting utterly unnerving. The stained glass did not depict traditional scenes of Christian divinity, but abject monstrosities in various, barbaric acts of devouring and mutilating human kind.

And yet, if those particular images were ignored, there was a strong sense of peace here, as if all noise from the outside world were eradicated. The idea of being surrounded by death, *memento mori*, was an interesting sentiment — it could be seen as a shrine to contemplate one's own place in the world and —

No. No, this wasn't right. Something about this place just wasn't right. Where had the bones come from, for starters? Had they been excavated, dug up from graves? Or was there fouler business afoot? Surely, the police would have to be notified about this. Human remains — in such a vast quantity! They'd have a field day.

Sophie gathered her wits and walked briskly out of the chapel and did not stop until she got home.

But Sophie did not call the police.

She thought about it, but determined to visit the place one more time, just to satisfy her own curiosity, before police and inspectors defiled the sanctuary, crawling all over it like ants.

That night she watched the phantasmagoria of lights rippling through the trees. Sleep came easily, for the first time in ages, and she awoke feeling refreshed.

In her mind, Sophie had told herself she was returning to take photographs, documentation to provide to the police, but the truth was she simply wanted to be there. To stand in that shrine and feel the power of that place again.

She snapped several pictures of the exterior. But when she entered to document the interior, she found she was not alone.

There was a man kneeling at the foot of the statue, whispering, praying.

She could not distinguish the words, neither could she bring herself to move closer. She felt she was intruding on a private ceremony. Obviously the man believed he was alone...

What was she supposed to do, wait her turn? A lurid hunger dug at her mind, urging her to enter.

"Excuse me?" She called, taking another step. Already she felt better. "Sorry, I didn't want to interrupt." *Yes I did, that's exactly what I wanted to do.*

The man turned, but was not angry. Instead, he smiled when he saw her. "You come seeking Dev Mogwül's blessing. He has many to give."

"Did you build this place?"

The man's grin grew, and he stood to face her. Sophie gasped when she saw that the man held a knife in his grime-covered hand. He laughed at her reaction, and slipped the knife into his coat. "No. No, it was built long ago. I come here to pray."

"Why do you pray to him?"

"Because he's here. And because he listens. And often, he answers. Can you say the same for your god?"

"I have no god." Sophie felt a stinging needle pricking her heart. Was that jealousy? Why should she be jealous of this poor old man who prayed to a slab of stone?

Because his god answers.

"Dez Mogwül is always willing to take on new acolytes." The man stepped up to Sophie and placed his hand on her shoulder. It was powerfully comforting, the first physical contact she'd had in weeks. "May your quest find its end at the great one's feet."

Then, with those words, the man departed.

Sophie walked up to the face of the stone god, looking deep into pockets of mineral rock. What had the man called him? Dis Mogwool? It wasn't English, whatever it was.

A strange thought fell on Sophie then, a sudden urge to pray. What did she have to lose at this point? A faster death? *Please God, kill me now.*

She laughed at that. Knelt. And began to whisper words she never thought she would ever speak.

"Dez Mogwül, or however the hell you say it...I ask you to cure me. Please."

It had been three weeks since Sophie had gone into complete remission, shocking the doctors and medical personnel who had deemed it necessary to run days worth of tests.

The results were clean.

Nada.

Zilch.

She was whole again. And she knew why.

She extended her lease on the cabin and found a remote job she could work from her laptop.

Each morning she started the day with a new ritual: visiting the chapel for prayer.

All her life she had longed to find a god of true power, a god who responded and acted like an actual freaking god!

Well, she'd found him.

Dez Mogwül.

With each visit, her devotion grew. She could feel, actually *feel* him reaching out to her — giving her strength. Wisdom. Abilities.

For example, she no longer needed her glasses.

Their connection continued throughout the day. Sometimes she thought she could hear him whispering to her. It wasn't creepy or off putting...it was just . . . nice to know he was there.

She continued to notice other things as well. Alien nests of vines and branches in the trees. Glimpses of movement just beyond her view. Eyes on her when she thought she was alone. But she knew it was her Lord, and that there was nothing to fear. It was just his influence spreading.

One day before leaving for her walk she felt an urge to bring a knife with her. Why? She didn't know. But she trusted Mogwül.

She expected an answer, and when she arrived at the chapel of bones she received one. How nice it was to actually expect and receive an answer!

Mogwül wanted to show her something, but he needed something from her in order to do that.

Nothing much.

Just a few drops of her blood.

Nothing she wouldn't miss. And a small price to pay to the being who saved her life.

Sophie didn't think twice about bringing the knife to her finger and digging the sharpened tip under her flesh. Crimson drops fell like rain into the dish at Mogwül's feet. She watched them roll down into the dark hole.

No sooner had the drops vanished, leaving a pristine and untainted dish, than a black vorpule sprang to life in a perfect orb above Mogwül's head. The black sphere rested on his hands, so it appeared he was holding it.

But this was no ordinary sphere, inside that circle she could see dancing color. Brighter and more surreal than any experience she'd ever had in her life. There were colors in that vortex she didn't even know existed. Then, as soon as it had opened, it was closed again, and a black bird was flapping its way across the chapel, out the door.

The experience had left her trembling, and like a half fulfilled orgasm, desperately craving more.

But she would have to wait.

●

Reports about deaths in the nearest town, a quaint hamlet by the name of Cadwich, reached Sophie's ears the following day. There had been several animal attacks in the area over the last few weeks, resulting in nine deaths and several more injuries and disappearances. The whole town was up in arms. Sophie couldn't have cared less.

Ever since she had left the chapel, she had one thought and one thought only: *get back.*

She had a dire need to look inside that portal again. The thought didn't even cross her mind that she had a god at her disposal and she could ask for anything she wanted. Eternal life. Wealth. A perfect lover. She only needed one thing. She had looked into heaven, and it had been the best moment of her life. She needed *more.*

Dez Mogwül had forbidden her to stay, and instructed her to come back to the chapel only once per day.

The next morning, she left at dawn. She gave more blood. She would have given him a finger, but instead she made a small incision on her wrist, allowing the blood to flow freely until she was commanded to stop.

Her connection to him was growing stronger. She could hear him now, in her head. It was more than just impressions, it was words. He was speaking to her! How blessed was she!

And she was aiding him in his mission; what exactly that was had not yet been revealed to her. He worked in mysterious ways. But today, she had allowed four of his servants to pass through into her world. Four! But she could give more. She knew she could give more — allow more servants to come through — keep that portal open longer so her eyes could look upon that world that was dazzling! Sublime! Defying all description.

And the next day she did. She gave blood until she grew faint.

She returned the day after, repeating the process for an entire week.

And each day, she felt his pleasure with her growing. His voice filled her with an ecstasy she had never imagined possible —

Sophie...you have honored me today...come back tomorrow...and I will reveal my secrets unto you...

The secrets spilled forth like lifegiving water from a fount...forgotten knowledge from before man was...

What a privilege...what an honor...

And of all the secrets she was told, the one she thought of the most was this: that the statue was not her Lord's true form. No man had ever had the privilege of seeing what he truly looked like.

She wanted to be the first.

She wanted to behold the Lord in all his glory and see him for what he truly was and shout praises to his holy name!

When the morning gasped its choking breath upon the world, Sophie was at the chapel's door dragging a frozen corpse behind her through the snow. It was only one of the many tasks he had asked her to complete over the days prior, and she had done them all gladly, without contestation.

She abandoned the sacrifice at the threshold and crawled her way over to the statue, kissing her Lord's stone feet. With her blade, she cut a stripe across her palm and watched the blood drip from her fist like she was squeezing a ball of blackberries. The black circle awakened, revealing a swirling window of madness within. She never knew what wonders she would behold through the window. Today she was flying over a desert of blue sand.

"Dez Mogwül," she called. "I wish to look upon your face. I wish to see you with my own eyes."

Patience, my daughter. I have many tasks for you yet to complete.

"I will do anything you ask. My body is weak, it fights me, it demands to see you, and I fear if I don't, I will lack the strength to continue."

An infinite silence. Then —

So be it.

The scene shifted and Sophie found herself soaring over a blackened wasteland marred by pits of green frothing substance and riddled with lumbering beasts too awful to describe.

She rose up a dark tower, to its pinnacle, and on a wizened throne sat Dez Mogwül in all his glory. It was nothing like she'd imagined. The thing before her could not be a god, it was simply too ghastly...*too monstrous.*

Blood poured from her ears in spurting streams. Her head burst into flames as her eyes melted, running down her face in boiling cascades of gore.

Sophie collapsed and the portal closed.

Just outside the chapel stood a ring of stoic figures, clad in elegant ceremonial crimson cloaks. Two strode out into the snow, leaving sweeping footprints behind them. She would be put to good use. Her blood would be drained and poured into the chalice. Her bones would be harvested and used to expand their church.

One of the bird-beasts perched above the chapel watched this process to its conclusion. Then, when there was nothing left, it gave an ear rending shriek, and fled into its new world.

STORY NOTES

THE SEED OF THIS story was the idea "What if there was a chapel made of bones?" I don't know where that came from, it was an image that got stuck in my mind. Religion can be a frustrating thing. Many pray and feel they don't receive an answer. They feel they hear nothing but silence. I finally found the story when I asked the question "What if there was a God who actually answered?"

r/AskReddit Post Title:

What is the most unexplainable thing that's ever happened to you? Serious Answers Only

Response posted by u/claireshepherd42 6 months ago

Response Title: **THE TRANSPARENT MAN**

Upon hearing the term "Transparent Man", readers today are most likely going to imagine that this is a reference to some superhero from the lesser searched rung of a dusty comic shop (and indeed it very well might be for all I know), but to me it means something else entirely. I first heard the expression, in the context of which I am currently using it, when I was working as a CNA at the Retirement Facility off of Benedict's Hollow down in Ingram, a sleepy town that rests beside the Long Island Sound in southern Connecticut. Previous to landing that job I had been a fickle minded young woman, hopping around from job to job, unsure of my future objectives and without a roadmap to show me the way. I suspect that I was like many youth are, lacking direction and after finding themselves suddenly thrust out of their parents' nests and into the real world, hesitant to voyage too far from home.

It was as I was thus employed that I first heard whisperings of the "Transparent Man". I had mentioned to Sandy Burke, one of the in-home residents, that the boy I was talking with at the time had just ghosted me, and she made a comment that I thought was rather odd.

"Cheer up, honey. You've been blessed with a pretty face, another tramp in trousers will come along soon," she said, or something to this effect, in an effort to cheer me up. "Besides, it can't be any worse than what happened to Tess Strang."

I recognized that name as one of the other residents of our facility. "What happened to her?"

Sandy cocked a tweezed eyebrow. "You know how most men have a tendency to disappear from our lives? Well, hers actually did, right in front of her eyes. *The transparent man. Ask her about the transparent man.*"

Naturally, this elicited a raised eyebrow of my own. Near the end of my shift once most of the residents had retired to bed I found my way to Theresa Strang's room, situated at the far end of the east wing, and discovered that she was still very much awake. I asked her about the comment made by Sandy, and recorded our conversation. Obviously I am in no position to verify any details of Theresa's story, and my cursory searches for official documentation or newspaper articles about her case only lend credence to the more realistic aspects of her report, and not the ones that stretched into the supernatural.

Make of it what you will. I present the audio file as well as the transcript of our dialogue here, for your perusing and enjoyment. More likely than not it is the attention seeking ramblings of a half demented senior citizen, but I'll never forget the look in her eyes or the somber tone in which she told me this story, with tears in her eyes. Regardless of whether the finer details of the account are true or not, it is a tragedy of the finest making.

OFFICIAL AUDIO TRANSCRIPT   October 15th, 2014

CS: Good evening, Ms. Strang. Do you remember me?

TS: Of course I do, dear. You're the one with the pretty nails. The only one brave enough to do that around here. I wish I could still go out and do that.

CS: Aw, well what's stopping you?

TS: A good pair of legs. Help me out of this chair, will you?

[Shuffling and grunting]

CS: I got them done again this week. Are you comfortable?

TS: Yes, thank you dear. Ah, look at that. You changed them already?

CS: I do them every two weeks.

TS: They must be paying you pretty good if you can afford to do that.

CS: Well, I don't have a boyfriend so I get to spend all my money on myself.

TS: Good. Don't rush into anything. You've got your whole life to spend with boys.

CS: Did you take your pills for the evening?

TS: You mean my horse tranquilisers? Not yet. Do I have to?

CS: Eventually. But maybe we can talk for a while first. Is it okay if I sit down?

TS: What am I gonna do, stop you? I can't even get out of bed.

CS: That's just what you want people to think. It's all a façade.

TS: Yeah, that's right.

CS: I heard Sandy mention something today that I wanted to ask you about.

TS: Sandy Burke? I thought you were smart, girl. You should know better than to trust anything that comes out of that cow's mouth.

CS: Well you'll have to tell me how true this is. She said your husband disappeared in front of your eyes. Something about a transparent man?

[Prolonged silence. The beeping from a monitor can be heard]

CS: I didn't mean to upset you. We don't have to talk about it if —

TS: Yes we do. Yes we do. It's been awhile since I've talked about it is all. After years of people calling me crazy, I learned to keep my trap shut.

CS: So it's true, you really did see him disappear?

TS: I did. That's the short story. The full story is much longer. How much time do you have?

CS: I get off at midnight.

TS: You wanna hear it?

CS: I would love to. Would you mind if I recorded it?

TS: You can do that?

CS: Yes. On my phone.

TS: I'll be dead soon anyway, do whatever the hell you want.

[aggressive coughing]

[Water pouring into a cup]

TS: Thank you dear. Now, I'll tell you my story. I've got to remember how it begins, is all. It's been so long — [drawn out sigh]. Okay. I've got it. When Roger and I were newly weds we lived out in Rhode Island. We bought a house from Roger's Uncle that he had bought from a Sears Catalog and put it together himself. You could do that back then. And we were happy. You never knew Roger, but everyone loved him. He was always smiling, always trying to help others. To the point where sometimes I became irritated with him. I would tell him not to stop and help folks stranded on the side of the road because he would always do that and make us late for dinner or wherever it was we were going. And he would always give me the same look and say "Tess, if we were the ones stuck, wouldn't you want someone to help?" And I'd always feel so guilty after that, but he would take my hand and reassure me that our destination didn't matter as much as the people we helped along the way. That was Roger.

Anyway, we had this strange neighbor who lived next door to us. An old man by the name of Josiah Sturgess. He was a bit of a recluse, and we didn't see much of him except when he would go out to get his mail. We tried reaching out a few times to get to know him a bit. We would make him dinner or invite him over for a social evening, but he would always either decline or not answer the door, in a rather judgmental way too. Strange man. I was content to let the old scrooge alone, let him rot away in solitude. After all, that's what he wanted, but Roger was more persistent. He saw Josiah's rejection as a challenge, and so one day when the old man failed to go out and collect his mail, Roger began bringing it to h im.

Day after day Roger would do this, and he would never get any response from the old man. We stopped seeing him, and the mail was piling up on his porch. So one day Roger decides that he's going to break into the man's house to make sure he is okay. I told him not to do it, that maybe the man was on vacation, or maybe he was ignoring us at last. But Roger only gave me that look. I caved. Maybe the old cronie really did need our help. So when Roger brought the crowbar up Josiah's front porch, I accompanied him.

CS: Naturally.

TS: Naturally. Well, wouldn't you? We didn't know what we were gonna find, and what we did find was so strange, Claire it really was. Roger cracked open the door and we called out for this man, Josiah, and no one answered. Immediately we noticed there was an awful smell. It smelled so bad, I can't even describe what it smelled like, but it made me want to vomit. It's been so long but I remember several details very vividly. I remember all the walls of the house were painted black, which I thought was so weird, because it was the sixties. Nothing was black in the sixties. There was one wall that had this writing on it, right on the wood in chalk. It wasn't English, it looked Egyptian, or something like that. I should have copied some of the characters down, maybe it could have helped us. Anyway, we searched the whole house, top to bottom and there is no sign of Josiah. He's just gone, like he abandoned the place. But the whole time I kept feeling like we needed to get out of there. Something was really telling me that we weren't supposed to be there. But I didn't want to leave Roger, and I knew he wasn't going to leave until he'd searched every room.

We got to the basement, and there was — it was the most bizarre thing I had ever seen up until that point in my life. There were plants growing on the walls. And the floor. And not like a garden, but I have to assume there were cracks in the concrete, I couldn't even see the concrete so I don't even know, but it looked like plants had grown up through the cracks and gotten out of control. Like no one had been down there in decades to clear them out.

CS: Whoa.

TS: I know. So bizarre.

CS: It sounds like Jumanji.

TS: [laughing] You know, it kinda was. Like a jungle in there. Well, finally we realize that we're not going to find this guy and as we're walking toward the door to leave I hear Roger kind of shout. I said "What's wrong?" And he says "I think that something just touched me on my arm." Well there was nothing there, so I said "Maybe it was a fly or a bee." And he said "No, no it can't be anything like that. This was like an arm or a hand. It grabbed me."

At the time I just said "Yeah, whatever. It was a bug." And we left. We decided there's nothing more we could do. We did our neighborly duty. It wasn't until that night when I noticed something was wrong. We were getting ready for bed and Roger was in the bathroom when I heard him call out. I rushed in, thinking maybe he cut himself while he was shaving, but he was just standing in front of the mirror with his shirt off.

That's when I realized what I was looking at. His skin was — well the only way to describe it is to say it was losing its color. Losing its pigmentation. Normally I could see some of the veins in his arms, but now I could see every vein, every line of blood snaking its way through his body was visible to our naked eyes. "It's the damnedest thing," he said. He just kept saying that over and over, staring at his own body. I asked him how he was feeling and he said fine, just dandy. We were bot h baffled by this. I asked him if he wanted to go to the hospital, and he said no, but I made him go anyway. It was a quick trip. They ran some tests, but didn't see anything wrong with him, so they sent us home. Nothing they could do, they said.

I don't think I have to explain why that night I didn't get a lick of sleep. Roger though, he didn't seem too worried about it, and I had him next to me snoring the whole night. All I could do was think that there was something wrong with him. When he finally did rise, I rose with him, and took him by the arm and dragged him right into the bathroom with me.

I don't think I've ever screamed so loud as I did then. Whatever process was running its course in his body had progressed exponentially over the night. To me, it looked like his skin was just gone. Like someone had removed his skin from his body. Can you imagine that? Have you ever seen in a doctor's office, one of those cutaway posters, where they show the organs and systems inside the body, how they all sit and work together, it was like looking at one of those, but it wasn't a poster, it was my Roger. He was a walking bag of muscle, organs, and bone — and I couldn't tell what was holding him together. He's just as scared as I am, and I can see — actually see, his heart beat faster when he looks at himself in the mirror.

I went to touch him, to see if his skin really was gone, and it was so bizarre, because I couldn't touch his heart or stomach, if I closed my eyes, I don't know if I could have known there was any difference. He felt just like he always did, I could even feel his wedding ring on his finger and the stubble on his chin. But to my eyes, it looked like it was just gone!

This time, it was Roger who demanded I take him to the hospital. He put a ski mask on over his head so people wouldn't give him strange looks. But I was the one who made him pause — to take a picture. I don't know why I felt like I had to do that, but I snapped it with my polaroid. Maybe it was because if for some reason all this went away, I didn't want the doctor thinking I was crazy and had made it up, they're like to think that of a woman, I've had it happen to me before.

But I had sense enough to pack a bag. I knew this wasn't going to be a quick trip to the hospital. Something was seriously wrong, anyone would know that — and I knew they weren't going to let him go till those doctors had figured out what the hell was going on. Will you help me over to the window, dear?

CS: Of course.

[Sounds of groaning and footsteps shuffling. A window opens]

TS: I need a cigarette.

CS: After what you've been through, I don't blame you.

TS: You don't think I'm crazy?

CS: Who am I to say? It didn't happen to me.

TS: You're damn right it didn't. And I hope it never does.

CS: Did they ever figure out what happened to him? What was going on?

TS: Those doctors pinched and prodded him, injected him with god knows what, burned him, electrocuted him...we transferred hospitals three times. Three! Each time adding another level of security, the last one was some kind of basement, I had to pitch a fit just so they let me stay with him....Every kind of specialist and expert on the planet was called in it seemed, and they all said the same thing. "We've never seen anything like this." So to answer your question, no, they never figured it out. But I know what it was.

CS: What was it?

TS: Well, I've got my theory. And it's better than any of the theories they came up with. It was that house. Our neighbor. Josiah Sturgess. Whatever he was doing in that house, whatever happened to him, it was connected to what happened to Roger. That's where it all started. And I sent them there, I told them about that place. They said they sent someone to check it out, but when they came back, they said they hadn't found anything and then when I got home the house was boarded up and taped off.

CS: But...why did it affect him and not you?

TS: Impossible to say for certain, but I always think back to whatever touched him in there, whatever grabbed him or brushed against him, that's what did it. It didn't touch me, it touched him. And set off this chain of events which tore him from me.

[Theresa becomes emotional.]

CS: Here.

TS: Thank you, dear.

[Theresa blows her nose]

TS: I suppose we better finish this story. It always breaks a piece of my heart to tell it.

CS: I'm sorry. I didn't mean to —

TS: Nonsense, dear, if I didn't want to tell it, by God I wouldn't. No one tells me what to do, not at ninety-three! No, the truth is I like telling it, even though it hurts. When I talk about what happened, I get to think about Roger, remember him, and it helps. I get to share what I went through, and even if the person I'm talking to can't possibly understand, hell, I don't even understand, just having someone else try to understand, it helps. So help me to my bed.

CS: Yes, ma'm.

[Theresa chuckles]

TS: Never get old, dear. Now, I have to think of how to tell this. We hated that hospital. All of them, but especially the last one. They finally decided to quarantine us in a windowless room, and whenever anyone came in, they would be wearing this bulky suit. Apparently they didn't want to catch whatever Roger had, and even though I loathed them for it at the time, I can't say that I blame them. But they didn't give me a suit.

CS: They didn't do any tests on you?

TS: They did. They wanted to keep us apart, but I wouldn't hear of it. I wouldn't have Roger go through that alone. Going through it was hard enough. And I had this sinking feeling...that I was going to lose him. It didn't take long, this process...Only three, four days. We hardly slept. Hardly ate. Bit by bit I watched as my husband's body faded away. His nervous system, his organs, his muscle and tissue...until all that was left was a skeleton, lying in bed next to me. By that point I knew the route this disease was going to take. He was going to disappear. Fully, completely. I was going to lose him forever.

So the next time a doctor tried to come in, I knocked him to the ground. We ran — we escaped from that damn building and we stole a car and we drove home and we didn't look back. Me and the skeleton by my side. Drove all the way back to Rhode Island. I don't fully comprehend it, but Roger wouldn't stop looking out the window. I held his hand, and he just kept screaming beside me. I would ask him what it was, and he would just say "There's something out there." But I would look and it would seem to me an ordinary world. Just green trees blurring by on the side of the road. But he saw something. He tried to describe it to me, something floating in the air. Many things, all around us, monsters, he said. By the time we got home, he was shaking. I sat on the couch and held him, and he just kept looking around.

He was the one who put it together, not me. He said that he felt like he was in another world. That everything around him was the same, the same space, the same buildings and people, but it was like there was another world overlaying the one he knew. That there were abominable creatures everywhere he looked, monstrous entities that curdled his flesh, clinging to the walls, floating through the air, and slithering across the ground. The closest thing he could compare it to was the revolting work of artist Jesse Hensley and his paintings of the Clinging Squobs. I said it didn't make sense, I thought he'd lost it. But he gripped me with his two bony hands and his eye sockets looked me right in the eye and he said "No, I've figured it out. I'm not just disappearing, I'm being transferred...from one plane of existence to another. Once I'm gone, I'll have to live in this universe of horrors!"

He sobbed and I held him. For a long time I held him. That's when we realized his bones were starting to become transparent as well. We wept together. And then I made dinner. Spaghetti and meatballs, his favorite. And we ate. There was nothing else to do. We went to bed. Made love. By the time we were done, I was holding an invisible man in my arms. We talked until we fell asleep, remembering the good times, telling each other how much we loved each other. He was so scared. I didn't know what to tell him. Eventually we fell asleep. When I woke up, I was in an empty bed.

The people from the hospital showed up with the police sometime in the night, wanting to know where he was, but I told them I didn't know, and that was the God's honest truth. They didn't arrest me as I thought they might, but they did interrogate me for several hours before finally leaving me alone to grieve. There was a car parked outside my house for a few weeks afterward, but eventually they left me alone.

I was a widow. I had to learn how to be one. Had to tell my family, and his. The doctors kept everything out of the papers, and so I had nothing to prove what I was saying was true. There were no articles or reports. Everyone thought I was crazy. And I did spend some time in Rock Harbor Hospital. For a time I really thought I might be crazy and imagined the whole thing, husband, marriage, disease, all of it. In the early days, there were times when I would feel something touch me in the dark, like a hand trying to take my own, but whenever I would turn around, there would be no one there. Sometimes I heard a voice calling my name. Was it a ghost? Was I imagining it? Whatever it was, those things stopped with time as well. My husband, as far as I was concerned, was gone. Was dead. He had transitioned to another plane. I don't know why. I don't know how. But I never saw him again.

CS: And Josiah Sturgess? Did he ever turn up?

TS: No. Not as far as I know. He was declared missing as well, and eventually his house was burned by vandals. Or at least, that's what the papers said. So what do you think? You think I'm crazy?

CS: Ms. Strang...who am I to say? You seem sane to me. All I know is that unexplained shit happens everyday, who am I to say what can and can't happen. If you say you saw your husband disappear, then I believe you. I wasn't there, you know?

TS: Well that's one of the more elegant responses I've heard in a while. So thank you, for not treating me like I'm some nutcase. All I can do is tell the truth as I know it. There have been times when I've doubted what I experienced, but the memories are always there. They never fade or shift to a 'reality' that I blocked out, like so many therapists have tried to tell me it would over the years. So I guess it must be true. Crazy world, huh?

CS: Yeah.

TS: Well, thanks for listening, anyhow.

CS: Are you kidding? I'd much rather sit here and listen to you then do my rounds.

TS: I hope I didn't get you in trouble.

CS: Eh, it'll be worth it. I should probably go check on Mr. Ellsbury, but I'll stop by tomorrow, okay? And it's time to take your horse tranquilisers.

TS: Okay, dear. You know where I'll be. Falling in love always ends the same way, which is to say, sooner or later it ends.

END OF TRANSCRIPT

Theresa Strang passed about six months later. Since she had no surviving relatives, I was given the task of going through her small assortment of belongings and donating or trashing the lot. She had a small photo album with pictures from her early life. Her wedding with Roger, their first home, and tucked into the back sleeve was an old polaroid stamped May 1861. It was the picture she had taken before bringing Roger to the hospital. The picture of a man sitting on a couch, all his inner organs and systems visible, like someone had just ripped the skin off his body. My first instinct was to try and get it verified as not having been doctored, even though I knew it wasn't. But even if it was verified, I knew people wouldn't believe. The government would probably try and bury it. I didn't want that. So I kept it in my own personal collection. I, at least, would always know what it was: the only surviving photo of the transparent man.

STORY NOTES

This was a fun one. I knew I wanted to play with form, an audio transcript. I thought it would be interesting to tell a cosmic horror love story. Of course, because it's cosmic horror, it wouldn't end well. But it was a fun challenge and I think it's unique. This story was inspired b y *The Invisible Man* by H.G. Wells and *From Beyond* by Lovecraft. I thought the idea of someone fading away was scary, but Roger didn't just fade away, he faded into somewhere new. Somewhere filled with indescribable terrors, and that, to me, is a terrifying idea.

THE WITCH LIGHTS OF GAMUN G'BAR

a novella

I

From the moment he was born, it seemed, the world had wished for Ned Pickman's destruction. And so, it seemed sensible that he should also seek to destroy the world. For most of his life he'd had no aspirations to do so, in fact his acts up until that fateful night could be described as a series of pathetic rejections by his peers and family. Eventually, it became clear that he did not belong. He'd *never* belong — even if by some miracle his neighbors managed to throw all judgments to the wind, he'd still know — every time he looked in the mirror — that he would never be "normal."

And that's why Ned tried to take his own life. He'd tried before, numerous times, but he had never really meant it, had never actually, down in the deep dark belly of his crippled soul, intended to follow through. To bid goodbye to his existence and welcome oblivion. But on that fateful night he had — he'd crushed the pills into a colored powder — mixed them into his water — and had been raising the bottle to his lips when the knock on his apartment door stopped him in his tracks.

The man at the door called himself Mr. Locke. The tall, gaunt man who always dressed and spoke so elegantly, coming just in the nick of time with ever so charming an offer.

Ned Pickman. . . would you like to destroy the world?

And now Ned was shuffling his boots down a street of African dust, eying a half starved prostitute who was posing for him beside an abandoned building of crumbling brick.

It was amazing, the places life took you.

Ned sauntered toward the woman, a bone thin thing in an oversized blue dress that billowed away from her skeletal body. She bit her cracked lips and drew near, eager to captivate her prey.

If only she knew.

"What you hiding behind that mask, handsome?"

Ned dug into his pocket. "How much for your services?"

The woman's smile faltered — a brief indication of hesitation — but she did not turn away. "For you? Discount. Five thousand."

He paid, the equivalent of five dollars in American currency. The woman couldn't take her eyes off him. His mask made him mysterious. His attire added to his bizarre persona — black gloves, long sleeved suit coat in the sweltering heat, and a dark cloak whipping at his back. It was a look that attracted attention. It was a look that exuded power.

The prostitute took Ned's gloved hand and led him into the decaying structure. Inside was a sparse room. A rusted bedframe and stained mattress — no sheets — and a few supplies which rested on a stool on the dirt floor. Just enough to get the job done.

The woman looked up at him, eyes trusting, trying to gauge the secrets that lay behind his façade. "Alright. Mask on or off?"

"On." He reached into his side bag and pulled out a clear bottle and needle. "You wanna have some fun?"

Ned inserted the needle into the tube and pulled the plunger. Once full, he flicked it to dispel all bubbles, and beckoned his guest closer. He trailed his finger along her arm and drove the needle gently into her flesh. She gasped, but he held her firm.

The morphine didn't take long to take effect. She wobbled, one hand holding her head. "What did you give to me?"

Ned ditched the needle but pocketed the morphine. "I need you to come with me." He took her by the arm, supporting her with his hand around her. She flopped limply, like a rag doll.

He guided her through town, and by the time they got to the train station she could barely stand. She mumbled something incoherent and Ned helped her sit on a shaded bench. People should think her a drunk.

"Is that the one you've chosen?"

Ned turned, startled, his heart pounding, to find Locke standing beside him in a dark suit. No matter how long they worked together, Ned had never gotten used to that. The way he just appeared and disappeared, as if by magic.

"Yeah," Ned said, "You got the tickets?"

The tall man extended a thin hand with two slips of paper, his bones protruding from his skin like someone had taken a vacuum hose to his mouth and sucked all the fat out of him. Ned hated the way Locke's eyes felt crawling over his body. Like they could see right through his mask. He tore his own away in search of anything else. The tracks. They were a reasonable thing to focus on. The train tracks seemed to stretch across the plains into infinity. There was no clock in this village. "Isn't it time yet?"

"Time is meaningless."

Ned rolled his eyes. "Maybe to you." All these years working for Locke and how much did he know about him? Almost nothing. The man was a sealed tomb. Not one for small talk.

He stood beside his boss and retreated into his thoughts to pass the time, mindful of a small crowd that was beginning to arrive.

At last Ned glimpsed the thin trail of smoke on the horizon — and watched as the train grew from a blur to a distant shape — until it pulled up before them, brakes screeching to a halt.

Ned glanced down at the woman. A globule of drool hung from her lip. She was dead asleep.

A small cluster of passengers emerged from the train's cars — but the throng of waiting citizens crowded around the doors, eager to board. A ticket master acted as gatekeeper, punching each ticket before waving them on.

"Board," Locke instructed.

Ned spread the tickets in his hand — only two. "You're not coming?"

"No." Locket must have sensed Ned's lingering as a dissatisfaction with his answer, because he added, "We're being followed."

Ned looked around at the faces on the platform. "How do you know? Where?"

"You know what to do. Perform the ritual. Open the gate."

Ned suddenly felt very alone. Very much like a child who was being told they would be home alone for the first time. "Yeah." He had been counting on not being by himself at the end of the world — but there was no changing that now. He knew how to open the gate, though this would be his first time doing it all on his own.

Ned hefted his cargo off the bench and joined the line. The ticket master frowned at him, with the mask and the unconscious woman — he had every right to be suspicious. But he asked no questions, punched their tickets, and Ned pulled the woman down a narrow aisle until he found an empty couple of seats.

The girl's head thumped against the window, but she did not wake.

A train whistle sounded. Ned looked out the window. Locke was gone.

Moments later, the train began to move.

II

"Stop the car."

The wheels on the paint-stripped cab screeched to a halt, the taxi rocking to a stop with an unexpected shudder. Dane Westwood brushed his sandy hair out of his eyes (a futile gesture as it immediately flopped back down). His thick fingers flipped through notes of local currency. He cursed under his breath, and with no true comprehension of the local exchange rate, handed the driver a spread of bills. "Are we square?"

The driver took the bills and flashed Dane a thumbs up. Dane searched the man's face for any indication of surprise or glee, but the man was smart and kept his reaction discreet.

Dane grimaced and turned to the woman next to him, a Peruvian girl named Fabiana, her hands resting serenely over her swollen belly. "Come on."

He stepped out of the car, but when Fabiana did not follow, he reached back in, seized her frail wrist, and pulled her out after him. She nearly fell into the dirt road, kept on her feet only by Dane's vice grip. She adjusted her black hooded cloak over her shorts and dirt stained tank top, which was not large enough to cover the growing child beneath. She was almost to term, but with no proper examination by a doctor it was impossible to say how close.

Dane shut the door and released her. "Stay. Right here." His fist thumped the trunk twice and it popped open. "There you are, sexy." Inside the car trunk sat Dane's own trunk — a modified antique traveler's case, sealed with an unprecedented amount of locks and latches. Everything in the world Dane Westwood professed to care about was either inside his bank account or inside this trunk.

Dane was a strong and muscular individual, but it took him a considerable amount of effort to heave the heavy trunk out of the car and place it onto the ground. He'd added a sturdy frame to the exterior, with wheels and an extendable handle like a modern travel suitcase, but wheels were much more useful on hard, flat surfaces — not loose sand. No, this would require some serious gruntwork.

Dane the Grunt.

Sweat was already dripping down his face and moistening his pits when he took Fabiana by the hand and began to lug both her and his trunk down the main "street" of this backwards bazaar of a town. He had better be sufficiently compensated for all the trouble, or the old man was gonna hear it.

Bring the girl to me.

Those had been his orders. Dane had been provided an address in the middle of nowhere Africa, and a promise of "sufficient compensation." No dollar amount had been mentioned.

But the old man had earned his trust. After all they'd been through together, after all Dane had *seen*, the old man had earned at least that. For the last five years he'd kept Dane on a golden lure. Dane didn't know where his mysterious benefactor had come into his seemingly bottomless fortune, and wasn't sure he wanted to. All he knew was that as long as the money kept flowing and he got to shoot things, he'd do whatever the old man asked.

Dane's double pistoled holster hung heavy around his chest as he rounded a corner and saw the train tracks at the end of the road. *Finally.* His head pounded in the infernal heat. The sun gleaming, like a divine vision above, sapped all energy like a magnet. He could not recall the last time he'd slept. They had flown from Rio — then traveled by train to Mzuzu, where they had caught a taxi. Dane didn't dare close his eyes, not around the girl. Victim or not, she'd been part of that cult, and if Dane had learned anything since being recruited by the old man — it was that cultists were not to be trusted.

The haze of desert waves snaking their way across his vision dissipated into oblivion and the train tracks became two immobile lines on the earth as Dane arrived at the "station" with his cargo in tow.

Beyond the tracks was nothing but wilderness. This was it. The edge of civilization.

Dane scanned the faces of the other waiting passengers, most of them clustered in scarce fragments of shade, until he found who he was looking for.

The old man.

Min Huang.

Dane lugged his trunk over to the canopy beneath which Min was standing. "Well, Min, I babysat this one halfway across the world for you, just like you asked. You gonna tell me why?" Dane hadn't noticed him until now, but there was an African boy, maybe twelve or thirteen, leaning against the building beside Min. A black cat was curled around his neck. "Scram, kid."

"He's with me," Min said, his tattooed hand snapped a pocket watch shut. "You were almost late."

"Well, I'm sorry Old Man — I can't control the traffic. I got here as fast as I could. She's your problem now."

Min took Fabiana by the hand, looked her in the eye, and with a twinkle in his own, kissed her. "Bienvenido, mi niño. I'm afraid that's about the extent of my Spanish."

"Where'd you pick up the kid?" Dane asked, finally setting his trunk down with a groan.

"This is Jabari. I found him in Mombasa. Or rather, he found me." Min watched Fabiana as she shuffled, one hand gripping her stomach, over to the wall and sat down, head bowed. "Has she said anything?"

"Not a peep the entire trip." Dane unstrapped his canteen and took a much needed drink.

"She's been through a lot."

"So have I," Dane said. "So, you gonna tell me what we're all doing out here in God's sand pit?"

"We'll get to that, on the train. We're still waiting for one more." Min smiled. The bastard was always smiling, like he knew something you didn't, and usually that was true.

"Who?"

"A professor from Oxford."

"So mysterious. Why do you have to be so damn mysterious all the time, Min? How much time do we got?"

"Until the train arrives."

Dane scoffed, looking around. His eyes halted on a set of open doors across the street. "I'm gonna get a drink. Watch my trunk, will ya?"

Without waiting for a reply, Dane walked back into the sweltering sun, praying the establishment harbored some kind of alcoholic relief.

He passed through the doors and audibly sighed, a sign of gratitude for the circulating air of the fans. All eyes were on him. He smiled and waved, reminded that he was probably the only white man within a hundred miles.

The shop was a mish mash of functions — a restaurant, convenience store, and bar among them. Yellowed advertisements covered any surface that wasn't exposed brick. A TV mounted to the wall played a football game, and flies hovered around tables of empty dishes.

Dane approached the counter, not wanting to spend any longer than he had to in this place. He greeted the man behind the counter with a grimace, thrumming his fingers on the glass. "Hi. You guys got any strong liquor?" He smiled wide in wishful anticipation.

The proprietor dipped down behind the counter and returned bearing a labelless bottle of amber liquid. Dane could already feel his mouth beginning to water. "Uh, what is that?"

"Thibarine."

"Thibarine? Uh, yeah, give me a glass of Thibarine."

The man poured a glass and Dane traded the glass for a bill, once again not bothering to ask for change. "Come to Papa." He hefted the glass, then swatted a fly away. He decided he wanted to enjoy it in a fly free environment — he turned —

And collided explosively with the idiot who had the audacity to walk in his turning bubble! The contents of Dane's glass showered his white shirt.

"Mother —"

"Oh! Sorry, I'm so sorry!" The woman in front of him was pulling a suitcase, looking very out of place in a white linen shirt, pressed tan pants and pristine boots. She spoke with a British accent, but her hair and skin were far too dark to suggest that she sprang from Anglo-Saxon stock.

"What the devil are you doing, lady?"

"I'm so so sorry. I was looking for someone — I *am* looking for someone. A gentleman by the name of Min Huang. I was going to ask that man at the counter if he had seen —"

"Wait a minute," Dane held up a hand to cut her off. "You're the Oxford professor?"

The woman's eyes went from frenzied to suspicious as she absorbed the question. "Well, why do you have to say it like that? '*You're the Oxford professor.*'" She did her best imitation of a husky American.

Dane frowned. If there was one thing he couldn't abide, it was being mocked. Especially by Oxford professors who had just spilled his drink. "Okay, first of all, I don't sound like that. And second of all, you bumped into me! And I didn't expect an Oxford professor to be so —"

"So what?"

Dane bit his tongue — his first inclination had been to call her pretty, which she was, striking in fact, with a well proportioned face, but his current desire was not to compliment her, so instead he said, "so clumsy!"

The woman's eyebrows coiled. "Charming. Well, you must be with Min too, then. I don't suppose it would be too much to ask for you to point me in his direction? Is he here?" She looked around, actively trying to avoid looking at Dane.

Dane took the woman by the shoulders and turned her toward the south door, then pointed across the road at Min. "Only Chinaman in town. Right over there."

"Okay."

"You see him?"

"Yes — I — thank you." She removed his hands from her shoulders. "Very much." She lifted her bag just as a thin whistle blew, signaling the train's arrival.

"You know you owe me a drink!" he called after her. The blur of the train rushed by the window, and Dane sighed and placed the empty cup on the bar. It was probably better to keep a clear head anyway.

Dane charged out the door, made his way across the street, and collected his trunk.

"Dane, this is Mona. She's the professor I was telling you about." Min motioned Mona to Dane.

The look she flashed him could be defined as nothing short of a death glare. But she falsified a polite smile for Min's sake. "Yes, we've met," she said, her dark eyes watching him from beneath heavy lashes. "What's your role in this party?"

"I shoot things and kill monsters."

Mona's lip fluttered into a half smile, genuine this time, then she gave him the cold shoulder. It was a smile of amusement. A smile of naivety. This was her first rodeo. No one could be prepared for what they would encounter when they got entangled with Min. She would be screaming soon enough. If the stakes weren't so dire, Dane would take more satisfaction in that thought.

Min clapped his hands. "Well, we're all here. I've already paid for our passage. We have an entire cab to ourselves. Mr. Westwood, please escort Fabiana aboard."

Dane grunted and helped Fabiana to her feet. "I better be adequately compensated for this, Min!" Min did not respond. He knew, as well as Dane, that Dane would receive all he wanted and more, and in return he would do whatever Min asked and put up with his clandestine mannerisms.

Dane once more lugged his trunk along with Fabiana to the train car that Min was now entering. He motioned to the ladder and then monitored the girl as she climbed, until she passed through the door. With tremendous effort, Dane hoisted his trunk up to the platform, then hopped up himself.

"What's in the trunk?" Jabari asked, his cat cradled in his arms.

Dane squinted down at the kid in the harsh light. "When it's time to know, you'll know."

Dane gripped the hand rail and shivered. A sensation of creeping dread was crawling up his spine. A feeling like he wasn't alone. . . a primordial instinct letting him know he was in danger. Dane had come to respect these impressions since working with Min — and his cautiousness had saved his life more than once. Dane let his eyes sweep the scattered faces around him — and then, the feeling faded, almost as if it knew, almost as if it sensed his awareness...

His fingers released around the holster of his pistol. He hadn't even realized he was holding it.

"Well are you going to stand there all day, or are you going to let us on?" Mona chirped from below.

Dane stood, gripping the handle of his trunk.

"Is all that for you?" Mona asked, eying his trunk. "You pack more than my sister."

"Trust me, we're going to need this trunk. Your sister I can do without."

After one final look around, Dane Westwood entered the train car.

III

As Mona Marzouk looked around the train car, at the rugged, worn seatbacks and tarnished brass, the cracked windows with gr-affiti etched upon their smudged surfaces, she thought about how strange it was to be here. She was not a stranger to Africa. Mona had been born in Egypt, had spent many years traveling back and forth between England and her mother's homeland. She was a child of Africa — but Africa was a big place. And she was far from home.

Mona made her way to the back of the train car, her hand bouncing along the seats as she went. A whole car to themselves. She had communicated with Min only through email before today. He had reached out to her, wanting to know more about her research into ancient religions. He was especially inquisitive about her paper on the V'Razis myth. She had been happy to oblige. After all, it wasn't every day someone reached out to discuss academic work on half forgotten myths. It wasn't like she was a pop star, throned by voracious fans. Opportunities to discuss her passions with attentive parties were rare. And when Min had offered her a chance to learn more about V'Razis, to join him on an expedition to a location where she might continue her research . . . to say she was intrigued would be an understatement. Even despite her initial hesitation, and Min's tight lippedness as to the details of their journey and the exact form this "research" might take, she could not turn down Min's fully funded offer. What did she have to lose? A few days in Africa?

Or your life, you ninny.

Mona swallowed and turned, realizing she had inadvertently distanced herself from the rest of the expedition members. The pregnant woman was seated on one of the padded benches. The boy was chasing his cat, which was hopping from bench to bench. The gruff mannered American was checking the locks on the windows, and the old man...

Was watching her.

The train shuddered, then began to move. They were heading north, into the wastelands. Hadn't Stephen King written a book about traveling on a train into the wastelands? She hoped this journey wouldn't end up being like one of his books.

"Jabari, help me draw the shades," Min instructed before motioning to Mona, "You too, Mona. Start at your end."

Mona did as she was told, and with each stretch of fabric she pulled shut, the car grew darker. In her office at Oxford the chance to head into the field, the thrill of adventure, had made her heart soar . . . yet now she felt woefully uneasy. She didn't know these people. The old man seemed nice, but his hands were covered in tattoos, and she could see them peeking out from under his shirt around his collar — as if his entire torso and arms were covered. What kind of a man did that? She tried to convince herself not to judge, but in this situation, wasn't it wise to consider all possibilities? Wasn't the stereotype that shifty, criminal types were the ones who more often then not covered themselves in tattoos?

And what was the American hiding in that trunk of his? He was the one she feared the most. Him and those guns hanging openly at his chest. He caught her looking at him and she glanced away. She didn't want to give the wrong impression. He'd been rude to her upon first meeting, another bad sign. Yet, she had spilled his drink. But despite their chilly introduction, she could not deny that he was well built, his face was far from an eye sore. And there was a sort of rugged sense of blunt energy to him that twisted her up inside.

The boy seemed benign enough. And the pregnant woman? Once she was finished with the shades Mona sat on the bench across from Fabiana, reached out, and took her hand. Fabiana winced at the contact but did not pull her hand away. The women were outnumbered here, they had to stick together. Even if the woman came from a different walk of life, surely she could recognize that?

With the final curtain pulled into place, they were left in near darkness. Min lit several candles, which he had pulled from a case, and set them on his table, securing them with tape from the constant movement.

Mona squeezed the woman's hand. Fabiana raised her dark eyes to meet Mona's gaze but did not return the gesture. The girl's flesh was cold and icy. It was like touching a cold mannequin. "How'd you get roped into all this?"

The woman only looked at her. She made no effort to even move her lips.

"Don't bother. She doesn't talk. Trust me, I've tried." Dane was leaning over the back of the seat behind Mona. She could smell his sweaty musk and once more found herself wishing he'd go away. Or at least back away. She didn't mind looking at him from a distance.

Without looking at him she said, "I can't imagine why she wouldn't want to talk to you. I mean, you're such an easy person to talk to."

"In my defense, me and her got off to a much smoother start. Of course, she didn't start by immediately tossing my drink all over me."

Now Mona did turn, and narrowed her eyes at the man's audacity. "You're never going to let that go, are you?"

Dane pulled at his damp shirt, which clung to his chest beneath. Mona felt herself momentarily unable to look away. "Well, at least not until my shirt dries."

Thankfully Min brought their exchange to an end. "I'd like to ask that you all join me around my table. We have much to discuss, and I'm sure you're all curious to learn more about my plan for our time together."

Fabiana rose and Mona helped her sit down on the bench across the aisle from Min. Dane filled the space across from Min and his eyes motioned for Mona to sit next to him, but instead she chose the seat across from Fabiana, smiling defiantly.

Jabari was busy chasing his cat around the darkened half of the train car. "Jabari, I'd like you to join us as well."

"As soon as I find Batman."

"Your cat will be fine back there. She'll return to you when she's ready. You need to hear this too."

Jabari hurried back to the light and took his seat beside Min, although he did cast one last look to the back of the train car, hoping his cat might appear.

The candlelight flickered ominously, lighting Min's whiskered face in a constant stream of shifting shadows. The train rocked and swayed beneath them. "I work for a group known as The Black Circle. For more than a thousand years, they have toiled ceaselessly to learn about the Old Gods, and to prevent their return." Min's hand rested on a book that was clothed in faded leather binding, the kind that signaled its ancient origin, with a packed cluster of yellowed pages between its tight lips. "Dane has heard this all before, but for those of you unfamiliar, we follow the writings of a man known as Solomon Cross. He was a knight of The Black Circle, and a sorcerer in his own right. He recorded his attempts, his successes, failures, and all the things he learned into a book. This is that book. The Key of Solomon."

The train jolted over a particularly sharp bump, sending them all rocking. Mona kept her skepticism pinned to her face and away from her lips, and she hoped that this was some kind of story, and not really what the old man believed. He had seemed reasonable in their exchanges and over the phone, but now...now he sounded like he was some kind of cult fanatic.

"Now I must speak to you about the object of our mission. There is a man named Ned Pickman. He serves the Old Gods, we've had eyes on him for awhile and monitored his comings and goings. We consulted the oracle and she saw that Ned would be attempting to open a gate near the Witch Lights of Gamun G'Bar. We must stop him before he unleashes the Children of V'Razis, who carry on their heels an eternal darkness which will consume the world."

Mona had managed to keep her mouth shut up to this point, but the more the man talked, the farther into gibberish his speech was descending, and finally her reaction burst from her like a gunpowder keg introduced to flame. "Okay. Pause. I'm going to need to backtrack. I'm new to all this, and to be honest, I'm a bit confused — I thought this was going to be an archaeological trip, or maybe a field study in meeting with a group who knew something about the Old Ways. Are you for real, here, because if you are, I'm going to feel really really uncomfortable."

Dane rubbed the ridge of his nose. "Here we go. Rip off the bandaid."

Min looked over at her, sincerity gleaming in his beady eyes. "Mona...I offered you an opportunity to learn more about V'Razis. What I didn't tell you, but I'm telling you now, is that he's real."

There was a long moment while Min allowed Mona time to digest his words. But the more she thought about it the more she came to the conclusion that "You're all crazy." Again the words poured from her mouth like honey. She stood, instinctively needing to get away, to put some space between her and this unwanted new truth.

"I am sorry, Mona, if I wasn't upfront about our intention," Min continued, "But if I'd been candid about everything, you'd never have come."

"Absolutely I wouldn't have come!" She turned to Dane, for the first time, looking to him for comfort, as the voice of reason. "Do you believe all of this?"

"Well, I've never heard of this V'Razis guy, but yeah, generally, everything else sounds about right. Monsters, Elder Gods, it's all real. Trust me, Min knows what he's talking about. I've seen them."

Mona's lip quivered and she stepped around Fabiana, moving toward the back of the car. Oh, she'd made a terrible, horrible mistake!

Now she was stuck here on this train in the middle of nowhere with a bunch of loons! She should have trusted her gut. Yet even despite her current situation, she had not been totally negligent in her preparation. Her hand fell to her waistline where she had tucked a miniature revolver in case she ever needed it. Panic was rising within her breast, unhindered, swelling — She didn't know what she was going to do, but she knew she needed to get out of here. She needed to get away. She needed —

Before she could stop herself, the revolver was in her hand and she was pointing it at the old man. It was a survival instinct — pure and simple — point the gun at the thing that's threatening you. "What do you really want with me?" She managed to stammer through heaving breaths.

In a sudden flurry of movement Dane leapt out of his seat, and into the path of her gun. Her mind froze, and she found herself petrified, unable to pull the trigger — as the man who was much larger than her descended upon her and plucked the gun from her hand before she could do anything about it. "Don't ever point a gun at Min. He's the only chance we've got at getting out of this alive." Dane had the gun on her now.

Mona felt herself melting — her life now on the line. "Please don't kill me. I didn't mean to —"

"I don't want to kill you. Come on, why don't you have a seat. You're here for a reason, okay. Min wouldn't invite you and initiate you in the way of unnameable horrors unless he thought you could help."

Dane backed up. He gripped Mona by the arm and steered her back into her seat next to Fabiana. She felt sufficiently chastised, like a petulant child. It was everything she could do not to burst into sobs. Dane stood between the seats, her gun clutched in his hand. "You're going to be fine, as long as you don't scream or call for help. You were saying, Min? Something about this vorayzees guy?"

"V'Razis," Min corrected. "A formless demon beyond our ability to see. The gate will unleash its children. Cover the world in darkness. Mona, you know the tales of V'Razis better than anyone. Even myself. This is a demon I've never faced. We need you."

Mona bit her lip, took a deep breath. They didn't want to kill her. Could it be possible that they really just wanted her to tell them about V'Razis? Maybe after she did that, they'd let her go? Then this nightmare of a role playing game would be over.

"Okay, spill sister," Dane casually commanded, as if holding a woman at gunpoint was a daily operation for him. "Who's this V'Razis guy?"

Mona placed her hands on her knees, finding herself, and forced her mouth to start moving. *It's just like teaching a class, right? Except you're teaching a group of crazy criminals who might kill you if they don't pass their test.* "There are only a few sources that mention him. One is the *Lex Tenebrarum*, but only fragments remain. There are also etchings on stone found in Mesopotamia, in the ruins of a buried city. It's a creation myth. About the division between light and darkness, kind of like the Bible. V'Razis existed — and when he retreated, light appeared, and life flourished. He is the darkness, in a sense. The absence of light." Mona swallowed, her throat dry. But now was not the time to stop and ask for water. Her audience was appeased for now. She had to give them what they wanted. She forced herself to continue. "Another myth from Egypt tells of his Children. Amun-Ra is light, he vanquished the eternal darkness and sent the beasts back into the black pit. It's interesting, I never thought of this until now, but the black pit is depicted as being a black circle. Perhaps there is a connection to the organization you mentioned. Anyway, this was found in the temple at Ka rnak."

"How did he do it? How did he send the children back into the darkness?" Min asked, eyes afire with curiosity, almost pleading.

Mona squinted, trying to remember. "He sent his own son into the pit. A sacrifice. The beasts followed him."

"That's kind of like the Bible too, God sending his only son into the pit," Dane added, scratching his chin.

Mona wouldn't have thought him capable of intellectual thought, but then again he hadn't made that far a logical leap. "These ancient myths all build off one another," she whispered. "That's about all I know." *Please let it be enough.*

She felt relieved when Dane and Min finally took their eyes off of her.

"Okay," Dane said loudly, clapping his hands, "So, to review. Our goal is to kill the monster, close the gate, and save the world."

"Yes, that's a very simplified version of events. Though it seems some kind of sacrifice might also be needed."

They're 4,000 year old myths, they're hardly reliable sources of information, Mona wanted to say, but instead she stayed silent. The less she said now, the better. She didn't want to anger them further.

She glanced over at Fabiana, and felt like she was truly seeing her now for the first time. She was a prisoner of these barbarians as well. They were all crazy, keeping two women at gunpoint. *How do I get out of here?*

Wait. That was the thought that came to her mind.

Wait. The moment to escape will come, and when it arrives, you'll take it.

IV

Ned fidgeted nervously in his seat. The girl shifted in her sleep and her head rolled onto his shoulder. A strange sensation rippled through his flesh. The touch of a woman. Of any human, was not something he'd felt often. She moaned softly. What was she dreaming about? Ned wrung his hands as a couple passed by in the aisle, their eyes drawn to his face. The man frowned in judgment, and then turned away. There was little privacy here, crammed into this car, like rows of cattle in a slaughterhouse. What he was doing was illicit, illegal, and he'd be punished if he was caught. But he wouldn't let it come to that. And what did he care if they stared? Let them stare! They'd all be dead soon anyway. The Quickening was almost upon them.

Ned did not move the girl's head from his shoulder. It was a tender connection with humanity, almost like a goodbye of sorts. He was human, after all, despite the cruelty he'd experienced by his fellow man.

He glanced out the window, eyes patrolling the passing savannah where man had not yet flung his corrupting hand. Then Ned caught his own reflection in the glass, and was harshly reminded of the face behind the mask, his true face — even the mask would not hide the truth from himself. From others, yes, but never from himself.

He reached out a gloved hand and yanked the curtain closed, shutting out the view. But it was too late to stop the swelling of pain within him, a pain which he did his best to choke back down — but not before reminding him of several objectionable facts.

That Ned had been born a child of deformity. His head mis-shapen, his eyes, always appearing to bulge forth from their sockets. A face no one could learn to love, not even his own parents. He had not lasted long in school. The ridicule had been too much.

That he'd lived most of his life in the shadows, barely surviving his adolescent years. He'd managed to land a remote job, where his face no longer mattered — but that did not quell his need for belonging or affection. Still, it enabled him to survive on hope. Hope that one day he would find acceptance. Hope that one day he would find someone who would love him as he was. Ned thrived in anonymity as he never had before. God bless the internet! There, in the tangled string of chat rooms, comment sections, and porn sites he had found some semblance of a connection to the beings who shared his world. At last he began to understand them, and as he did he understood just how strange he truly was. At first, he observed, but gradually he began to get involved, to integrate himself. A comment here, a like there.

That he'd started talking to someone. A girl. *Alicia*. Chatting, they called it. And it stirred all kinds of feelings within him, things he'd never felt before. Was this what it felt like to be loved? It was a high he'd never expected nor hoped for. A part of him knew it would never last. How could it? Eventually she asked to see him. He declined, politely. He knew he could never allow her to see his face, no matter how much he wanted it. She started begging. She grew angry, impatient. Not even a picture? He sent pictures of another face. One he found on the great, wide sea of faces. Lies built upon lies. He tried to ghost her, to abandon her. It was better than facing him directly, than learning what he truly was, but he could never stay away for long. She was his drug. She demanded to see him, gave him an ultimatum. She even offered to fly out to his remote home, but no, he couldn't ask her to do that. He went to see her. He couldn't bring himself to fly, to sit around all those judging eyes, so he rented a car. Drove for two days. And on that drive he thought. What if this was it? What if she saw his face and didn't care? Had he been sequestered away all these years for nothing? They said that sometimes on the TV programs, that it's what's inside that counts, that the outside doesn't really matter. He knocked on her door, heart hammering like those rabbits he'd seen on nature shows, thumping their feet. She opened the door . . . and screamed.

That he'd tried to kill himself. For real this time. That Mr. Locke had found him.

Ned Pickman...would you like to destroy the world?

Yes, I'd like that.

That night had marked the beginning of a formidable friendship, or at least that's what Ned called it. He'd done whatever dark deeds Locke requested of him. Terrible, unforgivable deeds. He should have seen the electric chair a hundred times over. Locke had shown him a different kind of thrill, of unnatural fulfillment — the thrill of power. The ecstasy of revenge. The indescribable sensation of squeezing the life out of someone with your bare hands.

And in return, Ned had seen horrors beyond his imagining. They had robbed him of sleep, ripped any semblance of youth from his countenance, and turned him to substance abuse of his own.

The girl beside Ned stirred again, her head lolling forward, her eyes fluttering, struggling against the morphine. Ned cursed under his breath, cast a wary eye up and down the aisle, then fumbled with the black case tucked into his jacket. He turned away from the aisle and injected a fresh stream into the girl's arm. She groaned, then relaxed, and within moments was dozing again.

Ned felt his jaw slacken. The tension in his muscles eased.

He turned once more and glanced out the window across the train car. The sun had passed its zenith. Each moment brought them all closer to the end. No one in this train realized that they were carrying their demise with them. The man who would erase humanity. The Quickening was coming.

Ned adjusted the girl's head so it rested against the window. He did not need her head on his shoulder. He did not want any complex feelings clouding his judgment. For when the time came a sacrifice would need to be made to open the gate.

She was it.

V

Fabiana could feel a geyser of anxiety building inside of her. This manifested in nervous fidgeting and a compulsive need to dig her fingernails of one hand under those of the other. Besides getting up once to use the restroom, she had not moved from her spot the entire train ride. She twirled her hands beneath the loose fabric of her dark cloak and folded them over her lap in an attempt to get herself to stop fidgeting.

She felt pressure in her belly as the baby lashed outward against her already expanded flesh. She could see it, clawing to break free. There was something alive in there. Was it a hand or a foot? A boy or a girl?

She had never given birth before, but it was not an experience to which she was looking forward. Fabiana had been taken from her family when she was only a child herself, and raised in a twisted world where children were only things to be offered up to unknowable gods. She had witnessed mothers pleading for their babies only to have them ripped from their hands. Part of her was glad that she was now free of that horror. Another part feared that she would now have to keep the child growing inside her.

What would she do with it? A child? She had no control over her future. No family. She was at the disposal of the old man and the American, who held no love for her.

Love.

It was a concept with which she was not extremely familiar. Only the other sister wives had shown her kindness and selflessness, and then, only when they could. She feared she couldn't love the child that grew within her. Not because she wasn't capable of love, but because it would always remind her of *him*. It belonged to *him*. It would carry his blood in its veins, and who knew — maybe it would turn out like *him* as well.

Might it not be better to cast it away and let it die? Let that part of her die as well, to spite him?

The others were talking now. About what, she couldn't say. She did not understand much English. McKarney would speak it sometimes, but she was only able to grasp a few words here and there, more than she let on, but not enough to communicate or understand fluently.

Her mind drifted. It always drifted. Focusing was hard, now that she was free of the drugs.

When she glanced up again, their conversation had ended and the group had abandoned their conference around the table. How much time had passed? Impossible to say. But she had not even seen them move. The boy was now playing with his cat. The old man was drawing on the walls with a piece of chalk. Symbols, shapes, and letters which she did not recognize, but it was almost like artwork, and that she understood. She was a gifted artist herself, though she had never had formal training or materials to truly pursue any kind of ambition. She had simply used it as a coping mechanism. An escape.

The American was playing with his gun. She was afraid of him. He had been rough with her. True, she had not made his job easier, but why should she? She would much rather have stayed with her sister wives. That was a world she knew, a world she understood — even if McKarney was no longer a part of it.

Fabiana glanced out the window. She did not know where else to look. The other woman edged into the seat across from her and spoke to her in English. Fabiana caught a couple of words, but failed to comprehend what it was she was saying. She shook her head at the woman, the universal body language for "I don't understand."

The woman grimaced, said something to the American, and then turned back to Fabiana.

"I'm Mona. What's your name?"

Fabiana raised an eyebrow. The woman was speaking to her in perfect Spanish.

"Do you understand what I'm saying?"

Fabiana nodded. The edge of her lip quivered, begging to rise into a smile, but Fabiana could not force the movement.

"Nod if you understand."

Fabiana nodded.

"That's good. Do you know...do you know why you're here? Where you're going?"

Fabiana shook her head. As far as she knew, she had been brought here by magic. Before a week ago she had never seen a plane or a train, and she had since traveled on both. There were boards and signs with writing, but she couldn't write or read. She had never been taught.

Fabiana desperately wanted to speak to the woman. The one with kindness in her eyes. The only one to whom she could actually communicate. So why couldn't she? What was wrong with her? *Why couldn't she talk?*

She used to be able to speak. When she was a child, she had spoken so much it annoyed the other wives. She had taken delight in this, and had taken to annoying them on purpose. But then her time had come. McKarney had called her to his tent. He had disrobed her. Served her sweet tasting drinks that made her head spin. And touched her in places she had never been touched before. He had been *inside* her. She had been powerless to stop him. Her mind had traveled to another place, another sphere. There she had seen marvelous things, but when she returned — she knew that something was different.

The process had been repeated, many times, until her bleeding had stopped. Then her belly began to grow. She was with child. *His* child. The white man, who led their compound. The man who had taught them to pray to his strange gods, the one who fed them and clothed them. There were times when she felt grateful for her life. She found solace with the other wives. Even joy, at times. The drugs they were provided gave her great pleasure. And she was not alone.

But they had lived in constant shadow of fear. The threat and knowledge that eventually McKarney would call them to his tent and fill them with his seed — they would bear children, and their children would be taken from them and sacrificed to McKarney's god. They would be cast into the dark pit, screaming, until they were silenced forever.

The Black Circle.

It was a place they were ordered to keep away from, and they did so gladly. Only McKarney was permitted to approach that dread-ridden abyss. It was a hole in the ground so deep that many believed it had no bottom. The only time they were allowed near was when they were required to pray to the dark thing within. She felt a power stir within her when she prayed. A desire aroused to give up and join herself to whatever lay deep down, in the unfathomable dark.

Fabiana had seen strange things while living in that camp. Wonderful things, and terrifying things. There were things that slunk around in the darkness. She would catch glimpses of them now and then out of the corner of her vision. Glowing eyes in the dark. Tracks in the dirt. A limb slithering out of view. Only at night did they appear. Fatima had vanished. They had found traces of blood on her tent, and when they questioned McKarney about it, he had only told them not to worry and to stay inside once it grew dark. When they failed to get their sacrifices, the old ones ventured forth from the pit, he said. They would all need to be strong. All who weren't pregnant were brought to his tent that night.

Fabiana had lived for months in fear of what would happen when her child was finally born. She already felt an attachment to the child she couldn't explain, or put in words even if she was able to speak. She did not want to throw the child to the beast. And yet what choice did she have? Many had tried to run away before, but with no knowledge of survival, the weakness of pregnancy, and the astuteness of McKarney and his guards — no one ever got far. Then there were the creatures that were said to roam the thick forests around them, Terrible beasts from another world.

Her choice was to live and give up her child, or die, and face the unknown.

At least this horror was known to her.

Then, in the midst of her despair, the unthinkable had happened.

A group of strangers had arrived. They entered her tent in the middle of the night. One of them, a white man, had handed her a knife. They told her, in Spanish, that they were going to set them free. That they were going to kill McKarney and put an end to his horrible sacrifices. Fabiana had led them to McKarney, who was in the middle of reading from that book of his, kneeling before an altar. Fabiana had not waited for the strangers to take action. With the knife in her hand and the strangers backing her up, Fabiana had plunged the dagger into McKarney herself. She would never forget the look of betrayal on McKarney's face. Nor the way his face appeared once all life had left it, still and pale, like it had been etched from stone.

The white man and his companions had fed them foreign food, and took her away from her sisters. The one with light hair, the leader, she assumed, had explained to her that she was going to be taken somewhere far away. They would help her start a new life. Her child would be safe. She had been given to the American, Dane, he had called him, who had brought her here.

But the darkness was not done with her yet. She still dreamed of the pit. And sometimes she could hear whispers that seemed to come from nowhere. They told her to do things. Terrible things. It was the voice of McKarney. She told herself it wasn't real, but even still, she could feel a curious feeling stirring inside her, a power begging to be let out. She covered her ears to shut them out, and still the whispers continued.

McKarney had carried a strange power with him. Simply by looking into his eyes, Fabiana would feel a desire to do whatever he asked of her. Whatever rebellion she had worked up inside herself would be instantly washed away.

Fabiana shivered. The other woman was no longer sitting across from her. She was standing near the door, talking to the American. The wall across from her was now nearly covered in the old man's writing, and the boy was slumped over, asleep in one of the booths.

Her stomach rumbled within her. She was hungry. How could she ask for food? Her body felt weak. This child was sucking the life out of her. Fabiana glanced to her left, out the window. Her breath caught in her throat. A strangled gasp tried to escape her, but it was unable to do so, as if some invisible hand was around her throat.

Two eyes were looking back at her from the window glass. The eyes of McKarney, blue and piercing, unmistakable. But how?

Immediately she felt a calming warmth, familiar and potent, spreading throughout her body. The feeling of giving herself over to his power. To his control. She resisted, tightening her muscles, but it was useless. The eyes laughed at her futile gesture.

In the glass, McKarney was seated next to her, watching her, asserting his control.

"Don't look away," his honey laced voice whispered. In the glass she watched as he pulled out a knife, the same one she had used to kill him, and placed it on the table before her.

She felt him nudge the handle underneath her fingers. But that was impossible, he wasn't truly here. Was he? She could not turn her head to look.

McKarney's eyes flashed and then he issued the order. "Kill the old man."

The image before her was gone, and the spell of paralysis lifted. Fabiana heaved deeply, breath she had been holding within her. She looked down and saw the knife resting under her fingers. She wrapped her fingers carefully around the gleaming blade. It was as real as the train around her.

She wanted to cast it away, but McKarney was inside her now. His voice in her head. His power pulsing through her veins.

Kill the old man.

Fabiana did not have a choice.

VI

Min's fingers cramped from writing. He dropped the chalk into his left hand and shook out his right, letting the ache pulse and subside. He stretched his fingers out, cracking each of the knuckles, then stepped back and admired his work. Artfully drawn runes, symbols, and shapes spanned in a line around the entire rectangular shape of the train car. More could be done. More could always be done. But this was a start. It would do much good.

"What are you writing?"

Min turned, half startled, to see Jabari standing by his side. The boy had crept up without so much as a footstep. Or Min had simply been so deeply concentrated that he hadn't noticed. Either way, his hearing wasn't what it used to be.

"It's a protection charm," Min explained with a smile. He rolled up his sleeves, revealing arms hidden beneath a layer of ink.

"What is it protecting us from?"

"Whatever's to come."

The boy seemed unsatisfied with that answer, but Min did not have a better one to give him. Better the truth than guesswork. Honestly, he did not know what dangers awaited them at the end of their road. There were limitless possibilities for how things might unfurl. And their job was to be prepared for as many of them as they could.

"I got a better question," Dane said, spinning his pistol around his finger like a gunslinger. "When are we getting off this caboose?"

Again, Min did not have an exact answer to give, so he resorted to a non-answer. "The conductor knows when to stop. I gave him the coordinates, and paid him for his loyalty."

A familiar shuffling reached Min's ears, and he turned, alert, to find Jabari leafing through his book which rested on the table in the booth beside him.

The boy is only curious. Do not react with emotion. He means no harm.

It was all Min could do to remain calm. That book was everything to him in the world. Without it, there was no hope of victory. He eased up closer to the table, within arms reach of the book so he could react if anything went wrong.

"What is this? Some kind of Bible?"

Min chuckled softly. "Something like that. It's called the *Key of Solomon*. It was written many years ago. Not quite as long ago as the Bible. But closer to their time than ours."

"What's it say?"

So many questions. He's only a child. Were you any different when you were his age? They do not understand the world, and so they must ask to know. "It says many things. It contains a history of a man named Solomon Cross, and his adventures. His quest to rid the world of evil. He was a knight of the Black Circle, and he fought the same evil we face. We need to close a gate. Gates have been closed before, but Cross is the only one I know of to record the process of how to do it."

"How *do* you do it?" Jabari's eyes were innocent, full of life.

Min pulled the book closer to himself. "Well, let me show you." He flipped through the ancient pages carefully, until he found the page he sought. *The Rite of Sigillum in Aeternum.* "Here. It describes the ritual we must perform. And after the gate is closed, this next page gives instructions for how to seal the land, so no more gates can be opened here."

"How come we don't just seal all the land? That way no gates can be opened anywhere?"

Min laughed, his voice full of merriment. "Oh, if only we could. When land is sealed against evil, it is also sealed against light. Nothing can grow there, nothing can thrive. The land is blighted. Do you understand? Useless. We only seal land when we must."

"And the Black Circle? What's that?"

"It's an organization. A group that was formed long ago to delay the return of the Old Ones, who would destroy our way of life, and take the planet for their own, dark purposes."

"What do you mean, delay?" Mona was kneeling on one of the train's benches, listening to their conversation.

"The Quickening cannot be stopped, not entirely." Min closed the book, and rested his hands upon it. "Only delayed."

"So, we can't even kill these gods? What's the point in even trying then?"

"They are gods," Min explained, fearing that any attempt to defend his position was pointless. *You must see to believe. You will see soon enough.* "If we did not try, everything you've ever loved, and everyone you've ever cared about, would be erased from existence. We hold back the dam."

"But eventually that dam is going to break? Dam's don't last forever."

"No," Min whispered, offering her the ghost of a smile. "They don't. But let us pray we'll all be long gone before that day comes."

He turned and placed his hand on Jabari's shoulder. "You have a warrior spirit. That's why I chose you. We need warriors in this fight. You are not just fighting for your family, or your village. You are fighting for all mankind. It is the most noble calling to which any of us could hope to aspire."

Min felt a pang of cramping in his legs and resolved to stretch them by walking to the back of the train car. He turned —

To find Fabiana standing right behind him, blocking his path. Pain reverberated outward from his abdomen. At first he thought it was a sudden intestinal pain, but as he looked down he realized the true source of the discomfort —

A dagger protruding from his gut.

Fabiana retracted the knife and thrust it at him once more before he could stop her. This time the knife jammed into his left shoulder, and a searing jolt of pain roared through his mind. His paralysis of shock broke and he reached up and took Fabiana's wrist in a viper's grip, restraining her so she could do no more damage.

Jabari screamed and lunged at Fabiana, pulling her away from Min and to the ground.

"Wait!" Mona screamed, chasing after Jabari, "Don't! Don't kill her!"

Blood pounded in Min's head, the rest of the world growing hazy and the voices of the others fading to distant murmurs, as if he were in a dream.

He felt hands pulling him back, away from the tussle. Dane's hands. He ushered Min onto a bench away from the chaos, and Min watched, as if from a body that was not his own, as Dane scrutinized the damage.

"Hold tight, old man."

Then Dane was gone, barking orders to the others. Min tried to rise to see what was going on, and managed to sit up with great effort. He watched as Dane threw Jabari aside and restrained Fabiana's wrists with a length of rope and tied her to a portion of bannister that ran between two seats. She appeared to be dazed, but otherwise unharmed. Min hoped her fall had not hurt the child.

Dane waved a finger at Mona. "You. Watch her. She tries anything, call for me. Don't let the kid near her." Dane then turned to Jabari, "You. Sit right here, you're in time out."

Dane hurried back to Min, kneeling before him. He dug into a side bag and pulled out a flask. "Okay, old man, you still with me? I was saving this for a special occasion, and I have to admit this was not exactly what I had in mind. I was hoping there would be more ladies. Maybe some music."

Min made an effort to hum a song, which made Dane exhale in amusement. "Not bad. You keep that up."

Dane next unfurled a makeshift first aid kit of his own design. He tore open Min's shirt, inspecting his stomach wound first. "This one's not too bad. Not too deep. I can't see inside, but we'll wrap this up and you'll be okay." He set to work wrapping several layers of bandage around Min's midsection. Min did what he could to help, holding himself up in a sitting position, which was not an easy feat with his failing strength and loss of blood.

After securing the bandage, Dane tore Min's shirt around his shoulder wound, the knife still protruding from it. "Okay. Now let's get a look at this guy." Dane gripped the knife and looked at Min. "Hey Min?"

"Yeah?"

Before waiting for a response, Dane yanked the dagger out of Min's shoulder, setting it on the floor, and held a portion of gauze to the wound. "Your arm will be sore for a while, and we'll need to get you to a hospital, but you won't die today. Not from this at least. But you're lucky. If she had driven the knife deeper into your abdomen or a few inches south of here, you'd be a goner."

Min's mouth was parched, his lips and mouth dry, but he did what he could to respond. "She was fighting it."

"Fighting it? What's *it*?"

"The power that binds her."

Dane scowled, and Min could see that he did not understand. "Binds her to what, her crazy? The girl's a psycho. Now I'm thinking about how she could have tried to off me on our way over here. I'm considering asking for a pay bump for escorting a murderer. You didn't tell me I'd be escorting a homicidal maniac. Why is she here?"

Min placed a weak hand on Dane's arm, allowing him to feel his honesty. "The oracle saw her among us, so she must be here. She must have a part to play in this mission yet."

"Yeah, well I hope she can play it with her hands tied, because that rope's not coming off."

Dane finished wrapping Min's shoulder, his hands now stained with drying blood. He brought Min his canteen, then went to the bathroom to wash up.

Min found that it was hard to keep his eyes open. But he did his best to fight the wave of exhaustion that was now pouring over him, the adrenaline and blood loss sapping his strength. When Dane returned he wiped as much of Min's blood from the dagger as he could then handed it to the kid. Jabari's scowl at being reprimanded disappeared, replaced with his usual sense of wonder. "Here, kid. You earned it. But it's only to be used in self defense, you hear?"

Jabari nodded, taking the knife in his hands with reverence, turning the sharp edged blade in his hands.

Min watched as Dane turned to Mona. "Is he gonna be all right?" Mona asked.

"I don't know about all right but he'll live." Dane placed his hand on the back of the seat that Mona was sitting in. "How's the girl?"

Fabiana sat on the ground, her hands raised, eyes staring at the floor.

"Nothing," Mona said, sadness rippling in her voice. "It's almost like she's a robot. I feel bad for her."

"Don't feel too bad. She did just try and kill your boss. Where'd she get that knife from, anyway? I brought her all the way across the ocean and she didn't have it."

Dane looked down at Mona, and she looked up at him. Min detected a glint of suspicion in his eyes. "She must have found it on the train," Mona said, half shrugging in an attempt to turn the suspicion from herself.

"Yeah. Or someone gave it to her."

"It doesn't matter," Min said, his voice hoarse and scratchy. "It's over now. It's done."

Min's eyes flashed down to Fabiana, who for the first time since the incident raised her head. Their eyes met — and Min sensed something in those eyes — and several impressions assaulted him at once.

The first was that the eyes were not her own. She was not herself. She was acting under the direction of another force. Min had already suspected this, the girl was susceptible to dark influences, this was not uncommon for recovering cultists. The second was a memory. A flash of a young boy, himself, standing before a burning hut. He was kneeling in a puddle of blood. Min shivered and shook off the memory. It was not one he wanted to relive.

And on the memory's wings came words. Words and impressions that chilled him to the bone.

He's here. Her eyes seemed to say.

Who?

You know who.

Min knew but he did not want to admit it.

He's on this train. Right now.

How is that possible?

The thing smiled — or seemed to smile. It was not going to answer that.

Min swallowed. He searched his own soul, reached out, to see if he could sense if what this thing was saying was true.

At first, he felt nothing, nothing but darkness and the pain in his shoulder. Then, beyond the protection of his charm, he felt it. Pulsing. Waiting. Lurking just out of sight. It had been here all along and he had not felt it. It had hidden itself from him.

The darkness that had destroyed his family, that had tried to destroy him — the daemon from beyond — the formless, bodiless entity that had hunted him ever since he was a boy.

It was here, now.

It had found him.

At last, Min accepted this bitter truth, though to do so sent his pulse racing.

At last he dared to speak its name, making his fate a reality.

Pandemonius.

That's when he knew...

He was going to die.

VII

Ned peered out the window of the moving train. The witch lights could not yet be seen, not until the sun sank below the horizon, but the location of the gate needed to be precise. He had instructions to disembark at a certain location, marked by a wall of vermillion cliffs. A passing shadow on the opposite side of the train drew Ned's attention. The horizon was no longer marked by endless plain, but by a towering rock formation a mile or two distant.

The cliffs.

Ned wasted no time. He reached his hand up and yanked hard on the emergency cord. A bell sounded and the train's brakes engaged, sending every passenger lurching forward. A man standing in the aisle tumbled to the ground.

Ned hoisted his captive up and threw her over his shoulder. She was a burden, but nothing he couldn't handle. Ned moved down the aisle, past startled and confused passengers who were leaning forward, chatting amongst themselves, eager for some kind of explanation. Ned ignored them. He made his way to the back of the car and forced the door open, then carefully stepped down onto the firm soil below.

As Ned made his way away from the train, the burden of carrying the girl weighed on him. The sun was beginning to make its descent. Soon it would be gone, and the witch lights would appear. But even if Ned couldn't see them, they were still there, even now. He would occasionally feel the ground grow hot beneath his feet and force himself to scamper sideways, followed by an impressive burst of heat and the smell of sulfur.

Ned quickly became drenched in sweat, but there was no way around that. He stopped only to drink what remained of his water, but kept a straight line for the cliffs. He had a long ways to go yet.

Eventually, the train behind him blew its whistle and continued on its way. It was Ned's last connection with humanity. He turned and watched them fade. *Good riddance.*

He became momentarily distracted by the setting sun. He would miss the sun. Of all the horrible things about this world, sunsets were not one of them.

Ned wiped his brow and pressed on.

As the space around him darkened, Ned began to grow anxious. He had been tasked with opening the gate, and he had been told to do so at the foot of the cliffs. But they were large cliffs. Did it matter precisely where it happened? Locke had failed to give him exact instructions.

Ned had no way of contacting his overseer, but decided that he would continue on until the air was so dark he couldn't see, then he would stop.

He did not have to wait long. Ned began to sense a power growing around him, an energy that was unmistakable and potent — the ground and air were abuzz with luminescence. He could feel it flowing through him, and though he couldn't explain what it was or what caused it, he knew this was the place. He knew this spot was special.

Ned set the girl on the ground, his aching shoulders grateful for the break, and pulled the electric lantern from his bag. He opened the heavy tome Locke had given him — the *Lex Tenebrarum*, and set to work performing the ritual. He carved a circle into the earth around the girl, and with his finger, wrote the symbols the book provided. Once it was finished Ned knelt, hands raised to the heavens, eying the empty space before him. His throat was dry. This was it. The moment he had been waiting for. His chance to turn his back on humanity.

Strangely, Ned felt no second thoughts. He had thought he might, but none now came. His mind was as clear as a starless sky. He breathed in, and whispered the words of the invocation.

Protho Ficaro Lodemi Althr! Lthuaw Orgol Magh Lithwagbr!

Ned's eyes snapped to attention as the woman in the circle burst into flames. He watched her body try to rise, before it sank back to the earth, a pile of melting flesh. There was no scream, no pain. She was drugged, he had made sure of that. The fire leapt higher, unnaturally high, swept upward by a swift, warm wind that curled itself around him. There was a deep, disembodied moan — as if it came from the earth itself — and then Ned perceived the colossal black hole that rested in the sky above his head. The edges swirled, a power forcing the sky apart, like a tear in the hull of a ship.

It is done.

The gate is opened.

VIII

The American fumbled with the locks on the exterior of his trunk. Jabari heard it as clear as a bell from six seats away and popped over to investigate. What could be inside? Treasure? The heads of his enemies? Holy artifacts?

Jabari attempted to lean in to get a front row seat but Dane swatted at him and glared. "Stand back, kid."

Dane's fingers opened the final latch and threw the lid open.

What lay inside was certainly not holy, but to Jabari's eyes — it was just as precious as treasure.

Guns.

The trunk was filled to the brim with various types of high-powered weaponry and ammunition. Similar to the kind the men in his village had toted — except these were better. Jabari could tell that just by looking at them.

Instinctively, Jabari leaned forward, earning him another swat on the hand from Dane. "Don't touch! These aren't toys."

"I know," Jabari said, withdrawing.

Dane picked up one of the guns, a handgun, and looked again at Jabari. "You ever shot a gun before?"

"No. But I want to." He tried to suppress his enthusiasm, but it was contagious. Guns had fascinated Jabari his entire life. In his world, those with guns were those who ruled. They were the powerful, and all too often the gun-toters would use that power to wreak havoc and strike fear into those they ruled with an iron fist. Oh, how often Jabari had wished for a gun of his own to fight back, to right the wrongs of his oppressors and to use that power to do good.

"I want to help."

"Good," Dane said, which was not the reaction Jabari was expecting. "We're gonna need ya. Now, while we have a few minutes, let's go over a little safety and operation training."

Dane raised the pistol, aiming it down the aisle. "Very simple. You're gonna want to use two hands, and even then it's gonna throw you. That's one thing they don't teach you in the movies. These things have a kickback like you wouldn't believe." Dane scratched his throat, adjusting his footing. "Right. Basic idea is point and shoot, but there's more to it than that. I wish we had time to practice. Okay, footing. You're going to want one foot in front of the other, firmly planted, because it's going to throw you back. Eyes on your target. Your hands will follow. This here is the safety. Flip it up, locked; down, unlocked. This button here releases the mag." Dane let an empty magazine fall into his hand. "Not loaded. Here. Get used to how this feels." He handed Jabari the gun.

Jabari took it, his hands immediately dropped. "It's heavy!"

"Uh, yeah. It's real." Dane tapped his head.

"Do I get one?" Mona stood in the aisle with her hands on her hips.

"Sure. Plenty to go around." Dane handed her a pistol.

"No bullets?"

Dane reached into his trunk and grabbed a full mag, but when Mona went to take it Dane pulled it away. "You'll get them, when the time is right."

"Whatever you say, Lord of the guns."

Dane threw his hands up. "They're my guns."

Jabari raised his pistol down the aisle like he'd seen Dane do. He imagined he was gunning down monsters, pulling the gun back as he 'fired.'

"Jabari. Come here."

Min was calling him. Jabari turned — but he did not have to ask to know what Min wanted to say. Colorful lights blazed out the window.

"The Witch Lights of Gamun G'Bar."

Jabari instinctively moved to the window and sensed the others do the same. Even Batman crawled up beside Jabari and hissed at the flashing lights.

The view before him was spellbinding. Jabari had never seen anything like it. In the distance, bursts of bluish-green flame would burst forth from the earth, spout flame for ten to fifteen seconds, and then vanish. There were almost always two or three flames burning at once, creating a constant light show.

"What makes it do that?" Jabari asked.

"It's a very unique phenomenon," Mona said, with her eyes still fixed on the lights. Jabari could see them dancing in her eyes. "This area has hundreds of pockets of natural gas, which mixes with the soil. A mineral gives the flame its color. Though scientists believe the area's electromagnetism may be a factor as well."

Jabari frowned. "Okay. So...science stuff."

"Of course, the legends surrounding the witch lights are infinitely more interesting," Min whispered with a wink thrown Jabari's way. "The locals shun this region. They say it is a gateway to hell, a breeding ground for devils, and that's why the ground shoots flame. And maybe they're right...More than a few have gone missing in the vicinity over the years."

"Of course, the noxious fumes emitted by the gas have nothing to do with that," Mona retorted.

"Well, it very well might. But that doesn't negate the fact that this area is a hot spot for occult activity. And now they've built this railroad right by it. Turned it into a tourist attraction. Pah!" Min sighed and handed his water bottle to Fabiana.

Jabari didn't understand the woman's words, but he did understand Min. He trusted the old man. He'd saved him from a life of living on the street. And among street rats — tales of magic and legend were plentiful. The lights sure looked like magic to him.

"And uh, what's that swirly thingy?" Dane asked, joining the conversation. His finger pointed toward a large hole in the sky, as if someone had torn open the air itself.

Jabari watched Min's expression change. For the first time he saw fear in his guardian's eyes. "The gate is open. We're too late."

IX

As if the train were reacting just as its passengers to the bizarre spectacle above the witch lights, the brakes engaged. The effect was immediate. Everyone in car number five was thrown sideways. Some were thrown into seat cushions. Fabiana, who was restrained by the wrists, was rolled so her head slammed against the wooden bench leg beside her. Dane had unfortunately stepped out into the aisle, and was sent staggering sideways into the train car door.

The brakes squealed beneath them, and gradually momentum caught up and Dane was tossed the other direction onto his hands and knees.

He sprang to his feet and immediately loaded an assault rifle. He noticed that Mona had gone pale. She was staring out at the gate, a doorway through space and time. "Look here," she said, attempting an air of authority, but failing to convince even herself. "What kind of joke is this? What is that out there? You've had your fun and I demand the truth."

"We told you," Dane said, "It's a gate."

"It's not a gate! That's impossible."

"Did your academic journals tell you that?" Dane pulled the magazine from his pocket and handed it to her. "It's time. You're gonna want this."

She took the weapon with limp fingers, no more assured.

She has to pass through the gauntlet. We all do. And not everyone makes it. Everyone would have to accept the reality of their world, that there were monsters and gods out there beyond their reckoning and comprehension. It was more difficult for rational minds than simple ones. He took one more look at Mona. Dane hoped she the realization didn't break her. He was just beginning to like her.

"Here kid." He tossed a magazine to him too, and the boy caught it with deft hands.

"What about Min?"

"Min doesn't use guns."

Jabari turned to Min. "Why not?"

"Because I have other ways of defending myself." Min smiled at the boy, but there was a sadness behind his eyes.

"Well," Dane declared, attempting to sound confident. "Guess this is our stop."

"Yes. But let us not be too hasty. We are protected here. Out there, we are vulnerable."

Dane shook his head at the professor. Sometimes he really didn't understand that man. "Yeah, but isn't the gate over there? So unless you have a magic way of moving this train over there, we've got to use our legs."

"Not yet," Min warned.

Dane knew better than to argue. "Alright, but something's up. I'm going to step out and take a look. Everyone else stay here." He looked right at Jabari, raising his eyebrows for emphasis. Then Dane pushed open the train car door and stepped out into the night.

The evening air was much colder than Dane was anticipating, and though he would never admit he needed a jacket, inside he wished he had one. His bravado would have to suffice. The smell of sulfur was much stronger out here, wafting across the plains from the witch lights. Dane threw his rifle strap over his shoulder and climbed the ladder up to the roof. He pulled himself over the edge of the train, mindful of his footing. Each step he took sounded loudly off the tin cover.

Once his footing was sure, Dane looked up and down the line of train cars but didn't see any movement. The plains were just as empty. A few yards from the tracks was a haggard barbed wire fence with signs reading KEEP OUT.

The familiar pong of footsteps on tin reached Dane's ears and he spun, his weapon at the ready, to find Jabari climbing up after him.

"Dammit, kid. I said stay put! I looked right at you."

"If you get in trouble, aren't two guns better than one?"

Dane relaxed slightly. "Can't argue with that." He turned and looked out over the sublime view, the chill air rushing at his face, whipping his loose hair all around him. "It's something, isn't it?"

"It's evil," the boy whispered.

Dane thought truer words had never been spoken.

Something caught Dane's eye — a flicker of movement, almost imperceptible against the crushing blackness swirling within the gate's eye. He squinted, and was able to make it out in the darkness. Something was moving away from the gate. Toward them.

"Get ready for action," Dane warned, taking a knee and keeping his gun trained on the movement. Jabari mimicked his exact actions, perhaps not realizing that his pistol would serve as a pitiful defense. "Don't fire until it gets close. Your range isn't as long as mine. I'll tell you when."

Jabari accepted the advice like a stoic.

The shape glided higher, backlit by the stars and shining moon — and then Dane could see its true form. It was nothing from the natural world — a daemon from the darkest abyss — a winged death with tentacle limbs flailing sickeningly beneath it.

"Oh dear," Dane exclaimed, dropping his weapon. He nudged Jabari back toward the ladder. "Get back inside get back inside get back inside!!!"

"I thought you said we were gonna shoot it! You said we were monster fighters!"

"First rule of monster fighting, kid. Know when to run."

Dane waited for Jabari to climb down the ladder and then he leaped to the deck below. He couldn't get back inside fast enough.

"Hi," he said with spent breath, addressing Min and Mona. "We got a problem. Or like, a million of them, headed our way."

"This is only the beginning," Min said, "We must find a way to overcome or pass by these creatures in order to shut that gate."

Dane beckoned for Mona. "Hey. Mona. I need your help. I need you to find the conductor. Tell him to get this train moving or all these people are going to die. Can you do that?" He placed his hands on her shoulders, taking the opportunity to look into her large brown eyes again.

Mona nodded, her eyes digging for strength. "Right through the cars," Dane advised, then he turned his sights on Min. "What's the plan? How do we beat these guys?"

"I'm going to stay here until the last possible second."

Dane fake smiled. "Okay. Great." He reached into his trunk and began filling his arms with guns. "Kid, I need your help. You wanted to kill some monsters? We need to be properly prepared."

Jabari grinned, and followed Dane back out the doors.

X

Even though the train was no longer moving, Mona felt like she was going to be sick. It was not the ground beneath her feet that was swaying, but her mind itself. The very reality she knew was teetering on the brink. Looking out the window, Mona knew what her mind was telling her she was seeing. It was the same thing everyone else was seeing. She had come to trust her eyes in the thirty five years of her life, and still part of her doubted what she was now seeing. How could it be real? It simply did not make sense!

Mona weighed the pistol Dane had given her, keeping it down by her side as she pushed her way into the adjacent train car. The task Dane had given her occupied her mind, gave her something to focus on other than the fact that she felt like she was going crazy, and for that she was grateful. However, she also realized that she was alone and vulnerable, away from those she knew in this foreign country. And if, heaven forbid, the lurking hole in the sky was real, then she was greatly downplaying the amount of danger she was in and leaving her party was even more of a risk. But best to focus on one thing at a time.

The passengers in the car were all pressed against the eastern wall of windows, fixated on the spinning lights and spectacle outside. Mona took advantage of their distraction to make her way down the aisle, keeping the gun out of sight.

She stepped out into the frigid air once more, her breathing expelled from her in a visible cloud, and cast a furtive look at the gate. There was something beautiful about it. Almost as if it were a black hole, but on earth. A feeling of dread crept through her chest, and she had the distinct impression that she was currently witnessing something she was not supposed to be seeing.

There was movement in the sky. Dark things on dark wings. Mona's heart fluttered and she threw open the door to the next car and leapt inside. She did not want to be out there with whatever that was pouring forth from the gate.

They were just legends. Just stories told by simple minded people long ago to explain the intricate workings of the universe.

Her chest tightened, and she wanted desperately to curl into a ball and disappear. *Keep going, Mona. Just keep walking.*

Had everything she'd ever been told, everything she'd ever known been a lie? Did the universe operate on different principles entirely than the ones currently accepted by science? What was more likely — that magic and cosmic demons were real or that they were witnessing some kind of optical illusion? Or perhaps the natural gas was causing their brains to react.

But would all their brains react exactly the same, and present the same visual phenomenon? Chances of that seem pretty low, Mona. But there has to be some kind of explanation!

Dammit all.

Best to ignore the looming elephant in the sky for right now.

Mona pushed her way out into the night, finally arriving at the engine car. She reached out a numb hand and pulled the latch on the door. It was open.

"Hello?" Mona called out as she stepped into the darkened car. A fire roared in the combustion engine, and a pile of coal filled half the room.

There was a soft moan and Mona noticed the conductor, half bent over in the corner, his body rigid and shaking.

"Oh my goodness, are you all right? Everyone's worried." She kept the pistol behind her back.

The conductor turned, and in the dim lighting she could see that he was not all right. "It's inside me," he managed to sputter, spittle flying from his cracked lips. He grasped his head with two rigid hands.

"I don't understand," Mona managed to say. "People are scared. We need to get this train moving. Is there someone we can call? I can try and find a doc—"

In a sudden flash of movement the conductor grabbed the coal shovel and swung it at Mona's head. She stepped backward, but not in time, and the corner of the shovel caught the side of her head, knocking her sideways.

Her head rang and stars shimmered across her vision. Mona shook off the shock just in time to realize the man was once more raising the shovel to swing it at her.

This time Mona dove out of the way. She saw that the exit door was in reach, and forgetting that she held in her hands a gun, and not mentally prepared to use it, she leaped off the train, into the darkness beyond.

XI

Min opened his eyes. He could feel the darkness brewing around them.

Pandemonius was here. He could sense him. Though it really wasn't a him but an *it*. A formless entity who only desired their freedom and to wreak destruction among the souls of men. Memories assaulted his senses — visceral and clear. He had come up against Pandemonius before.

When Min was a young boy, only seven or eight, his mother had begun coming home late at night. Sometimes she would bring home a strange man and sequester herself in her room. She swore Min to secrecy, but the man did not seem to care. He would leave clues, items, things his father would later find. Min's father was not a dumb man and soon caught on to what was happening. He confronted his wife one night. Min would never forget the fear he felt at hearing them raise their voices, at hearing his mother assault his father, and at hearing his father beat his mother to death, and then take his own life.

A kind man in the village helped Min, and after seeing to his physical needs, provided him with a protection talisman. Min hung it in the window, and when his mother's strange lover came back for him, he found that he could not enter the house. The man wailed and threatened Min, but Min would not listen. That's when he saw Pandemonius' true form. The man changed before Min's very eyes into a cloud of crimson-red dust.

It was only later that Min would learn what it truly was that he had seen. What force had broken his family and left him an orphan. Min wandered many years before finally joining the Black Circle, where he had spent the rest of his days, learning...and waiting for Pandemonius to come back.

And now he had.

Min glanced out the window at the cloud of dark wings moving toward them and felt a pang of despair. How could they defeat such wretched abominations? No matter how well they fought, the end was inevitable. He knew this. He had accepted this years ago. He had rationalized the situation in his mind — he was fighting to extend humanity's life and reach, not save it. With luck, humanity would not end for generations after Min had passed on. But today he could not see even that hope.

Here, alone with Fabiana, he felt vulnerable. He felt alone.

Min was startled out of his reverie by a sharp rapping on the glass. He turned, and saw the train conductor standing behind the door. Without thinking, Min made his way (painfully) toward the man and extended his blood stained hand toward the door handle...then paused.

He looked at the conductor and smiled. "How can I help you?"

The conductor motioned to the door handle. "Open the door."

"It's not locked."

The conductor's frown turned into a hideous grimace. He pointed at the woman. "What's going on here? Why is that woman tied up?"

"That is private business. But I assure you she is unharmed. If you have anything you wish to say to me, say it here. I can hear you quite clearly. Otherwise I ask that you please leave us in peace. We paid for the exclusive use of this car, and you agreed to our terms."

The conductor growled, but did not leave. "That's before I knew you were tying up women. Now open the door, or I'll have no choice but to contact the authorities."

Min returned to his bench, reached into his satchel, and pulled out a wooden box of curious workmanship. It was a puzzle box of his own design, modeled after one described in the Key of Solomon. He held it up for the conductor to see. "Do you know what this is?"

The conductor's eyes flared, but he did not speak.

"Ah, yes. I see that you remember it." Min took a step forward. "I'm going to open the door. I'm going to open the door and you're going to get a full demonstration. Just like old times."

Min took another step.

Gunfire erupted from the top of the train car, momentarily distracting Min.

When he turned back to the door, the conductor was gone.

XII

The closer the creatures got, the harder Dane's heart pounded. They were still out of range. Dane had just enough time to set up his M2HB Browning machine gun on its tripod. "Cover your ears, kid," he warned, before pulling his finger tight against the trigger. A barrage of bullets lit up the sky. Dane swept the weapon along the path of his moving target and heard a high pitched scream that assaulted his senses, nearly shattering his eardrums, pierce the night sky.

Hold down on the trigger. Just hold down on the trigger. His clip emptied, but as he went to change it he realized the beasts were within range to attack with close range weaponry. However all that was put on hold as his eyes beheld the monstrosities before him.

They were made of oozing putrescent flesh, large bat-like wings sprang forth from their backs. Gaping mouths filled with thousands of razor sharp teeth hung from their bodies. Tentacles, their only limbs, twirled from their corpulent frames, reaching outward to grasp at prey.

"Plan B," Dane quipped, fully aware that now was not the time for quipping. He couldn't help himself, it was his defense mechanism. He raced to his next weapon — a flame thrower, tossed the straps on his back, threw the safety, and pulled the trigger just as one of the tentacled beasts descended upon them. Flame exploded forth from the end of the barrel — and the beast was kept at bay only by the force of the fire. The night beast squealed, and in the added light, Dane could see that the tentacles also contained eyes running up and down their fibrous, boneless limbs. Dane shivered, his stomach retched, the popping sound of overcooked eyes and burning flesh sent his hair spiking, then the beast fell to the earth where it rested, an inert pyre of abomination and flame.

Dane and Jabari both looked at each other in disgust. "Can I shoot now?" Jabari asked.

Dane nodded. "Yeah."

Dane let loose, and his bursts of flame were accompanied by pops of Jabari's handgun beside him. Dane swept the sky, keeping the monsters away, charring any who dared to come close. Some hovered just beyond the reach of his flame, as if they were waiting for the inevitable moment where he would run out of fuel. The others attached themselves to the other train cars, and began reaching their tentacles inside, pulling passengers out through the windows.

Dammit all to hell! There was no way he could save everyone on this train. They were simply too few against too many. And why the hell wasn't the train moving??

"Stay here," Dane ordered, as he threw a rifle over his back and launched himself over to the adjacent train car. The beast leered in Dane's direction, and Dane waved at it before burning it to hell. The tentacles writhed and swung about in a desperate defense. One of them caught Dane on his shoulder, nearly knocking him off the roof.

Another beast swooped out of the sky and went crashing into the train car. Tentacles sprouted from the windows and Dane began burning. There was a roar from below and the tentacles made desperate grabs for Dane which he did his best to dodge.

He burned as many as he could before hopping down to the deck below and kicking in the door. He swung his rifle down into his hands and fired until the mass of flesh stopped moving.

Just because they ain't from this world doesn't mean they can't be killed by a gun.

Dane nodded to the surviving passengers, who were huddled amidst indescribable carnage. He felt something squeeze his waist, but by the time he looked down it was too late. He was pulled out the door by the tentacles of another unseen monstrosity.

Man, these guys just keep comin'!

From his vantage point in the sky Dane got a good look at a view filled with winged beasts swarming the train, covering it like moths on a lamp. Dane pointed his rifle downward and fired at the one holding him hostage. As the tentacle loosened and he began to fall, Dane realized that the train was rocking back and forth.

Dear God, he had time to think, *they're tearing the train from its tracks.*

XIII

Jabari fired his gun at anything that moved. Dane had been right, the recoil of the weapon was fierce, and his wrists and forearms ached terribly — but there was no way he could stop. His small handgun was just barely managing to keep the creatures off of himself, let alone help anybody else. He should have been filled with despair at this frightening predicament. He was caught, cornered, there was no way out and he would eventually run out of ammo.

But that is not what Jabari was thinking. He was thinking how thrilling this was — the moment when he finally was allowed to fire a gun! The power he felt was indescribable. Pop! Pop! Pop! He laughed as he squeezed the trigger, sending a night beast flailing downward. Provided with enough ammo, Jabari was certain he could do this all night. This was living! This was fun! This was —

The train rocked beneath him and Jabari found himself falling toward the ground. His body slammed hard, his hand lost his gun, and his chest screamed for air. The wind had been knocked out of him. He lay amidst the carnage of burning bodies that he and Dane had sent to the earth. In the flickering witch lights Jabari searched for his gun and found it a moment later, only to immediately have his attention ripped away to a familiar scream.

A female scream. He had never heard it before, but somehow he knew who it belonged to, he didn't know how but he just knew, like a sixth sense.

Jabari turned and saw that one of the night beasts had Mona by the leg, its tentacle raking her across the rocky soil toward its chasmous mouth. Left unhindered it would soon reel her in and slash her skin to ribbons. Jabari could not allow that to happen.

He leapt into action, hopping over a flaming pyre of flesh and fell to one knee. Taking careful aim, he fired his handgun into the monster's body until his gun clicked empty.

Mona wriggled free from the dying creature's grasp and flew to Jabari's side.

Her hair was a mess, her skin no longer immaculate, but stained with dirt and blood. There was a half crazed look behind her eyes. "We're all going to die. We're all going to die." She repeated the phrase over and over.

Jabari didn't know what to do. He hadn't been trained on how to handle mumbling professors, just how to point and shoot. He took her hand. "Come on," then pulled her along after him.

The train was overrun with night beasts. They perched on top of the overturned train, digging their tentacles through the open windows and pulling survivors to their doom. The air was filled with their death cries as one by one they were found and devoured. Jabari found Min's train car and inserted a new magazine, his last one. He used the bullets to scatter the monsters around the car, then flung the car door open.

Min was on his hands and knees, crawling through broken glass. Fabiana was still tied to the post, a fresh wound on her head, her hair now matted with drying blood.

Jabari shook Mona, forcing her to look at him. "Can you get the girl? I can't do this alone."

When there was no response, Jabari shook her again. "Can you get the girl?"

"Y-yes."

It would have to do. Jabari climbed inside, and then watched to make sure Mona climbed in after him. Jabari went for Min, helping the old man to his feet.

"Thank you, my boy. My book. Don't forget my book."

Jabari searched in the dim light for the fallen book, and found it resting atop a window. He threw his arm under Min and helped him walk to the doors. Mona used one of Dane's knives to cut Fabiana free. Together, they ushered their injured party out into the war zone.

Jabari sensed movement to his left and instinctively turned and pulled the trigger. But the shot was only one handed and went wide.

Dane raised his hands in surrender. "Kid! Don't shoot me!"

"Sorry," Jabari said, though he did not drop his gun.

"Well, what about now, Min? Can we leave the train now?" Dane took over for Jabari, allowing Min to rest upon his larger frame.

Min's face was paler than Jabari remembered, or maybe it was just the dim light, but a blossom of blood was spreading from Min's shoulder. "Yes. We must...get to the gate. We must close that gate..or die trying."

XIV

Ned watched the night beasts pour forth from the gate, his eyes as wide and amazed as a child on Christmas morning. The creatures moved so quickly they were a blur. And there were so many. Thousands, even. He had seen marvelous things in the service of Mr. Locke, but never anything like this. This was the stuff nightmares were made of.

He felt the burden of his mission ease off his shoulders. The gate was open. His task was complete. Now he could sit back and watch the world burn. Humanity would get what was coming to it.

Ned hunkered back to the side of the gate. Up until this point, the night beasts had been so eager to get out that they had not bothered to look sideways. But eventually one of the creatures had flown high, and after surveying the scene, had honed in on Ned as possible prey. It was swooping down for him now.

His skin prickled at the sight of the hideous thing heading his way. There was nothing beautiful about it...it was alien, unnatural, an abomination.

Isn't that what they called you? Isn't that what you are? Something hideous. Something that shouldn't exist?

His attempt at comparing himself to the creature did not make him love it any more, and instead heaped more self loathing upon his head. *Is that how others feel when they look upon your face, Ned? Something so awful that they wish it did not exist?*

He felt no pity for this thing, this beast which had landed on the ground and was now slithering toward him in eerie, snake-like motions.

A wave of emotion swept across him as he perceived what other humans must have felt when they looked on his own face. Seeing this embodied form of evil did not make him feel good. It made him feel dirty. Guilty, even. He could do nothing for it.

Ned extended his hand. He wasn't sure if it was an invitation for the beast to sniff his hand, a token of friendship and peaceful intentions, or if it was a warning hand, meant to keep the beast at bay.

A thousand knives tore into his flesh and as the beast ripped his arm in two. Ned sank to his knees, screaming, too shocked to retaliate.

He watched as the creature devoured his arm, his own blood dripping down its pungent flesh. He did the only thing he could think to do. He called for help.

"MASTERRRR! MASTER SAVE ME!"

Blood poured in waves from what was left of his arm. The scene before him was like watching a dream. He could feel pain, but he was detached from it all. Perhaps that was for the best. With his only remaining hand he unclasped his belt, then tightened it around his upper arm to stop the bleeding.

By the time he was done he was feeling lightheaded and weak. A shadow swept over him and Ned realized that Mr. Locke was standing beside him, and his heart rejoiced.

"Locke. That thing bit my arm off! Look!"

He raised the stump for Locke to see, but the gaunt man only glanced down apathetically, uncaring and unsurprised. "What do you want from me?"

Ned's eyebrows raised in surprise. "Kill it! Make me a new arm! All the above, haven't I earned your help?"

"I never said you would be spared," Locke sneered coldly. "You wanted to end humanity. That includes you." Then, in afterthought he continued. "The children must feed."

Locke turned and walked away, leaving Ned to his fate.

The creature was finished devouring his arm now, and it was inching toward him again. Ned drew his pistol and fired, the bullets sending bits of flesh flying.

The thing shivered to a halt only a few feet before him.

Even though the immediate threat was gone, Ned felt no better. A void had opened inside him that was irreparable. He had been betrayed by the one person he trusted.

What was the point?

There was none. No point at all.

Ned laughed. He laughed harder than he ever had. It was all a joke! This thing called life. Ned turned the gun on himself and pulled the trigger.

The gun clicked.

Empty.

Ned laughed.

XV

Dane did the best he could to lead his intrepid troupe across no man's land, toward the hovering portal in the distance. Without his trunk he had limited ammo. All he had left was his rifle, a few bursts from the flame thrower, and a pair of pistols. With those meager weapons, he paved the way through a field of dead monsters. A torrent of night beasts flocked above, but somehow they were no longer swarming after them. Perhaps the myriad of dead bodies masked their scent, perhaps now that they were on the ground, and carried no light, they were no longer as visible. Dane didn't care. He was grateful to preserve ammo.

They didn't need to carry a light, either. The illumination from the witch lights was enough to mark their path. As they drew closer to the arena of flashing lights Dane could see that there was a cloud of creatures hovering above the lights, seemingly drawn to them. And they were bewitching, there was no doubt about that. Many a man had lost his life after falling prey to their entrancing power.

The ground under Dane's feet grew warm and he ushered the rest of his party along. "Come on! Ground's gonna blow."

Jabari, who brought up the rear, had only taken a couple of steps past Dane's initial location when a towering burst of teal flame erupted from the earth. The heat was so intense Dane could feel waves of it washing over him. Any closer and he'd have lost his eyebrows.

Note to self: beware of hot ground.

Dane plucked one of the pistols from his holster and offered it to Mona, hoping she could help defend them against the monsters that would surely attack them as they grew closer. "Here. Hold onto this, you're gonna need it."

But Mona only looked at the gun weakly, as if she wasn't quite sure what to do with it. It was only now that Dane could see that Mona was swaying on her feet. She appeared pale, nearly catatonic.

"Hello? Earth to Mona?" He turned to Min for answers. "What's wrong with her?"

"Not everyone is built to handle the ignominious truth."

"Speak English!" Dane demanded.

"I'm afraid the girl may have lost her mind."

Dane grimaced. He hoped this was a temporary losing the of the mind kind of situation, instead of permanent, but there was no use dwelling on the issue now. The practical effect of this new information was that Mona was going to be no help in a fight. Dane gripped her hand, an act which sent a torrent of emotions sweeping through his flesh — he was at once aroused, hardened, and depressed — as he realized that she might not ever be the same again and whatever seed of hope he had held of getting to know her better after all this was over was instantly swept away. This was all intensified by the fact that up until now he hadn't been aware that he had been harboring a secret hope to get to know her better.

Dane led the group in a weaving path through the lights, though it was impossible to tell how long a particular flame would last or where and when another would appear. As they moved around one of these pillars of fire, it promptly vanished, leaving them totally exposed.

One of the creatures above, who must have seen them in the light, dove down in their direction. Several more followed suit. Dane used his flame thrower to roast two before it ran out of fuel. He ditched the heavy tank, heaving it at another beast as he slid it off his shoulders, then unleashed a fury of bullets. He could feel warmth spreading beneath his feet and waved at Min and the others to keep back. Several creatures converged on his location.

Dane waited for as long as he dared before he dove out of the way. Of course, the monstrosities followed him. A powerful flame shot from the ground, crisping the creatures. Dane couldn't stop himself from cheering out loud.

"Dane! He's got Batman!"

Dane turned to see one of the tentacled beasties bearing a hissing cat. Dane took aim but by the time he had his sight lined up, the cat had been dropped into a labyrinth of razor sharp teeth.

The commotion had caused quite a scene, and as Dane looked around, he could see that night beasts were converging on their location from all directions.

"I'm running out of bullets, Min!" Dane called, but he could already see Min was on his knees, drawing with chalk in the dirt. He was making a circle. He only hoped that Min could finish it in time.

"Get in the circle," Dane ordered, pulling Mona and Fabiana along with him.

Jabari fired a few bullets into the crowd. "Save your bullets, kid," Dane advised. Min completed the circle and set to work drawing various runes and symbols inside the outer ring, muttering to himself as he went.

"There are too many," Jabari said.

"Yeah. I know. Sorry about your cat."

There were tears in Jabari's eyes. Not tears of despair and lost hope, but of anger. That spark encouraged Dane. The creatures closed in. One of them tried to reach a tentacle toward Min, but as if it were shocked by some invisible spark, pulled back. The creatures could not breach the boundary of the circle.

But that did not change the fact that there was a sea of gnashing teeth and writhing bodies surrounding them. There was no way out of this. There was nowhere to go.

It was over.

They were trapped.

There was no way they were going to be able to close that gate.

XVI

The world around Min was growing dark. He looked above the seething creatures to the gate where the darkness was pouring forth into their world, just as he had predicted. If they did not close that gate, their world would be consumed. They did not have much time.

Min turned to Dane and Jabari now, raising his voice so it could be heard above the din of the night beasts. "Did I ever tell you about Pandemonius?"

Dane's eyes were concentrated on the threat at hand, short-sighted, but Min could not blame him. "I don't think this is the best time for stories, my guy."

Min ignored him. "He is one of the vilest elder gods. Formless. A shapeshifter. He delights in seeing humanity flounder. He was exiled here to earth by his sister, V'Razis, and he wants desperately to escape. He opened the gateway, inviting her children to feed on the husks of men, in an effort to gain her favor."

"So, it's a family thing, huh?" Dane pivoted as a large tentacle lashed out, but the monster roared and leaped backward when it realized it could not penetrate the circle.

Min pulled the puzzle box from his satchel, turning the sleek woodwork in his bloodied hand. Jabari eyed it with interest. "What's that?"

"Solomon Cross, before he vanished, was developing a box that could ensnare Pandemonius, temporarily."

"Temporarily? How temporarily are we talking?"

"Long enough to hurl him into the dark abyss. Once, long ago, Pandemonius developed some kind of positive feelings for another — the black witch Tamaris, whose soul was more wicked than his own. She was the offspring of Elbozra, and therefore half elder god. When he saw her in her forest lair, amidst a graveyard of web-entombed corpses, some still wriggling in their netted cages, he entered a human body so he could have a physical form, and together they searched for a way to extend her life. She would need to transfer her consciousness to another body, as she was mortal. They completed the ritual — and it worked — but now she was wholly human. It was Solomon Cross who slayed her in this weakened state. Pandemonius has hunted Cross' prodigy ever since, seeking his revenge. There is an ancient prophecy that Cross' children are destined to torment Pandemonius forever. In order to ensure this prophecy was fulfilled, Cross sired as many children as he could, making it nearly impossible to eradicate his entire bloodline." Min turned toward the gate and in a voice that was magnified by some supernatural power, declared above the din "THE BLOOD OF SOLOMON CROSS FLOWS IN MY VEINS, DAEMON, AND I HAVE COME TO TORMENT THEE!"

A wretched screech filled the air, sending them all to their knees, clamping their hands over their ears. Min managed to keep his eyes open and watched as the children of V'Razis began to retreat. A pathway opened in their midst, like the parting of the Red Sea. Witch lights still burned around them, but even the power of their light was fading in the thickening darkness.

Yet out there, in the field, Min could distinguish the familiar shape of a thin man, with his arms extended, his feet raised off the ground.

An involuntary shiver ran down Min's spine as he gazed upon the creature that had destroyed his family.

Come to me.

The voice was not spoken by lips, and was not in his mind, but reverberated in the air around them.

Min felt a tugging at his sleeve. "Don't go," Jabari warned.

In a sense, the boy was right, to go would be foolish. But that was his destiny. He had been trained, bred, for this singular purpose: to defend the world of men. Stepping out to confront this wretched evil was his duty, whether it led to his death or not.

Min put his hand on the boy's shoulder and smiled. "You are special, Jabari. Never stop fighting. Find the Black Circle. Do not mourn for me. When I am gone, take this box, and throw it into the gate."

The Key of Solomon, Min handed to Dane. "Complete the ritual. Close the gate."

Dane accepted the book in silence, as if sensing the truth. "Good luck out there, Min."

Min held his hand out and shook Dane's hand. Then he turned, and stepped outside the circle.

XVII

The world around Fabiana was a mad blur of monsters and horrors. She wanted desperately to close her eyes, to simply be gone from this nightmare. Min's voice sounded around her, a power for light and goodness, and miraculously the evil began to withdraw. There was something else growing though, a shape taking form out there, just beyond the ring of light. She squinted, trying to make sense of it.

The face in the shape became clear and Fabiana gasped.

It was McKarney.

He floated there, hovering above the ground, his arms outstretched in invitation. How was he here? How could he be here when she had seen his dead body herself?

Don't look into his eyes.

But it was too late. His sea-blue eyes flared, and the movement caught her attention. She once again found herself riveted to that trance-like stare, once again felt the division inside herself — part of her wanted to resist, the other wanted to give in, to simply let McKarney take over.

She could feel herself once more under his spell, could feel herself once more enter that dreamworld where her body was not her own.

She could see what McKarney wanted her to do in her mind's eye and shuddered, the horror of the task nearly enough to draw her out of her reverie, but not quite. While the others were distracted, watching Min walk out toward McKarney, Fabiana felt herself reach forward and remove the loaded pistol from Mona's hands. Then she stepped outside the circle.

She had no fear that she would be harmed. McKarney had promised to protect her.

Finish the job. Kill the old man.

Min was halfway to McKarney right now. She could hear Min muttering to himself, no doubt trying to offer some form of protection charm. It would not work.

There was something in his hand, no gun or weapon, but a box. Yet it was this box which McKarney feared. Before the others could stop her, before they even realized what was going on, Fabiana started walking out toward Min. She gained on him quickly, as Min was taking his time, putting one foot in front of the other, as if he were walking against a great wind.

The deed was over before she had time to blink. She took the handgun, raised it to the level of Min's chest, and pulled the trigger. The first shot missed, her hands surprised at the force of the kickback. She pulled it twice more and the second bullet pierced the flesh of his back. She felt him cry out, falter. Still, even with the pain and shock he was still muttering to himself.

As soon as the bullet entered Min, Fabiana felt McKarney leave her. She had her mind back, and had a full recollection of everything he'd made her do. She was here, with a smoking gun in her shaking hands.

She screamed. Dropped the weapon in horror, but it was too late. Dark blood ran from the wound, turning the old man's white shirt scarlet.

But instead of retaliating, Min turned to her, on his knees. He took her hand, as if to say it was okay. "Can you lift my arm?"

She did not understand the words, but understood his gesture, and she slipped her arm around him, helping the old man to rise to his feet. She could feel warm blood running down her side. Together, they pressed on. McKarney was still waiting there. He opened his mouth as if in a silent scream, but the gape of his jaw was unnaturally large.

Min continued his muttering, in some tongue which Fabiana did not know. He twisted the box in his hands and its lid popped open. With a final effort, Min shouted the last words of the incantation and thrust the box toward McKarney.

McKarney wailed, and as if he were made of smoke, his form began to be drawn toward the open box. His semblance melted before Fabiana's eyes, as her tormentor was forced out of his disguise, sucked into Min's box — and once he was gone, the lid snapped shut.

They had him.

XVIII

Dane raised his gun to kill Fabiana, but Jabari knocked him aside, and the bullet went wide, grazing her shoulder.

"Stay off me, kid. I've had enough of this girl's attempts to murder my boss."

"She's helping him. Look!" Jabari pleaded, pointing to her arm around Min.

"Yeah, after she tried to kill him. You know what? Screw this." Dane left the circle, rushing out to meet Min. Jabari looked back at Mona. She was sitting on the ground in a fetal position muttering to herself.

Stay here. The old man said to say here. We're safe within the circle.

Jabari felt the ground grow hot beneath his feet.

Jabari took Mona's arm and helped her to stand. "Come on." He pulled her out of the circle just as a barrage of face melting flame broke from the ground.

Apparently the circle did not protect against witch fire.

There were squeals from above as the fire sent the night beasts scattering. They had a few moments of unmolested peace.

Jabari pulled Mona's hand behind him until they reached Min's side. Min was lying on his back in the dirt now. His eyes were still moving. Jabari knelt by his side and took his hand. Min placed the wooden box into Jabari's fingers. "Toss it...into the gate."

"I will," Jabari promised.

Min's breathing was slowing. He smiled at them. "I go at last to the dreamlands."

Min's chest rose and fell, and did not rise again. Jabari felt a wave of emotion rise up within him. The man who he had promised to follow, who he really thought would change his life forever, was now dead. Just like everyone else he had ever known or cared about. The world was a cruel mistress. What in the hell was he supposed to do now?

After a moment Dane squeezed Jabari's shoulder and pulled him to his feet. "Come on, kid. We've got to finish what we started. What Min started. We've got to close that gate."

Jabari nodded. Dane was right. This wasn't over. Jabari took Fabiana's hand and Dane took Mona's, and together they raced through the darkness across the grassfield.

The gate was incredible from far away but it was unbelievable up close. All Jabari could do was gawk in awe as straggling night beasts crawled forth from the abyss. Jabari felt the box torn from his hands and watched as Fabiana hurled it through the hole in the sky. The box passed through the black circle and fell through into the other side.

Into another world.

That's when he noticed movement out of the corner of his eye. A sniveling shape hunched below the gate.

A man in a dark cloak and mask, wielding a dagger. Dane saw him at the same time and swung his gun at the stranger.

"Whoa. Don't move, buddy. Show us your hands."

"Kill me. Kill me, isn't that what you want?"

"Who are you?" Dane demanded.

"I'm the one who opened the gate. I'm the one who caused all this madness. Kill me! Let me rot in hell for eternity."

"Throw down the knife," Jabari ordered, but the man did not listen.

Instead, he reached up a hand and tore the mask free from his head, revealing the most hideously deformed excuse for a face Jabari had ever seen. His jaw dropped. His stomach retched. He almost pulled the trigger just for the fear the image struck in him. Instincts told him to run from a thing like this.

"You see this? This is what I am. A monster. So kill me, damn you! KILL ME!"

Without warning the man raced at Jabari, and Jabari pulled the trigger.

XIX

Fabiana was free of McKarney. He had been trapped inside that box. And now he was far away. He couldn't trouble her again. But in order to make sure that really happened...they had to close the gate.

Ned rushed at Jabari, and one bullet from Jabari's gun sent Ned to his knees. A shot to the midsection.

Jabari rushed forward and kicked the knife from Ned's grasp. Fabiana stepped forward. The American said something, probably telling her to get away, but she did not listen. She took Ned's hand and held it up, observing the image she thought she had seen on his wrist. It was a brand. An ancient symbol, meant to mark him as an elder god's property. She had a different brand on her wrist, but it meant the same thing. This man, however disgusting he appeared, was a victim, just as she was.

She held out her wrist so Ned could see it.

"You? You served them too?"

Fabiana nodded.

"They lied to us," Ned sniffed, wiping his nose across his arm.

Fabiana squeezed his hand.

"You want revenge?" She asked in her native tongue, surprised at the sound of her own voice. "We need your help."

Ned replied to her in broken Spanish. "What can I possibly do to help?"

"You can help fix your mistake. We need to close the gate, but we need someone to pass through to the other side. A sacrifice."

Ned looked back at the swirling eye. "What will happen to me?"

Fabiana smiled at him. "I don't know."

Ned picked up the knife. "I'm sorry." He sliced the blade across his palm and flicked drops of blood at the ground before the gate.

Fabiana repeated the words she had heard McKarney repeat so often before sacrificing one of his young.

Then, without looking back, Ned rushed forward and leaped into the void.

Fabiana turned to Dane. "You must read the incantation. You must close the gate!" She motioned to the book.

Dane did not speak Spanish. But he understood her meaning well enough. He opened the book to the marked page, and began to read.

XX

Dane did his best to pronounce the foreign words of the incantation. He kept his eyes focused on the pages of the book, trying to block out the world around him, the pain he felt for Min and Mona, and even the gate itself. He had to be here. He had to be present.

Dane finished and glanced up, only to find that he was not where he had been standing only a moment before. He was no longer standing in a field in Africa, but in the interior hall of what appeared to be a poorly lit temple. The carvings on the wall indicated some kind of ancient worship. The vaulted ceilings, stone pillars, and majestic architecture left Dane speechless. No man had ever created something so pure or so stirring.

Dane knew not how long he stood there gaping in awe, the grimoire still clutched in his sweaty palms. A hooded figure in a dark cloak glided toward him from the shadows. The face was hidden beneath the cavernous hood. A hand, pale as death, extended from the robes and cast something skittering across the floor. The object, or objects, as it turned out, came to rest at Dane's feet. He glanced down and saw that they were a series of smooth white stones with runes etched upon their surfaces.

"What is that?" Dane asked, surprised at the timbre of his voice in the spacious chamber.

The faceless figure tilted its head, and in a voice scarred by ages said "The stones speak the truth. About who you really are, and about the path that lays before you."

"And what do they say about me?" Dane asked, reaching for his gun and realizing that somehow his weapon was no longer attached to his body.

The figure scrutinized the stones a moment longer. "That you are selfish. Unwieldy. That you fear more than you let on."

"Yeah, well thanks for the fortune cookie, but with all due respect, I'm here to close a gate, so do you have any idea how I do that? Because if not I'm going to try and find someone who does. And where the hell am I, by the way? The old man didn't say anything about...anything like this. He just said to read from the book."

"If you wish to close the gate...a sacrifice must be made."

"We did make a sacrifice. That disfigured guy."

The cloaked figure tsked and swept toward Dane, his hand pointed at Dane, inches from his chest. Even though it was just a finger, Dane withdrew. He peered into the chasmous hood, searching for any sign of flesh or face, and found nothing but blackness.

"The girl's mind is gone."

Dane held his ground. "The price some must pay."

"And what about your price?"

Dane held his silence. He decided he was going to play this man's game.

"If you wish to close the gate, a sacrifice must be made."

"What do I gotta do?"

"Lend me your finger."

Dane held out his right hand. The man drew out a slim dagger and Dane's muscles tightened, a sudden fear swelling in his chest that the man was going to slice off his finger, but he did not. He pricked the tip in one swift motion, drawing forth blood which rained down on the stone at their feet. Dane's eyes grew wide and his heartbeat quickened. The man's other hand was...all wrong. It was inhuman. Ribbed and rough, almost insectlike. It was with this hand that he collected a sample of Dane's blood and brought it to his unseen mouth beneath the hood, his lips smacking together as they tasted it.

Not another word passed between the two men. The mist thickened around them, swirling, as if propelled by some sudden wind — and the image of the man before him was lost. Dane looked around him. Visibility was zero.

He wandered around, waving his arms in the fog.

"Dane! Dane?"

It was the boy's voice, though he could not see him.

"I'm here," Dane called. He followed the sound of the boy's voice. The mist retreated around him and he saw that he was back in the field.

What a trip. Min could have warned me I'd be whisked to some mystical realm.

The boy ran to him and embraced him. "We did it," he said.

Dane looked up, and sure enough, the gate was gone.

"Well, I'll be damned."

Fabiana was kneeling on the ground, clutching her belly. She held Mona's hands. The features of her face were etched in fear, and Dane could see that there was no intelligent thought occurring behind her eyes.

He sighed.

"What do we do now?" Jabari asked.

They had completed the task, but Min had left Dane with the cleanup. He wasn't a clean up guy, he was used to solving all his problems with bullets. Why should it be his problem? He should leave, find some way to contact the Black Circle, collect his bounty, and leave the others to fend for themselves.

Yet another part of him resisted. This other part of him insisted he owed it to Min, if nothing else, to see that the rest of their party at least made it to safety. Dane wrestled with this for a few moments before realizing that the boy was still watching him, waiting for an answer. "First, we bury Min."

Dane led them back through the cemetery of deceased night beasts, that horror had not gone away, but there were none in the sky — they had flown to greener pastures and could be dealt with later. Jabari stayed with the women while Dane searched the train for supplies. He found some packaged food and water, and though there was no shovel, he did find a flat headed spear of metal that he figured would be almost as good.

Dane used the metal to dig a hole in the earth. Thankfully it was soft. He dug down several feet, and by the time he was done his hands were blistered and the sun was peeping over the mountains. He carried Min's body himself, and placed it down inside the pit. "Rest in peace, Min," Dane muttered as he filled the hole back in. It was a pathetic excuse for a funeral. Not what the old man deserved, but Dane had nothing else to give him. He was a killer, not a priest.

Another train arrived less than an hour later. The tracks were clear, but the conductor radioed in to report the incident, and agreed to carry Dane and the others to the nearest city.

As they rode, Dane finally took the time to fill his stomach with snacks from the train cart. Fabiana and Mona had fallen asleep. It was just him and Jabari. "You got somewhere you can go?" Dane asked.

Jabari only looked at him.

They arrived in Mzimba midafternoon, and Dane still had not figured out what to do. He could try and figure out how to contact social services, if this country even had such a thing, and leave them all in their hands. But Dane knew that whatever care they received would be abysmal. He couldn't bring them back with him to the US, trying to get them all to pass through customs would be a nightmare.

He was getting a headache. He had a safehouse in Morocco. He could transport them there until he figured out what to do. And this was the decision Dane ended up going with. He bought four train tickets for Kinshasa, and from there they traveled north. They arrived at his safe house a few days later.

The place was not large. It contained only two bedrooms, and sparse furnishings. Dane slept on the floor until he was able to buy another mattress. They lived there for several weeks, the semblance of a small family. Dane had enough money to get by for quite some time, and food here was cheap. He had hoped Mona's condition would improve, but she remained incoherent. She would mumble to herself occasionally, but nothing in the way of actual communication.

It was Fabiana he had to focus on now, though. He was no expert, but he knew enough to know that the girl was due any day. One of the first things he did was find a doctor to come and check her out. He assured Dane that the baby was alive, and told him to call him again when the water broke, which could occur any time. He would assist with the birth, for a fee. Dane grumbled but took the man's information.

Not a week passed before Dane was awoken in the middle of the night by a frightened Jabari. "Dane. Dane! I think Fabiana is having her baby!"

Dane told Jabari to hold down the fort while he went out and found the doctor. The doctor also was not happy about being woken up in the witching hour, but Dane assured him he would be well paid for his trouble. *How the tables have turned*, Dane thought as he guided the man through the winding streets of sapphire blue houses, *once I was the one taking the money, now I'm the one promising it.*

The doctor, however primitive his education might have been, made good on his word. He coached Fabiana through the birth, and even though he did not speak English, Dane was glad the man was there. He would have been useless.

The baby's wail greeted Dane's ears, a grating, uncomfortable sound, and he was told it was a boy. By all accounts, healthy. Dane paid the doctor for his services (once again, probably overpaying), and the doctor agreed to find someone who spoke Spanish to help coach Fabiana through breastfeeding and baby care.

Dane spent the next several weeks being woken in the middle of the night by the infant's wailing, a situation that caused him to lose his temper more than once and hold the pillow to his ears. *I need some ear plugs. Or better yet, a hotel.*

During one of these nights, when the baby was particularly fussy, Mona came to him, distraught. It was the first real sign of cognizance she had showed in weeks. He held her, like he would a child during a thunderstorm, and did his best to reassure her everything would be okay. He had the passing thought that perhaps she would be interested in some nocturnal activity, but the wiser part of him shoved that thought away. She was not in her right mind. Taking advantage of her position, no matter how attractive her body was, and no matter how horny he felt, would be wrong. She fell asleep in his arms.

Days turned into weeks, and finally, as he was out searching for work, Dane had the thought to reach out to Sloane. Sloane was a contact Dane had in the Black Circle. He might be able to connect Fabiana back with her cult sisters, wherever they were now. Hell, he might even take Jabari. It was worth a shot.

Dane called him and Sloane, although irritated at the thought of assisting with something so trivial when he was trying to hunt down night beasts and generally speaking, save the world, agreed to send out a representative to see what they could do.

Two weeks later, a woman arrived on Dane's doorstep. Her name was Cynthia Ramirez, and after Dane explained everything that had happened, and she had met the rest of their party, she assured Dane she could escort Fabiana back to Peru to be with her sisters who were being provided financial assistance and recovery, courtesy of the Black Circle. She explained all this to Fabiana, who seemed overjoyed at the prospect of returning to Peru with those she knew and loved. "Thank you, Dane," she said, as they parted, and kissed him on the cheek. They had been working on her English.

That night, while Cynthia stayed in a nearby hotel, Dane took Jabari up to the roof and spoke with him. He popped open a beer and offered one to the kid as well, who seemed surprised, but took it nonetheless.

"Kid, there's something I need to talk to you about," he began, suddenly feeling like a father. "This lady, Cynthia, works for the Black Circle. She's offered to take you with her. You can join them, they can teach you, provide for you, train you to carry on Min's work, just like you wanted. So I guess what I'm asking is...is that what you want?"

"Yeah," Jabari said, his smile wide, "But what about you?"

"I don't know. I suppose I'll keep fighting monsters, same as you. Maybe we can even work together. Just gotta figure out what to do with Mona first."

When Cynthia returned the next day, Dane pulled her into Mona's room and asked her about what could be done to help Mona. Cynthia pursed her lips, like a nurse about to deliver terminal news. "The Black Circle can pay to put her in a hospital. But as far as helping her regain her mind, there's nothing we can do that a hospital can't. She's suffering a mental breakdown. There's no way to know if she'll ever return to the way she was before."

Dane nodded, and told her he'd think about it. He spent the day walking around the city. On one side, he didn't want to be trapped with a crazy woman. He wanted to fight monsters and earn filthy amounts of money doing so. But on the other hand, he couldn't bear the thought of Mona living in a hospital. Hospitals were places where people that weren't wanted were sent. And Dane recalled vividly how he had felt during the brief time Mona had been herself. He had sensed chemistry between them, and hoped that might develop into something larger.

Even if it never did, Dane decided that he wanted to keep her around. At least for a while, to see if anything would change.

That evening, Cynthia announced that it was time for her to go. Dane said goodbye to Jabari and Fabiana and the baby. He watched them from the doorway, feeling a sudden absence of wholeness. Despite his mantra that he was only out for himself, Dane had come to care about these people after spending time with them.

That night for the first time in years, Dane wept.

He debated over what to do next. Mona seemed content to just watch TV and stare out the window. She was able to eat, but often Dane had to help her, even spoon feed her at times to make sure she got enough. And he had taken to putting her in diapers because she was no longer aware enough to use the toilet on her own. *It's like taking care of an old person*, Dane thought to himself one night as he was wiping excrement from Mona's legs, *except they're not old*.

Weeks turned into months and they fell into a routine. They would go for walks, eat, sleep, repeat. Dane spent a lot of time exploring, and showing Mona the world, hoping something would spark inside her mind, though nothing ever did. He eventually got a library card and started teaching himself about psychology, hoping he might learn something that he could use to help Mona. He ran through mental exercises with her, tried teaching her words like he would a child, tried teaching her basic physical skills — all met with infuriating indifference.

In the beginning, Dane lost his temper often. He even struck Mona once, out of anger, but also half hoping it might jog her mind like beating an old computer. But all it did was leave a bruise on her face. Dane felt terrible. He asked for her forgiveness, and for a time, Mona shunned him.

Eventually that faded, and things returned to the way they were. Dane resolved to be better after that. He began to be involved with the community, joined a service organization. He spent stints of time teaching gun safety courses and English lessons, though he was much more proficient in the former. He had social needs that had to be met, but beyond that he was well provided for. The Black Circle assisted them financially. Eventually Dane had to admit that he was never going back to his old way of life. This was his life now.

Mona was his life.

Jabari came to visit. He was a man grown now. When had that happened? He entertained Dane late into the night with stories of monsters they had fought or missions he had completed for The Black Circle. The stories reminded Dane of his own, and he told many to Jabari, now that he was old enough to appreciate them. It was good to reflect, to remember, and it made Dane miss the old days.

As their conversation died down, Jabari posed the question he had known was coming. "So, when are you going to join me? The Black Circle could use you. Your experience. Your skills. You can't hide out here forever."

"Why not?" Dane asked, and watched the crestfallen look cross Jabari's face.

"Because you need it. You need the life The Black Circle offers."

Dane sipped his beer and ran a hand through his thinning hair. "Perhaps once. But that is a young man's game."

"Min was not a young man."

"No. You're right. But I'm needed here." He motioned to the back room where Mona slept.

"Put her in a hospital. She'll be well cared for," Jabari insisted.

"Would you want to be in a hospital?"

"I'd be insane, I wouldn't care!" Jabari declared, and Dane grinned.

"Maybe not, but I like to think I'm making a difference."

"Whatever difference you are making here is infinitesimal in comparison with the difference you could be making with us. You'd be saving humanity. Mona's just one person."

"It makes a difference to Mona," Dane said. "And I've saved humanity, time and time again. Humanity will always need to be saved, and the work will never be done. But what I'm doing here...well, one day, when you're older, you'll understand. Changing the world, saving humanity...it's work that's done by small people, everyday, one person at a time."

They parted on good terms, but Dane never saw Jabari again. Months turned into years. Dane never remarried, though he did have romantic flings with women he met around the city. Some lasted longer than others. They were more ways to satiate his libido and need for companionship than they were for love. But perhaps that's what love was. Eventually, those faded as well, and it was just Dane and Mona.

He picked up the habit of talking out loud, talking to her, as if she could hear him or understand. He hoped she could. But if not, then it was a way to fill the silence.

Dane grew fat, and added daily exercise into his routine. Eventually, Mona's hair began to thin and she stopped eating. She was old. He had to accept that. He didn't want to accept it, but he had to. He was old too. What would happen to them after they died? Dane had seen horrors beyond his imagining, and he'd also seen humans fighting back. For the first time in his life, Dane allowed himself to explore religion. He visited several churches, and had ministers form various faiths visit him and Mona in their home, but he never found one that stuck.

Mona grew weaker by the day. She took to laying in bed, and Dane had a doctor come and see her, but they only told him what he already knew — she was dying.

He could have taken her to a hospital, could have tried to preserve her life for a few months, or maybe years, but for what? She had lived a long life. She needed to rest.

Dane took to sleeping by her side, an old man's wordless way of showing his affection, his gratitude for a lifetime of companionship. She passed in the night. Dane's body knew the moment it happened. He sensed the unfamiliar stillness and he woke from a light sleep to find her body.

Dane did not have time to mourn. There was someone else in the room with them.

A dark figure, faceless, in a dark cloak, stood in the corner of the room, watching over their bed.

Is this death? Dane wondered. *Has he come for Mona?*

"The price has been paid," the stranger said, and in that moment Dane knew that the figure was no stranger at all but the same man he had seen all those years ago when he had attempted to close the gate. "The sacrifice, accepted."

Dane felt his heart begin to slow. He reached out and grasped Mona's hand. Wherever she was, he would soon be joining her. He was comforted by that thought. And in his final moments, Dane felt joy in the idea that he would still be with her.

Then everything went black.

XXI

A chorus of night beasts flew off into the evening sky. Jabari watched them go. With a tremendous rushing of wind, the gate before them closed, sucked back into itself like a black hole. The world was back to the way it was supposed to be.

Except for one thing.

Dane was gone.

He had been standing there, right in front of the gate, only a moment ago. But now he was nowhere to be found.

Fabiana cried out, hissing in Spanish. Jabari turned to her, and saw that Mona was gone as well.

Where had they gone? And why had he and Fabiana been allowed to remain?

Questions. Questions that would never be answered. At least not in this life.

Min's book lay in the dirt by Jabari's feet and he picked it up. The book brought back to memory the old man's instructions — the ground would need to be sealed.

Jabari would have to do it. He was the only one who could.

He helped Fabiana to her feet and walked her back to the train, where she was able to get some food and water. Jabari was exhausted and had no light to see the book, except the witch lights and they were sporadic. He slept, Fabiana's head resting on his shoulder, and awoke to the noon sun gleaming down in his eyes.

Jabari immediately opened the book and scanned the pages, finding the page Min had marked.

He left Fabiana and scoured the field until he found a four foot high standing stone that would suffice for his needs. Using a hammer and screwdriver he found in the train, Jabari set to work chiseling the prescribed words into the rock, creating a marker that would sit here for generations and keep any gates from opening here.

Once he was finished, Jabari knelt before the marker and read the ritual words to seal the ground and marker. A chorus of whispers echoed in his ears, and then faded in the wind. That was the only sign his task was complete. He hoped he had done it right.

But Jabari's work was not done. He spent the next several hours burying Min's body. He cried over the grave. He had made a promise to the old man, that he would fight with him. In his mind, that promise was still valid. It was more than a singular deed, it was a direction. He had seen horrors beyond imagining, and there was no ignoring that fact. They were still out there. More would arise. The fight would have to go on.

The train arrived and offered to bring them to the next city. Jabari searched Dane's trunk, took what weapons he could carry, along with a stash of money that he hoped would be enough to get him where he needed to go.

He and Fabiana boarded the train. There was no doubt in his mind as to his destination. He would find the Black Circle, no matter how long it took.

STORY NOTES

I WANTED TO WRITE a story inspired by the Eldritch Horror board game, filled with monster battles and a group of diverse characters working together to try and close gates to save the world. This was the result.

THE BLACK CIRCLE: PART TWO

I

The chamber Marcus found himself in was narrow, hardly more than a closet. The walls were not stone, but metal. *Lead*. At first, as he stepped into the chamber, he thought it to be empty, as his candle instantly illuminated the confines within, but upon further inspection, he saw that there was a small chest, carved of the finest cedar, resting on the floor at the bottom of the far wall. As Marcus knelt, he observed that the lid was open, and inside rested an ornately crafted golden eye.

He had been right after all. They were guarding something precious, something he could steal. Feeling validated and filled with gold-lust, Marcus wondered if all this seclusion and security were really necessary; it was, after all, just a single jewel. Yet they were guarding it as if it were worth a fortune. How much could it really be worth? Marcus was about to find out.

He reached out his hand to take the jewel —

And was shocked to find that his hand passed right through the image as if it weren't really there at all! He tried to grab it again, with the same result. His eyes told him there was a jewel, but his flesh told him otherwise.

On the brink of madness, Marcus fell back as a merciless laughter of lecherous delight echoed throughout the small chamber.

Then, he watched in horror as the golden eye and cedar chest became translucent, forming into a cloud-like substance, which seemed to pulse and crackle with electricity. The cloud rose and seemed to stretch impossibly from floor to ceiling into the shape of a towering personage: the indescribably terrible face of Pandemonius, wrapped in his crimson cloak.

The horror, Marcus thought fleetingly, *not in all my days of war did I ever look upon a face so incongruent and alien...*

"*You don't know true horror...not yet,*" the thing said in a silk-soaked voice, reading his thoughts. The wicked being wailed, and Marcus slammed his hands over his ears to prevent his brain from scrambling. He felt a rush of wind, and saw the luminous cloud flit past him and down the hall. Marcus was momentarily paralyzed. The impossibly ruined face of Pandemonius was frozen like a painting in his mind, and would be for years to come. He retched, recalling the dream he had had, the one that had shown him the way. It had been a trap, he realized in that moment, and he had fallen right into it.

If there were any scales of doubt remaining over Marcus' eyes, they fell away at that moment. He knew every word of Rowe's story was real, and that there were unspeakable horrors populating this world. He also knew he needed to get the hell out of here before anyone else realized what he'd done.

Marcus scrambled to his feet and staggered down the hall toward the stairs. As soon as he rounded the corner, he was met with a host blocking his escape. Rowe, Helen (of course), and a small legion of armed rogues gazed upon his shocked face with unbridled fury.

One of the rogues thrust a spear, breaking the skin of Marcus' left side. "Ow!"

"He's real," the guard spat.

Marcus drew his own sword and took a step back. "There'll be no more of that."

He caught sight of Rowe's blank expression, staring forlornly into the empty lead cage at the far end of the hall. "Marcus, do you know what you have done?" His face was pale, his breath weak.

"I know you were right, Rowe. I saw that evil with my own eyes."

"And set him free!"

"I am sorry...I did not know..."

The nun seethed. "I cannot listen to this insolent pig a moment longer. For his crimes, he must hang!"

"I will atone. I will serve thee to my dying breath. Please, Rowe." Marcus knew he could fight his way out of here if he needed to, but he did not think he could live with himself if he did. His opinion of himself had already dropped precipitously in the last few minutes.

But Rowe only shook his head. "I wish I could trust you. If you are truly penitent, throw down your sword, and let your maker judge your deeds."

A battle raged inside Marcus then. A veritable struggle between his desire for self preservation and self loathing. The face of Pandemonius flashed again in his mind, and he heard the clink of metal as his sword fell from his fingers. "Well, it's been a good run." He smiled, a futile attempt to lighten the mood.

Then, they seized him.

Marcus was dragged out into the forest by an incensed mob. It seemed all occupants in their stone fortress were present for the occasion. *Lucky me, a spectacle event.* Many bore torches, and all glared at him, as a rogue who reeked of filth tossed a rope over a branch.

The noose was thrown over his head (rather roughly). Marcus proceeded to sing an old song of wayfaring he'd learned long ago, which earned him a thwap to the back of his head.

"Any last words, traitor?" The question came from Helen, hellfire reflected in her sunken eyes, though Marcus doubted she really cared about his final words at all.

"Only this!" He cried, "So listen, and listen well! Before today, I didn't know evils such as Pandemonius existed in this world. You lot had the right of it. And since you refused my penance, the only thing I have left to say is that in a mad world such as this, the only sensible way to live one's life lies in a couplet I learned while serving in the holy wars: Love women, drink wine, for we all live too short a time!"

"Hang him!" roared the nun.

Rowe's face was a cast of disappointment, *the face of the father I never had*, thought Marcus. Then the noose was tightened, and he was hoisted off the ground.

The pain was instantaneous. He could feel his windpipe being crushed. A cheer went up from the crowd as his body began to convulse, instinctively trying to escape. Many spat at him in his death throes.

"Rot in hell!"

"His body will be a sign of what comes of them who trespass against The Black Circle!"

And then, as his body was still wriggling, they tied off the rope, and left him for dead.

II

Marcus hadn't prayed in years, but he cast a desperate prayer in that moment to the heavens. *Please God, I know I've sinned, I know I'm a dirty scoundrel, but you know my heart. Spare me, and I will work to right this wrong til my dying day...*

A thought struck him like a lightning bolt the moment he finished his prayer. It was an image of the knife that still rested inside his boot...

Marcus raised his feet, putting even more pressure on his compressed windpipe, and managed to slip the knife from his boot with his bound hands before blacking out. Had the knife been dull, Marcus would have perished in the next few moments, but he had learned in the military never to carry a dull blade. It was razor sharp. He swung upward and severed the thick rope in two strong hacks.

Marcus hit the ground hard and collapsed onto his side. It took several minutes before he could manage anything more than choking gasps, and until his vision cleared.

He used the tree to climb to his feet, wholly conscious of the choice that now lay before him. He could run. Flee. Save his sorry hide, and live a lonely life of destitution and thievery. Or he could keep his promise, return to the fortress (or castle), and offer up his life. Perhaps they would kill him again, and if that were to happen, he was resigned to it, but if not, he foresaw a life of meaning, and perhaps redemption, at least in his eyes, of hunting the foul thing that betrayed him.

Perhaps the old Marcus Brown would have run, but to this new Marcus Brown, baptized in a hangman's noose, it was no choice at all. He had sworn an oath to his creator, and he intended to keep it. Reality struck him with startling clarity, and he realized he had been searching for a purpose his entire life and now, divinely appointed or not, he had finally found one worth his while.

He made his way back staggering down the darkened trail, toward the blurry lights in the distance. He moved slow, as nearly dead men do, until he found himself standing in front of two heavy wooden doors.

He raised a leaden arm and knocked thrice.

"Who goes there?"

"Tis the ghost of Marcus Brown, come back to haunt you." He was surprised at how coarse his voice sounded. Perhaps it added to the effect, though it pained him beyond description to speak.

There was a flurry of hushed, anxious voices, then the doors were swung open, and Marcus found himself facing the tips of twin swords.

The faces of the guardsmen paled the second they lay eyes on him. "You're supposed to be dead!"

"I am dead," Marcus growled, then stepped past them and into a dirt courtyard without any resistance.

He spun his head, turning around, until he laid eyes on Rowe, standing above him in the battlements. "Hullo, Rowe."

Rowe turned, as did Helen, and Marcus was aware of a multitude of eyes on him, a multitude of eyes closing in.

"Marcus!" cried Rowe. "How is this possible?"

"A miracle, nothing short of it."

Helen's jaw hung open in stupefied wonder. "Get him! We'll hang him again!"

"You did that once, it didn't work, do you really need to try again to understand that you won't be rid of me so easily?"

"Perhaps a sword, then!" She muttered, searching for a blade, but Rowe called her to peace with a hand on her shoulder. He stood before Marcus now, with a look of bewilderment on his face.

"Why did you come back?"

"That is a question for the good Lord and all his Holy Angels. Can't explain what happened. I died, woke up on my back, brought back to life by the Almighty, and I understood what I needed to do." Perhaps not entirely accurate, but he had to speak in terms these people could understand. "Your devil, Pandemonius, deceived me in a dream, told me where to go. It could have happened to anyone, Rowe."

Rowe nodded, acceptance and understanding dawning behind his glassy eyes. "Yes. And would have happened, and kept happening again and again, until he was free."

A man grabbed Marcus roughly by the rope that still hung around his neck. "I'm sick of listening to this dog talk!"

"The door!" cried Marcus, quieting the bloodthirsty crowd. "Why didn't you brick up the door? Anyone could have opened it, but not if you sealed it underground, forever to rest in an infernal tomb."

A light rose in the eyes of some, and he knew he was winning them over. That they could see the logic in his words.

Marcus tore the noose from his neck, flinging it with abandon at the man behind him, and knelt in the mud before Rowe, arms raised at his sides. "My work on this Earth is not yet done, and I swear to you, Rowe...I will serve you in this cause to my dying breath. I will fight whatever horrors you see fit and hunt whatever foul abominations you wish me to hunt. Else why have I been spared?"

Rowe looked down on Marcus with an expression of grim pride, and a pinch of pity. "You do not know true horror...not yet." He pulled a sword from his scabbard, and spoke to the others. "We could use Marcus' keen mind, and his trained sword. He has paid the price for his sins, and been sent back to us, reborn. There will be no contestation of this decree, Marcus Brown, with all his faults, has perished." He smiled now, and rested the tip of his sword upon each of Marcus' shoulders in turn. "I accept thy pledge, and bid thee rise, no longer as Marcus Brown, but as Solomon Cross, knight of the Black Circle."

Solomon stood, gazing at the many torchlit faces of his new kin. There were many who did not seem pleased with Rowe's decision, and he knew he had a long and difficult road to walk in order to win their hearts, but it was a road he was determined to travel.

"I always wanted to be a Templar Knight, but I suppose this shall have to do," said Solomon with a smirk. "So, about this Pandemoni us...how did you catch him the first time?"

"With occult spells and deception, tricks that I'd wager won't work a second time." Rowe sheathed his sword. Rain began to fall on them as the heaven's broke.

"Well, then we'll find a new way," assured Solomon, following after Rowe and the others, who had turned to seek shelter inside.

"You do not know of what you speak," Helen snapped with spite.

"Aye, I suppose I don't. But I shall learn. What about finding him? That ought to be the first issue."

"Where evil flourishes," Rowe said, stepping into the safety of the castle, and turning to face Cross, "that's where we'll find him."

"France, then," Solomon replied, and was disappointed to hear no one laugh. "Very well, then, we seek evil tidings." He pulled the door shut behind him, sealing him into his new home, "Let the hunt b egin."

I LIKE TO THINK that this story ends things on a slightly positive note, if there can be such a thing as positivity in cosmic horror. I wanted to end here because I wanted the reader to get a sense that they've come full circle with the Black Circle — pun intended. We started with Marcus Brown, and now we get to watch him transform into someone else, someone we've heard referenced throughout these pages — the hero Solomon Cross, whose name I partially stole from Robert E. Howard's Solomon Kane.

In cosmic horror, traditionally, there is no way to win. We are facing threats that are incomprehensible and impossible to "defeat" in any traditional sense. That's why they're so freaking scary and why you're just as likely to lose your mind as die if you encounter them. But I like to think if humanity was ever to encounter something so vast and terrifying that people would band together and *try* to fight back. Even if the odds were a zillion to one. That trying to me is something worth writing about, because no matter how bad things get, you can always try to find your way out.

DH

Acknowledgements

My immense appreciation and gratitude to those who have continually supported me in my writing and cheered me on. This is not an exhaustive list by any means and is not in any order of significance, but includes the following individuals: My wife Shannon, Jenny Whitcomb, Tate Prothero, Cody Perkins, Midori Ansai, Coy Hall, Tali, Alex Porter, M.E. Grey, William Sterling, Tasha Reynolds, my friends at the Lunatic Radio Hour Podcast, Danni Vinson, Hamelin Bird, Kyle J. Durrant, Kenlon Clark, Tori Phillips, Elizabeth Day, Damien Casey, Brittany Johnson, Anne Taylor, Emily Marie, Thomas Gloom, and of course all the Hutch Siblings and my wonderful parents.

OTHER WORKS BY DEREK HUTCHINS

The Undertaker and Other Macabre Tales
The Darkness

About the Author

Derek Hutchins is a screenwriter, director, and author of the novella *The Darkness* and of a collection of short horror stories *The Undertaker and Other Macabre Tales,* as well as numerous short stories published in various anthologies. Raised in Connecticut, (the most haunted state), he developed a love for horror and the fantastic at an early age. Derek has an MFA in Writing for Film and Television from Emerson College and lives with his wife and daughters in Utah. Follow him on Instagram @themanwhoknewjustenough or (X) @derekmhutchins for updates.